In Times of Trouble

In Times of
of

In Times of Trouble

YOLONDA TONETTE SANDERS

SBI

STREBOR BOOKS

NEW YORK LONDON TORONTO SYDNEY

Strebor Books
P.O. Box 6505
Largo, MD 20792
http://www.streborbooks.com

This book is a work of fiction. Names, characters, places and incidents are products of the author's imagination or are used fictitiously. Any resemblance to actual events or locales or persons, living or dead, is entirely coincidental.

ISBN 978-1-59309-471-3
ISBN 978-1-4516-9563-2 (ebook)
LCCN 2012951358

First Strebor Books trade paperback edition April 2013

Cover design: www.mariondesigns.com
Cover photograph: © Keith Saunders/Marion Designs

10 9 8 7 6 5 4 3 2 1

Manufactured in the United States of America

For information regarding special discounts for bulk purchases, please contact Simon & Schuster Special Sales at 1-866-506-1949 or business@simonandschuster.com

The Simon & Schuster Speakers Bureau can bring authors to your live event. For more information or to book an event, contact the Simon & Schuster Speakers Bureau at 1-866-248-3049 or visit our website at www.simonspeakers.com.

*This book is dedicated to my cousin, Tyrell Jones.
I love you more than you could ever know.*

Acknowledgments

First, I want to thank Jesus for loving, molding, stretching, challenging, correcting, and forgiving me. No matter how close I came to giving up or how many times I failed You, You never let me go. May my life bring glory to Your Name!

David, I could use all the pages in this book and more to express my love and appreciation for you. We have an amazing testimony! I'm grateful for both the good and the bad times we've endured. All has worked together to shape *us!* I love you, baby!

To Tre and Tia, my heart is open to many children, but no one comes close to matching the love I have for each of you and the joy I have from being your mother.

To my parents, Wilene and Eddie, in addition to David and the kids, you are my biggest supporters. Thank you for believing in me and cheering me on.

To Carla Laskey, Teresa Lewis, LaKesha Raynor, and Janice Sanders who took the time to proofread this story before it ever reached the desk of an agent or publisher. Your feedback was invaluable and I appreciate and love you ladies very much.

To Dan Schofield, I have never forgotten your kindness!

To my family (both biological and in Christ), friends, book clubs, stores, and members of *Yo Notes* who have supported me over the years, I thank you all very much!

To Torry Cornett, Tiffany Croom, Mata Elliott, Kim Hahn, Selvy Hall, Kayla Hollins, Tyree Ayers, Michelle (Graham) Jones, Yolanda Knox, Cheryle Lewis (wife of Joe Lewis in Cincinnati, OH ☺), Shinerr Parker, Donald Schwind, Jennifer Scwhind, Leslie J. Sherrod, MaRita Teague, Robin Thornton, Suzy Tobin, and Clarke Tobin, I sincerely thank each of you for the assistance you provided. No matter how "big" or "small" a part you feel you played, your role was important to my completing this story.

A HUGE thank you goes to Tifani Kendrick for reminding me that I have a voice!

To Megan Yenni, I kept my promise to name a character in this book after you. ☺

Tyra, you may be fully grown, but you will always be my "baby!" I love you!

To my longest friend, Vicki Wismer, I know you'll always be there.

To Rell, I dedicated this book to you because I believe in God's sovereignty over genetic health conditions. May you find comfort in His word.

To Sara (and Stephen), THANK YOU for believing in me! May this be the beginning of a long, happy, and prosperous partnership.

To everyone who works for or with Simon & Schuster and Strebor, thank you for your part in putting together the complete package.

If I have neglected to mention anyone, I must be having a brain fart at the time. Please forgive me!

To you, the reader, thank you for your support. I pray that this story is a blessing to you. Trust that God's power is not limited by life's circumstances.

Much Love & Many Blessings,

Yolonda

www.yoproductions.net
www.facebook.com/yoproductions
I can also be found on Twitter @ ytsanders

CHAPTER 1
A Minor Issue

I t took Lisa a few minutes to fully regain consciousness when she woke up and found herself in the living room. She hadn't meant to fall asleep. Tucked away in an eastern suburb of Columbus, the Hampton household had been relatively quiet last night. With her mother and daughter out, Lisa took advantage of the solitary Saturday evening and just relaxed. Considering the many late nights she'd worked the previous week, she needed the break. Lisa spent the evening in her blue satin pajamas curled up on her cream plush sofa where she had apparently fallen asleep.

The sound of snow humming on her flat television screen was irritating and she quickly used the remote to turn it off. Noticing the time was 12:49 a.m., Lisa leapt up and ran through the kitchen to see if her car was in the garage. Nope, just her mother's car, which meant that Chanelle, her seventeen-year-old daughter, had missed her midnight curfew!

"Don't jump to conclusions," Lisa said to herself as she reached for the phone, flipping through the Caller ID. She hoped Chanelle had tried to call when she was asleep, but was disheartened to find no evidence supporting her theory. She quickly dialed Chanelle's cell phone, hearing the hip-hop music selection that preceded her daughter's voice mail. She didn't bother leaving a message.

Dashing up the stairs, Lisa knocked on her mother's bedroom door as a courtesy, but didn't wait for a response. "Mama?" She peeked inside.

Hattie lay like Sleeping Beauty underneath a tan comforter that blended in perfectly with her light skin tone. She looked so peaceful that Lisa really didn't want to disturb her. She stood for a split second, admiring her mother's beauty. Though she was in her mid-sixties, Lisa's mother looked great—still-mostly-black hair, a shapely size ten figure and no wrinkles. Lisa hoped she'd inherited her mother's genes and would also age gracefully. So far so good, but if Chanelle kept working her nerves, she'd surely look old and gray within a few years.

"Mama!" Lisa spoke with more force.

"Huh?"

"Sorry to wake you...I want to know if you've heard from Chanelle."

"No, why? She's not home yet?"

"No, but don't worry. I'll find her."

Her mother quickly sat up. "Did you call Jareeka? Maybe Chanelle accidentally dozed off over there."

The girl's name was actually Gericka, like *Erika*, but Lisa didn't bother correcting her mother, who was notorious for renaming people. "Calling there is my next step. I wanted to check with you first."

Lisa ran back down to the kitchen where Chanelle's best friend's telephone number was posted on the small magnetic bulletin board attached to the refrigerator. By now it was a few minutes shy of one.

The phone rang several times before Marlon Young, Gericka's father, answered.

"Hi! I'm sorry to call your house so late. This is Lisa."

"Yes, what can I do for you?"

"Is Chanelle there?

"No, why do you ask?"

Lisa's throat tightened. "She's not here yet. Do you know what time she brought Gericka home from the movies?"

"I don't know what Chanelle told you, but she didn't go to the movies with Gericka," Marlon firmly stated. "Gericka and Karen went to Louisville on Friday to spend the weekend with my mother-in-law."

"I'm sorry...I thought. Never mind. I'm sorry I woke you."

"It's okay. I'm sure you're concerned about your daughter. I pray she gets home safely," he said, before hanging up.

With no other options, Lisa reluctantly dialed RJ's number, which she had unfortunately memorized by now. She *hated* calling her ex-husband, but figured the situation warranted such an action. It was a waste of time because he hadn't seen or heard from Chanelle either. As if his presence would calm Lisa's nerves, RJ had offered to come over and wait with her until Chanelle arrived.

"No, thanks!" Lisa quickly declined. He always seemed to be looking for an excuse to be near her, but the only man occupying her time was Minister Freeman, whom she had been out to dinner with on several occasions.

"Please let me know the minute you hear from her," RJ requested.

"I will," she assured.

He had some nerve, acting like a concerned father when he was the reason why she and Chanelle had left Baltimore and come to Ohio in the first place. Had she known several summers ago when she moved here that he would follow, she would have accepted another job elsewhere.

Feeling her blood pressure rise with each passing second, she went back into the living room and sat on the couch. She began fiddling with the charm on the necklace she never took off, which had become a habit whenever she became nervous or angry. The time was exactly 1:07 a.m. and that meant her daughter was now sixty-seven minutes past curfew. Lisa was fuming!

Though the "God, please don't let anything bad happen to her" prayer cycled through Lisa's head a few times, she honestly didn't feel a need to panic. For some reason, Lisa knew Chanelle was okay—wherever she was. Chanelle was okay now, but Lisa couldn't promise that she'd be later when she finally brought her behind home and parental justice kicked in.

She did not understand why Chanelle would intentionally lie and violate her curfew. She was fresh off of punishment for talking back earlier that week. Lisa had asked Chanelle to get off the computer so she could type some information for work, but Chanelle had defiantly replied, "No!"—as if Lisa had really given her an option. Already stressed because of her work challenges, Lisa controlled the urge to snatch Chanelle out of the chair by her ponytail and threatened that if she didn't move of her own accord, she would be moved. Chanelle got up without further objection but her attitude had struck Lisa's nerve, so Chanelle had been placed on punishment.

Hearing the sound of her mother's footsteps descending the hardwood stairs, Lisa leaned back on the sofa so as not to appear overly anxious.

"Chanelle still hasn't made it home?" Her mother's wire-framed glasses rested at the tip of her nose while a large green robe concealed her body.

"Nope…"

"Did you call Jareeka's?"

"Yes, her father said that she and her mother are away for the weekend." She felt herself tensing with every word.

"What about RJ? Have you called him?"

"He hasn't seen her either."

"Well, don't come down too hard on her. Maybe she didn't know Jareeka was out of town and when she found out, she decided to hang with one of her other friends instead. Now she should've at least called and told you, but she was probably so happy to get out the house that she forgot. Poor thing; it seems like she's always on punishment. Sometimes I think you're too hard on that girl. I don't want to meddle—"

"Then please don't," the thirty-eight-year-old interjected in the most respectful tone that she could conjure up with a clenched jaw.

"All right. I'll keep my opinion to myself, but I was merely going to say that you may want to consider extending Chanelle's curfew. She's practically an adult and it's time you start treating her like one. Maybe then you'd be less likely to run into this problem."

An electrifying jolt shot through Lisa's body. The way she disciplined Chanelle had become a constant point of contention between her and her mother. Thank goodness Hattie would soon be moving into her own apartment! Lisa could not wait!

"That makes absolutely no sense!" she fired back. "What she is, is irresponsible. Why should I reward her for not being able to honor her curfew? And anyhow, she wouldn't have been on punishment recently had she not been so smart at the mouth."

"I wonder where she got it from…" her mother replied cynically, quickly disappearing into the kitchen and returning moments later. "Good night."

"The same to you," Lisa replied, continuing to stew as the clock read 1:21 a.m. The only other noise she heard was the emptying of the automatic ice machine until ten minutes or so later when a car pulled into the driveway. Lisa's heart began racing when she saw flashing blue and red lights from the window. It wasn't her car as she had thought, but a police cruiser. A gut-wrenching fear fell over her. Had something horrible happened to Chanelle? She felt guilty about being so angry and the missed curfew was now a minor issue compared to the concern that her baby might be lying in the hospital somewhere. Lisa was horrified by the unlimited possibilities of things that could've happened to her daughter. The pit of her stomach knotted as she sprang from the couch and raced to the front door.

CHAPTER 2
The Perfect Match

Callie Jamison lay curled up in her waterbed. She'd barricaded herself in her room several days ago. Since the day she'd gotten the devastating news, she hadn't eaten, slept or done much of anything except stare at the sky gray walls. She felt ashamed. But why? *She* hadn't done anything. Still, she tried to bury her pain in the depth of her heart, but her anger was so overwhelming that it kept resurrecting and she found herself hating everything and everyone…including God.

Her Bible lay next to the bed on the oak nightstand, secured in its black leather case. Until a few days ago, she used to read it regularly. Having read the Bible from the time she was a child until her late-forties, she figured she knew just about everything it said. She could name all the books in order, quote scripture verbatim and over the course of many years, she had written a synopsis of every book for her own personal benefit. Because she was so well-studied, Callie had been prepared to deal with everything life threw her way…or so she'd thought. Nothing she'd read between the pages of those sixty-six books had prepared her for this!

"Mom," Bryan called, gently tapping on her bedroom door.

If it weren't for him, Callie probably would've lost her mind or killed herself by now. Thankfully, Bryan had dropped everything at a moment's notice and driven nearly six hours from LA to Sacramento to be by her side. She wondered what was going through his mind as he raced across the interstate. She realized that he was hurting in his own way. Both of them were still grieving the loss of his father, Marvin, who had committed suicide seven months ago, but Callie had been the only one in therapy over the situation. She had always felt guilty and negligent. As his wife, shouldn't she have seen the warning signs? The suicide note Marvin had left behind offered no explanation. It simply read, "I'm so sorry." Recently, new developments had surfaced, shedding more light on the incident.

"Mom!" Bryan yelled again.

"Come in," she finally said.

"I'm getting ready to go to bed. I wanted to make sure you didn't need anything." His voice was low and shaky—definitely not the sound of a prominent attorney who had recently made junior partner at his law firm. Even his appearance lacked confidence. Bryan's bulky frame normally stood about six-one, like his father's, but his slumped shoulders and drooping head made him seem shorter.

Callie shook her head. "Unless you have a bag of miracles, I can't think of anything else I need," she said in an 'I'm-trying-to-make-a-joke-but-I'm-really-not-in-a-laughing-mood' sort of way.

Bryan walked over and sat next to her on the bed. "I wish I could perform miracles," he whispered.

His sincerity caused Callie's eyes to well with tears. She didn't think any had escaped until Bryan wiped her cheek.

"I'm so sorry this happened to you..." He took her hand, squeezing it gently and staring at her, sadly. She could feel the energy of his love through his firm grip. Looking into his big brown eyes, she was reminded of the five-year-old who'd won her heart way before Marvin ever did. They had become the perfect match. He was the child she could never carry and she was the mother figure that he'd longed for.

It was as if Marvin was the stepparent and not her. People who didn't know the circumstances would sometimes comment on how much they looked alike. Besides their mocha-colored skin, Callie didn't see the resemblance between Bryan and herself, but she definitely didn't mind the comparison. They had an unbreakable bond with one another. If it weren't for him, Callie would've wished the last twenty-four years of her life away.

"This is a time when we must lean on God more than ever," Bryan said, interrupting Callie's nostalgic moment. "Lord knows, I don't understand why this has happened to you. The only scripture that comes to mind right now is Proverbs 3:4-5. That's what we have to stand on."

Callie quickly mulled the scripture over in her mind. *Trust in the Lord with all your heart and lean not on your own understanding.* Callie was so angry with God that she wanted to severely admonish Bryan for his advice. How in the world could she trust God when He was the One who had let this happen?

"What time are you leaving tomorrow?" She purposely changed the subject to avoid the possibility of further biblical instruction.

"I'll probably take off around ten or so. I'll be back on Thursday."

"What about your workload?"

"It'll be taken care of. I've spoken to one of the senior partners and he said I can take all the time I need. I want to wrap up a few things, but I'll be back."

"Thanks, honey, but I don't want you to take too much time off for me. Save some of your time so you can spend it with Tyra after the baby gets here."

"Don't worry…Tyra knows I'll be there when she needs me. Have you given any more thought to coming to stay with us?"

"I don't know…we'll see."

"When I mentioned the idea to Tyra, she didn't seem to mind. She'd enjoy dragging you to Lamaze classes and out baby shopping."

"Like I said…we'll see. I appreciate the offer, but I'm fine, really."

Bryan frowned. "This is what you call fine? Being locked in your bedroom for days without eating or socializing with the outside world?"

"I needed time to process everything."

"I know…but you're worrying me…especially since you're not eating."

"I have eaten— "

"I'm not convinced forcing a pack of peanut butter crackers down your throat while I'm watching can technically be considered eating. How about we get up early in the morning so I can take you out for some mouth-watering buttermilk pancakes?"

Callie couldn't help but smile; he knew she had a weakness for pancakes. "Thanks, but I'll pass. Maybe next time."

"Are you going to church in the morning?"

"I wasn't planning on it," she answered simply, though she really had a much stronger response in mind—a two-word phrase that began with the letter "h" and ended with the word "no."

"You may want to touch base with Sister Ellis. She's called several times. She sounded a bit concerned since she hasn't heard from you in a few weeks. She mentioned a women's retreat you two are planning."

"Helping her get that retreat together is the least of my concerns right now. She'll eventually figure that out because I'm not calling her or anyone else."

"Have you talked to Lisa?"

Callie sighed. "Not since all of this came out. The last time we spoke was about me coming to Chanelle's graduation party. I should call and let her know I'm not going to make it."

Nine years Lisa's senior, the two weren't close, but shared a cordial relationship. It was most likely the blood connection that kept them together, because they were complete opposites. Callie thought her sister could be a bit pretentious at times. No matter how many fallouts they had, their relationship remained intact.

They didn't really look like siblings. Far from inheriting their mother's light skin tone and hourglass figure, Callie's dark frame was more pear-shaped than anything else; and she hadn't worn any size lower than a sixteen since graduating high school. Lisa had always been the lucky one.

"Don't call and cancel," said Bryan. "Chanelle's graduation is still a month away. You may feel differently by then. I would go, but I hate to leave Tyra by herself so close to her delivery date."

"I'm not in the right mindset to be around Lisa and Mama. This is hard enough to deal with as it is. The less people know, the better."

"But they aren't just people, Mom. They're family. I recognize this is hard for you, but Lisa and Grandma Hattie will support you in any way they can."

"I don't need support right now, Bryan. I need to be left alone!" she snapped, then realized her harshness. "I'm sorry...you're only trying to help... I'm just so angry. This is too much to bear. I feel so..." She burst into tears.

Bryan bent down and cradled her. "Shhh...It's okay. We'll take it one day at a time," he whispered.

CHAPTER 3
Serves Her Right

"What in the...?" Lisa choked on her words, seeing her daughter escorted up to the front porch by a dark-haired, Caucasian police officer. Her daughter was dressed like she was a dancer on some gold-toothed rapper's video.

"Ma'am, I'm Officer Kendrick," he said, dropping Chanelle's arm and flashing his badge. "I'm here because this young lady was picked up at a party for underage drinking."

"She *what?*" Chanelle, holding a pair of black stilettos, nervously tugged at her micro mini skirt and avoided eye contact with her mother. "She was supposed to be at a movie," Lisa growled.

"I don't know about the movie, ma'am, but I do know your daughter was one of several minors we found intoxicated at the scene. I thought I'd bring her home instead of getting you folks entangled in the legal system."

"Go up to your room, now!" hollered Lisa. With mascara-stained cheeks, Chanelle looked at the officer one last time as though she wished he'd take her with him and then brushed past Lisa. Though it had been several years since Lisa's own run-in with the law, the wounds still felt fresh and she was truly grateful that Officer Kendrick had spared Chanelle from having any blemishes on her record. "Thank you so much, sir, for bringing her home."

"You're welcome. I tried talking to your daughter on the way over. You might want to reinforce that Cleveland Avenue isn't the safest place for a teenage girl to be late at night. I don't know how closely you watch the news, but a nineteen-year-old girl was found murdered in an alley off Cleveland the other day. It's only the first week of May and already we've had twenty-nine murders this year. I didn't want to lecture her, but she needs to choose neighborhoods wisely."

"I understand. Thank you so much. Rest assured, I will reinforce everything you said and then some."

"On the way here, your daughter said that she had driven to the party. Is that correct?"

"Yes. Did you happen to notice a silver Pontiac G6 anywhere near the location?"

"There were cars parked up and down the street. It may have been among them, but I can't say for sure. So much for attention to detail, huh?" He laughed.

"Would you mind giving me the address where this party was held? I'll have my mother take me to get it later."

"Just check with your daughter to confirm that it, in fact, is there. I won't mind taking you to get it if you'd like."

"No, that's okay. I don't want to inconvenience you."

"It won't be an inconvenience."

Lisa wasn't sure what to make of Officer Kendrick's overly nice gestures. First, he went out of his way to bring Chanelle home and now he was offering to give her a ride to her car. His actions seemed a little suspect. "Are you sure you won't mind taking me?"

"Not at all."

"Okay. Let me see what my daughter says. Give me a few minutes." She motioned for him to step inside the house and ran upstairs, bumping into Chanelle in the hall. "Is my car at the place you were picked up?"

Holding her hand over her mouth, Chanelle nodded yes and jetted into the bathroom. *Serves her right*, Lisa thought, hearing vomiting sounds followed by aching moans. Lisa was more than ready to go off, but thought it would be wise to allow her temper to cool first.

"What's going on?" Her mother poked her head from her bedroom, squinting without her glasses.

"Chanelle got picked up by the police for underage drinking. I'll be back. The officer is going to take me to get my car."

Lisa rushed into her own room. After stripping out of her pajamas and into a pair of blue jean capris and a t-shirt, she removed her scarf and quickly ran her fingers through her hair. Though the likelihood that she'd see a familiar face this time of night was slim to none, she had been taught to never leave the house without looking presentable. No matter how small the errand, Lisa wouldn't be caught in public wearing night scarves, hair rollers, raggedy clothes or anything else that she would be embarrassed about if photographed.

On her way back downstairs, Lisa stood in the bathroom doorway for a moment and watched reluctantly as her mother hovered over her daughter. Grandma to the rescue, as always! The smell of liquor oozed from her daughter's pores and floated through the air. Chanelle looked up with vomit-traced lips. "Mama, I'm sorry," she slurred.

That had to be the alcohol talking, because the girl rarely apologized for anything. "Just lie down and get some rest. We'll talk about this in the morning."

CHAPTER 4
A Flying Firecracker

The next morning, Lisa searched for something to wear to church and settled on a soft, yellow, short-sleeved dress with a pair of white, open-toed sandals, accessorized with studded earrings and, of course, her gold necklace. It was about five after ten when she made it to the kitchen, which wasn't bad considering that she'd gotten up at nine and spent at least twenty minutes fussing with Chanelle to get her hung-over behind up and ready. Usually they were out the door by that time so they could make it to Sunday school, but Lisa had overslept this morning and would probably still be sleep had it not been for her mother waking her to "discuss" Chanelle's punishment.

As always, her mother severely disagreed about what should happen with Chanelle and fought viciously with words to keep her from being punished. Though Lisa would probably never do cartwheels about his move to Columbus, one thing that worked in RJ's favor was that he stood behind any disciplinary actions Lisa took against their daughter. When she called and updated him on everything last night, he was just as livid as she was and didn't make excuses for Chanelle. For him to be a point of sanity for Lisa said a lot, especially after all he'd put her through.

"Show a little mercy," her mother had argued. *"Drunk or not, you should be thankful she came home last night and didn't run off and get married like someone else I know who didn't have the decency to invite her own mother to the ceremony."* Lisa would be the first to admit that eloping with RJ when they were only eighteen was not the wisest move; and she had paid dearly for her mistake. But her marriage and Chanelle's drinking weren't even comparable, and the fact that her mother brought it up didn't sit well. Needless to say, when her mother left for church, Lisa had a serious attitude.

After putting a pot of water on the stove and starting the coffee maker, she sat at the kitchen table while the argument with her mother continuously cycled through her mind. Was she really being unmerciful? She couldn't very well allow Chanelle to go unpunished, could she? She thought about Hebrews 12:5-6, which states how the Lord disciplines those that He loves and began praying silently. *Father, I don't like the feeling of being perceived as a mean disciplinarian. But, that's how it seems my mother and daughter view me. I love Chanelle! I know You hold me accountable for her. Help me do what is right and just. God, I don't want to be unfair or overly harsh. I'm looking to You for—*

Before Lisa could finish, the teapot began whistling and she heard Chanelle trotting down the stairs. Lisa wiped the dangling teardrop from her eye, taking a quick glance at the clock. It was only 10:23 am; service didn't start for another hour. There was still plenty of time for her to address Chanelle's behavior.

Chanelle dragged in the kitchen wearing a light blue jean jumper with a short-sleeved red shirt underneath. Though a little wrinkled, her outfit would pass, but her hair looked a mess with braids desperately in need of moisturizing lotion. Like her mother had done with her, Lisa had taught Chanelle to take care in her appearance. Was she really feeling that bad or was this a ploy to earn sympathy and stay home from church?

"I can't believe you're making me go to church." Chanelle plopped down at the table across from her mother.

Concluding that it was sympathy her daughter was after, Lisa got up to turn off the stove. "Yes, I am. If there's time when we finish talking, I'd suggest you touch up your appearance. Remember, you represent a long line of Johnson women." Johnson was her mother's maiden name. "We don't leave the house looking crazy."

"But, Jesus said to come as you are and I look how I feel."

"Well, if being electrocuted is the look you're going for, then it works." Lisa turned and gave her daughter a cunning I'm-not-gonna-play-your-game smile. Setting the cup of tea in front of Chanelle, she said, "Drink this. It may make you feel better."

Chanelle sniffed the cup. "What is it?"

"Some kind of herbal tea your grandmother bought."

"Is it good?"

"I don't know. I figured it would be better for you than coffee, though," Lisa took a sip of her latte. The tea she'd made Chanelle must not have been bad because Chanelle began to drink it slowly. "So...what happened last night?"

"I thought the officer told you."

"He did, but now I want to hear from you."

"Instead of going to the movies, Gericka and I went to a party."

"Really? Gericka was with you?"

"Yeah, I told you I'd be out with her," Chanelle answered matter-of-factly. "We met up with one of her cousins there. At the time we decided to go, we didn't know there would be alcohol involved."

"Then why didn't you tell me about the party?"

"Because sometimes you be trippin'. I didn't want the static. We didn't go there intending to drink. One thing led to another and we got caught up in the hype. When the cops showed up, we realized we'd made a big mistake. They would've let us go if we hadn't been drinking."

"So Officer Kendrick took Gericka home, too?"

"Yeah…"

Curious about how far her daughter would carry out this farce, Lisa said, "Maybe I'll call Karen and Marlon to see how they handled things with Gericka. Since you girls committed the same offense, it's only fair that you receive the same punishment."

"Um… Now that I think about it, the cops didn't take Gericka home at all…what had happened was she managed to sneak out of there and left with her cousin. Her cousin took her home…not the cops. My bad…some details of last night are still sort of fuzzy because of…well, you know. Mama, I learned my lesson last night. I promise I won't do it again."

"Do what again: lie or drink?"

"Both."

"If you intend to keep that promise, then you need to start by telling me who you were really with last night."

"I told you already," Chanelle insisted.

"No, what you told me is a bald-faced lie. You're not remorseful at all."

"What—"

"I've heard enough, Chanelle! Your fabricated story about last night makes me sick. I spoke with Gericka's father already, so I know you weren't with her."

Chanelle's expression turned blank and she chewed her bottom lip.

"I'm going to ask you one last time and you'd better tell me the truth if you know what's good for you. *Who were you with?*" Silence gripped the air. "Answer me!"

"I was with a friend of mine named Kyle Lewis."

"Who is he?"

Chanelle shrugged her shoulders like it was no big deal. "Someone I met a few weeks ago at the skating rink."

"How old is this boy?"

"We're the same age...seventeen."

"What in the world are you doing hanging out with another boy? You've only been given permission to date Justin."

"The problem is I don't like Justin the way you want me to."

"You sure liked him enough to drop his name with the police officer last night. I couldn't figure out why that man was being so nice until I got in the cruiser and he asked me if I could get him tickets to a football game." Lisa had taken his number and told him she'd see what she could do, though there was no doubt that she'd be able to get the tickets.

"I didn't say anything about Justin. The officer searched my purse and found the picture on my keychain of you and Miss Olivia. He asked me who y'all were and I told him. I didn't bribe him into bringing me home. He did that on his own."

"Well, the bottom line is I have the final say of who you can or cannot go out with."

"You're not willing to approve anyone except Justin and that's because Miss Olivia is your best friend."

"That may be true, but I know for sure he comes from good stock. You would've never been in that position last night if you were with Justin. That boy has a good head on his shoulders. Not many college football stars have a grade-point average as high as his."

Lisa really loved Justin. He was currently finishing up his sophomore year at Ohio State and, in addition to maintaining good grades, he was a dynamic football player. He broke the record for the most rushing yards by a freshman his first year of college and scored twenty touchdowns that season. This past season, Justin once again broke college records. Per NFL regulations, Justin had one more season to play before he would be eligible for the pros, and both he and his parents were gearing up for it. Lisa was happy for him, but more than being impressed by his athletic abilities, she admired how dedicated he was to his schoolwork as well.

"I doubt this Kyle character will even make it to college," she scoffed.

"How can you say that? You don't even know him."

"And based on last night, I don't have a desire to. I don't want you hanging out with him again."

"Why not? We're just friends."

"Well, not anymore. He sounds like bad news."

"But—"

"I don't want to hear it. I'd better not hear anything about you and him again. Do I make myself clear?"

"Yeah..."

"Excuse me?"

"Yes, ma'am."

"Because of this stunt you pulled, you won't get a taste of freedom until graduation day. So for the next month, there will be no TV, no telephone, no computer, no video games, no nothing! I hate to be like this, but had you told me the truth from the beginning, things could have been less severe. You know that I'm not going to tolerate lying under any circumstances."

"Can I still go to King's Island with Gericka on Memorial Day?"

"No. If you really wanted to go, you should have thought about that before last night."

Chanelle grunted.

"And give me your cell phone."

"Why? It was a Christmas present from Grandma. She's paying the bill; shouldn't she be the one to take it from me? I'm gonna be grown soon and you're still treating me like a child."

Lisa ordered herself to stay cool so she'd keep from laying hands on Chanelle. "You think turning eighteen this summer will make you grown? Grown folk pay for their own stuff. I don't give a flying firecracker who bought it. I said give it here and that's exactly what I mean."

Chanelle grudgingly reached down in her purse and shoved the phone toward Lisa.

"Since you'll have a lot of time on your hands, I suggest you use it to find yourself a summer job and save up enough bus fare for when you start college. If I can't trust you with my car while you're living in my house, there's no way I'm going to be able to trust you with it when you go to college. Because of your irresponsibility, you will not be driving my car all summer."

Chanelle had applied to and already been accepted by a local college. Since Chanelle was planning to live in the dorms, Lisa had considered buying her a car for graduation, but not anymore. Not after this! Maybe Lisa would reconsider and get it before Chanelle officially started school, but she was going to make her bus it all summer, for sure. "Anything could've happened to you last night while you were out dressed like a li'l hoochie. The officer told me that they'd just found a body in an alley over there. He escorted me to my car and I still didn't feel completely safe. All those people hanging outside on the corners...what in the world were you thinking? I guess that's the whole point...you weren't thinking. Well, I've said everything I have to say. Is there anything else you'd like to add?"

"Would it matter if there was?"

"Hurry up and finish drinking that tea so we can get to church. The sanctuary is the safest place for you right now because your smart mouth is really working my nerves!"

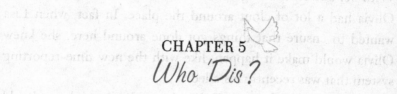

CHAPTER 5
Who 'Dis?

"Hey, I wanted to let you know that I'm back home now." Olivia called Lisa late Monday afternoon.

"How was the trip?"

"Great. I wish Isaac could've come back with me; I miss him already."

"How long is he going to be in New York?"

"Until his case is over, which could be at least another month." Olivia's husband was a very well-known and established attorney with a law business that was continually growing. "To whom much is given, much is required. I miss my baby, but I try not to complain about all the traveling he has to do. Girl, I remember when the brotha couldn't pay someone to hire him. Now he has law firms in seven states!"

"That's great."

"Naw, girl, that's God! In just three months this new office in New York has already earned him retainers of one-point-two million dollars from clients. Now you know that's nothing but the favor of God."

"Ain't that the truth!"

"I considered returning late last night or early this morning because of the weekly board meeting, but I figured no one would die if I missed this one. I didn't feel like rushing back."

"I'm sure they survived." Olivia was one of the board members of Brentson Technologies, the company where Lisa worked. With her and Isaac being large investors in the company as well, Olivia had a lot of clout around the place. In fact, when Lisa wanted to ensure that things got done around here, she knew Olivia would make it happen, like with the new time-reporting system that was recently installed.

With a name like Brentson Technologies, Lisa's employer should have done away with antiquated time sheets and implemented a computer-based reporting system long ago, but last Monday was the first day that employees were introduced to the "new way of doing things." As Head of the Human Resources Department, Lisa was forced to work a lot of overtime last week, dealing with training sessions, computer glitches, and staff complaints. She had been pushing for the new system for quite some time, but her proposals continued to get "tabled." Telling Olivia about the situation was all it took to expedite things. What Lisa had been trying to do for months was settled within a few short days once Olivia got involved, proving how much of an impact she had on what did and did not get done around here.

"How was church yesterday?" Olivia asked.

"It was good....guess. To be honest, I was zoning in and out a little."

"Why? Were you tired?"

"I was tired and stressed." Lisa filled Olivia in about the weekend's events.

"Chanelle knows better. Teenagers can surely put us through some stuff. Isaac and I had our share of issues with Justin. We got through it and so will you. Before you know it, this incident will be a distant memory."

"You think?"

"Trust me...it gets better."

"Girl, I hope so because that child is driving me up a wall."

Olivia laughed. "She'll be all right. She's strong-willed and one day that'll come in handy when dealing with people. One thing I like about Chanelle is that the sistah is not fazed by Justin's popularity. I don't want Justin to get big-headed because you know once he's drafted all kinds of little sluts will be throwing panties at him. Maybe hooking up with Chanelle can be what he needs to stay humble, but we can't force a match. If they get together, it'll have to be on their own."

"Yeah, I know..." Lisa was starting to lose hope. Justin was perfect for Chanelle, but she couldn't see it. "Girl, let me get off this phone and finish my work so I can get out of here. Minister Freeman and I are having dinner at six."

"Again? Y'all are getting awfully cozy. It's four o'clock already; you should be heading out now. What you really should've done was leave early."

"I thought about it, but I have an IT presentation in the morning and I didn't want to take work home with me. I'm going to leave from here and meet Minister Freeman at the restaurant."

"I don't see why you keep calling him Minister Freeman instead of his name."

"Because that's how he was introduced to me and he hasn't told me anything different. You call him by his first name, but you've known him longer than I have."

"Yeah, well, it sounds like you may be getting to know him much *better* than I do," she teased.

"Shut up. We're just having dinner, that's all."

"So you say...I suspect before long, we'll hear wedding bells. Just make sure you invite me to the wedding."

"Why would the matron of honor need an invitation?"

Now the very best of friends, Lisa and Olivia initially met under frightening circumstances only a few months after Lisa first moved to Ohio. They were trapped on an elevator when the electricity went out. Confined for hours and not knowing whether or not they'd live to tell about it, they'd shared many personal things with each other that day and bonded in a way that Lisa had never done before with any other female—not even her biological sister. Despite their eleven-year age difference, their friendship was so solid that one would think it stemmed from childhood. No matter what the situation, Olivia never failed to have Lisa's back and vice versa.

Lisa's assistant poked her head through the door. "Liv, I have to go, Megan needs me."

"All right, but tell your man I said 'hey.' Call me afterwards so I can start planning the bridal shower."

"Bye, you nut! I'll talk to you later." She hung up, laughing. "Olivia is so silly."

"I'm sorry. I didn't mean to interrupt. I wanted to see if there was anything you needed before I go."

Lisa loved Megan, who had been working as her administrative assistant since Lisa's first day at Brentson Technologies. She was a quiet person and always willing to go the extra mile. She looked almost Albino with her pale skin and stringy blond hair. Though Megan always wore a smile, her sadness shone through her eyes. Her sorrow was a result of having lost her husband while he served in Iraq. Now Megan was left to raise their young son on her own.

"Thanks, Meg, but I don't need anything. You can go now if you want. Lord knows you've earned the right with all the overtime you put in. I appreciate you staying over with me last week."

"You're welcome."

"Things should be a breeze from here on out."

"I can already tell a difference today. I don't know what you said to Olivia, but whatever it was, thank you. She really got the ball rolling with this new system."

Lisa smiled, slyly. "It pays to have friends in persuasive positions."

"I know…it's so cool that my boss is best friends with Olivia Scott. Her husband is like *the* go-to attorney for any and every-one on the A-list throughout the country. And I swear she has to be on almost every important committee or board in Columbus. I'm surprised they're still around here. The media always reports him in some other part of the country working on a case."

"Yeah, well as you know, they both have strong family ties here."

"Either way, I'm in awe. Olivia is like the Oprah Winfrey of Columbus. And you're…you're like her Gayle."

"Thanks, but we have our own identities. I'd prefer to be called Lisa." She chuckled.

As Lisa's assistant, Megan enjoyed many of the perks that having Olivia on the board of Brentson Technologies brought with it. Like Lisa, Megan took advantage of things like paid time off work without officially having to submit leave slips or extended lunches. Usually such fringe benefits only extended to company execs, but thanks to Olivia, Lisa—and Megan—got access to special privileges.

"Well, I guess I'll go ahead and get out of here."

"Okay, you have a good evening and I'll see you tomorrow."

It was about ten after four when Megan spun out of the office and Lisa tried calling home. Surprised that no one answered the phone, she tried calling Chanelle's cell phone and busted out laughing when it vibrated in her purse. Duh…she'd taken it from her. Lisa tried her mother's cell phone.

"Mama, is Chanelle with you?"

"No. She's at home."

"I just called there and she didn't answer the phone."

"Maybe she's in the bathroom or something, but she's there. I only left a few minutes ago."

"I was calling to say that I'm not going to be home until late. I'm meeting someone from church."

The advantage of her and her mother attending different churches was that her mother never inquired about whom she was "meeting" with or for what. The disadvantage was that the church her mother had chosen to join was led by RJ's dad's best friend. Since his relocation to Columbus, RJ has been attending there also. Truthfully, Lisa had attended Pastor Burlington's church initially when she moved here. That was only because it was a safety net until she could learn more about the churches in the city. She never had intentions of being a permanent member.

Thankfully, Lisa met Olivia who introduced her to Abundant in Christ Church, which had many affluent members in the congregation such as the Scotts. Olivia was very active in the church, overseeing several key ministries. She was the one who got Lisa involved with the Pastor's Anniversary Committee that gave Lisa the chance to work closely with Minister Freeman whom she was going out with tonight.

"I'm just going to go to my meeting from work."

"That's fine. I won't be gone long. I only have a few errands to run. I'll fix dinner when I get back. I had a taste for smothered pork chops anyhow."

"Thanks, Mama."

"No problem...I'll see you tonight."

Lisa resumed working and a few minutes later, Chanelle's phone vibrated again. Initially Lisa ignored the phone, but when several calls came back-to-back, she was compelled to see who it was. When the words "My Boo" flashed across the screen, Lisa couldn't keep curiosity from getting the best of her and she answered.

"Hey, shorty, what's up? Baby, I hope you didn't get in too much trouble Saturday. "

"This must be Kyle," she said accusingly. If they were only "friends" like Chanelle had stated, then why in the world was he calling her baby!

"Who 'dis?"

"*This* is Chanelle's mother."

"Aw man, my bad…for real."

"How old are you, Kyle?"

"Seventeen."

At least Chanelle had told the truth about his age. "I assume you're aware that the legal drinking age is twenty-one, right?"

"Um…can you just tell Chanelle to hit me up later?"

"I most certainly will not. I never want you calling my daughter again. Do you understand me?"

Lisa listened a few seconds for Kyle's response, then she noticed that he had hung up. Furious about his lack of respect, she tried calling home again. Still, no answer, but this time she decided to leave a message. "Mama said you were home. Why aren't you picking up? I want you to know that I just answered a call from your *boo*. The little hoodlum hung up on me. I meant what I said, Chanelle. I don't want you ever talking with or seeing that boy again! Oh…and by the way, I'll be home late tonight."

CHAPTER 6
A Different Perspective

Lisa and Minister Freeman decided to drive to a park after dinner. As they strolled through the walkway, her hair blew in sync with the light spring breeze flowing through the air. Lisa gently kicked pebbles along the way, finishing her soda. If she had been with Olivia, she would have slurped the last few drops of liquid from between the ice with her straw. But, while in the minister's presence, she chose the more lady-like option and threw the cup in a nearby trashcan. She immediately began shuffling through her purse.

"What are you looking for?"

"This." She pulled her lipstick out. "I saw most of it on my straw so I'm guessing it's time for a refresher."

He grabbed her arm gently, just as she was about to apply it. "I think you have a beautiful natural smile. Don't hide it with that stuff." He took a handkerchief from his back pocket and tenderly wiped the remaining residue from her lips. "Sister Lisa, I don't think I've ever been this close to such a gorgeous woman."

Had Lisa been just a few shades lighter, she would have turned bright red. Flattered, she put her lipstick away and the only thing she could think to say was "Please, just call me Lisa."

"Okay, *Lisa*....I hope I'm not being too forward. That wasn't a come-on line. I do think you're beautiful."

"Thank you, Minister Freeman."

"It's okay to call me by my name. It's Eric, in case you didn't know."

She laughed, suspiciously. "Have you spoken to Olivia anytime recently?"

"No, why do you ask?"

"Just wondering...Are you sure you don't mind being on a first name basis with me?"

He frowned. "Why would I? It's not like being a minister makes me any better than you. You asked me to call you Lisa, so I'm asking you to call me Eric."

"I don't want to be disrespectful."

"Look, some people get ordained and it goes to their heads, but I'm not on any kind of ego trip. Minister Freeman sounds so Sunday morning-ish. I never understood why brothers and sisters in Christ feel the need to be so formal with one another. We're not taking titles with us to Heaven, so why do we press the issue down here? Besides that, I want you to get to know me— Eric Freeman—and not be stuck on the fact that I'm a minister. You do want to get to know me, don't you?"

Oh, yes! Of course I do! Lisa prayed those words wouldn't slip from her mouth. "Yes, Eric, that would be great," she said as though she was trying the name out.

"Then that settles it." He took Lisa's hand, sending an adrenaline rush through her veins as they continued their journey through the park. "So...how's planning for your daughter's graduation party coming along?"

"Fine. The big day is just a few weeks away."

"Am I invited?"

"I...um, didn't think you'd be interested in coming."

"Are you kidding? I'd love to be there. It would give me a chance to get to know Chanelle outside of church; and of course, I'm looking forward to meeting your mother."

"I don't know...a graduation party isn't really a good setting for you to get to know them well." Lisa wasn't intending to invite him. RJ would be there and it would be awkward enough avoiding him on her own. She didn't want to drag Eric in the middle.

"You're right; perhaps I can come over for dinner one night soon. I'll still come to the party, but if we're going to tell them about our relationship we should do it before then. Don't you think it's time they knew about us."

"Okay..." she said, cautiously. She didn't know that they had officially become an "us." Part of her thought Minister Freeman—Eric—was moving way too fast but, then again, perhaps it was simply her fears taking over. Though she may have entertained one or two dinner invitations after her divorce, they were nothing really serious. Getting involved in a relationship had always been the furthest thing from her mind. RJ was her first everything! They'd known each other since junior high and eloped within weeks of graduating high school. After years of thinking that she knew him and then for having his true colors to show, really put a damper on Lisa wanting to trust anyone else. But, somehow Eric had caught her attention. Even if she wanted to, Lisa couldn't suppress the magnetism drawing her towards him.

It wasn't as much a physical attraction as it was a spiritual one. His barely-average appearance wasn't anything she'd brag about. Men in their early forties with spots of gray and receding hairlines were a dime a dozen. He wasn't excessively tall or ridiculously short, nor did he have a muscular, mouth-watering physique. He was, in all meanings of the word, "okay." He wasn't someone that would cause a woman to do a double take but because they worked so closely together on the Pastor's Anniversary Committee, Lisa got a chance to observe the way he carried himself. There was no doubt that Eric truly loved the Lord, and that alone made him more desirable than anyone named on *People* magazine's list of "Sexiest Men Alive." Eric genuinely walked according to the Word, unlike RJ who had been a wolf in sheep's clothing.

If Eric didn't push for things to go to the next level, Lisa would probably keep things like they were and continue finding creative ways to tell the truth to her mother and daughter without actually lying. Like tonight when she categorized this date as a "meeting." It wasn't so much as she didn't want them to meet Eric, but rather she was hesitant about him meeting them. She, her mother and Chanelle weren't exactly the Huxtables. If Dysfunctional were a last name, it would likely be theirs. The nerve of Chanelle getting drunk! And then—

"Yoohoo…Earth to Lisa," Eric called out, waving his hand in front of her face.

"I'm sorry; did you say something?"

"Yes. I *said* we are very blessed to be part of one of the greatest churches in the city."

"Um hmm…"

"Abundant in Christ is virtually incomparable to any other church in Columbus. Pastor Ross is really doing some great things. One of my dreams is to start my own church and be a shepherd of God's people."

"Um hmm…"

"Am I boring you?"

"No, it's not you. I'm sorry. My mind is elsewhere."

"Would you like to talk about whatever is troubling you?"

"Thanks, but I'll pass." Eric was a single man with no children.

The last thing Lisa wanted to do was scare him off with horror stories about her daughter. "There's no need to burden you with my concerns. I'm sure you have more important matters on your mind."

"Currently you're the important matter on my mind. Galatians 6:2 instructs us to bear one another's burdens and as a servant of the Lord, your problem is my problem. Being concerned about you is one of my obligations."

"Thanks, but I really don't feel like talking right now."

"That's okay. Do you want to continue this evening another time? It's obvious that I've lost your attention."

"I'm sorry; I feel horrible."

"Don't. I'm not offended. You probably just need a little quiet time. The best thing you can do right now is talk to our Father. He'll definitely have the solution to your problem. As a matter of fact, would you mind if I prayed with you before we leave?"

"No, not at all."

Right there in the middle of the park walkway, they turned and held hands while Eric proceeded. "Father God, I ask in the Name of Jesus that you be with Lisa. Lord, let not her heart be troubled. Whatever is concerning her, deal with it and take the burden off her mind. Give her peace about each and every situation in her life. In the Name of Jesus, I pray...Amen."

After the prayer, they walked silently back to their cars, still holding hands. "I'm glad we agreed to have dinner at your place next Monday. I'm looking forward to it, but I hope I don't have to wait until then to see you again."

What in the world was he talking about! Lisa didn't recall such an agreement. He must've mentioned it when she'd drifted off mentally. Lisa imagined that she said something like "Sure, okay," without really paying attention to what she was answering. Lisa wasn't ready to take this step, but Eric was standing there with a wide grin on his face and Lisa didn't know how to politely cancel without offending him.

It was a little after nine when Lisa got home. She walked in to find her mother and daughter at the kitchen table playing cards. "Hey guys…"

"Hey, how was the meeting?"

"It was great. Chanelle, are you going to speak?"

"I said hi when you walked in."

"I'm sorry, I didn't hear you."

"UNO!" Chanelle shouted.

"Nuh-uh…" Hattie smirked, throwing a Draw Four card on the table.

"How was school today?" Lisa asked.

"Fine…"

"I tried calling to let you know I'd be late."

"I know…"

"Why didn't you answer the phone?"

"Because I'm on punishment…I'm not supposed to talk on the phone, remember? You took away my cell phone for that very purpose," Chanelle said with such a snide attitude that Lisa could've smacked her.

"Go to your room!" she ordered.

"Why?"

"C'mon, Lisa, we're in the middle of a game," her mother jumped in.

"I don't care, Mama. She's not going to get smart with me."

"I can't say or do anything around here!" Chanelle ranted, smashing her cards down on the table and storming out of the kitchen.

"Say something else and see if I don't come upstairs and hold your butt accountable for your smart mouth!" Lisa yelled after her.

"Why are you always threatening that girl?"

"Mama, don't start with me. I'm not in the mood." Lisa slumped into Chanelle's chair and began rubbing her aching feet.

"Don't you think you were a little harsh?"

"No, I don't."

"She's almost grown. When are you going to start cutting her some slack?"

"You don't seem to think Chanelle should get in trouble for anything. You're always taking up for her and making excuses when she's wrong."

"*I am not*," Hattie said defiantly, gathering all the UNO cards. "I see things from a different perspective and I'm trying to get you to understand that every offense doesn't necessarily deserve punishment."

"Living in this house it does; especially when lying is involved."

"Fine, Lisa. I've said all I have to say. No one can tell you anything. I raised two children already, but apparently you know more than I do, so I'll just leave you be. But, if it were my child—"

"Chanelle's not your child; that's the whole point! The sooner you realize that *I'm* her mother and *you're* her grandmother, the better off we'll all be."

"What's that supposed to mean?"

"I'm just saying, Mama. You need to let me raise her, even if you don't agree with the decisions I make. Whether I'm right or wrong, Chanelle needs to obey me. It'll be much easier for her to do so without you always undermining my authority."

"So are you saying that I somehow contributed to her going out and getting drunk Saturday night?"

"No. Chanelle is no angel, but things have never been this bad.

Things seemed to have gotten worse since you moved up here."

Her mother stood up with her hand on her hip, cocked her head to the side and looked at her like she was crazy. "Let's remember that you are the one who begged me to move up here. I had a home and was just fine with my living arrangements."

Lisa stood as well. "For the record, I asked, not begged you to move here with me. Excuse me for caring about you getting beat up all the time."

She watched as her mother's cheeks burned with fire. Lisa didn't really want to go there, but how dare her mother be so ungrateful!

"Make no mistake about it… I'm a grown woman. I didn't need you to look after me. I could've handled your father by myself."

Lisa ignored her conscience telling her to defuse the situation by walking away. "Yeah, you could handle him all right. That's why I kept getting three a.m. phone calls every time he blackened your eye."

Her mother's glare deepened. "I didn't have to move here. I chose to."

Seeing the tears in her mother's eyes, remorse began to overshadow Lisa's anger. "Mama, I'm sorry for what I said." Though Lisa had softened her tone and resumed her seat, her mother hadn't changed her stance at all. "I merely want peace in my home…I want to be able to discipline my daughter without having to explain myself all the time. I'm sure you don't like this tension between us any more than I do."

"I appreciate you letting me stay here, but don't think I'm dependent on you. In case you have forgotten, I'm moving out at the end of this month. If that's not soon enough for you, I'll find somewhere else to stay until then."

Like Chanelle, Hattie also stormed out of Lisa's presence.

Lisa plopped her head down on the table in despair. It didn't feel good coming home to a hostile household. She had to find some way of getting out of this dinner date with Eric next Monday. There was no way she could invite him into her home with so much chaos brewing.

RJ said good night to the Burlingtons, got himself a bottle of water and headed off to the guest bedroom that had served as his quarters since his transition to Columbus four months ago. RJ was speechless when Pastor Burlington called and offered him the director's position at Hope Ministries Rehabilitation Center. At the time RJ was living in a poor, run-down apartment building in Baltimore working whatever odds and ends jobs he could find. Grateful that the Lord had delivered him from those issues that led to the death of his marriage, he was also living with a huge hole in his heart because of the loss of his family. He jumped at the opportunity Pastor Burlington presented to him. Not only did moving to Columbus allow him a chance to be closer to Lisa and Chanelle, but it also provided him with a decent salary and stable employment. Since he and Lisa had first separated, he'd been struggling to find both.

RJ had originally planned to have his own place by now, but the Burlingtons repeatedly told him that he was welcome to stay indefinitely. Having never had children of their own, it seemed like they really enjoyed his company. He extended his plan to leave within a few months and resolved to stay a year, or two at the max, and use this time to save up. If things went well, hopefully he'd be able to buy his own home. He definitely needed to rebuild his credit. He'd recently purchased a used vehicle, on which he was paying a very high interest rate. Initially the Burlingtons absolutely refused to accept any money from him, but RJ wasn't in the business of freeloading and insisted on sharing the household financial responsibilities. Pastor Burlington was like a father figure to him and RJ thanked the Lord for allowing Pastor Burlington to trust him with such an influential position, despite all of his past mistakes.

RJ lay in bed, slowly drifting to sleep, when a call from his brother on his cell phone brought him to full alertness.

"I'm sorry, did I wake you?" David asked.

"Not really...I was sort of going in and out."

"I'm sorry, man. I hadn't talked to you in a couple weeks and wanted to check on you. How are things going at the center?"

"Things are good. We have about three more weeks before the residents move in. I'm looking forward to it, too. Of all people, who'd ever thought that I would be the director of a center that counsels former drug addicts?" RJ chuckled slightly.

"It just goes to show the power of God and how He can promote us despite anything we've done in the past."

"Let me guess...you're giving me a summary of the sermon you preached yesterday, huh?"

"Naw, bruh...simply testifying about God's goodness."

"You know you fill the shoes of our father very well?" RJ and his brother grew up under the preaching of their father, the late Robert James Hampton, Sr. As the older of the two brothers and their father's namesake, RJ had originally taken over as pastor when their father passed away because that's what he'd always been expected to do. After the mess he'd gotten himself into in Baltimore, no one could argue that David was the one truly called to the preaching ministry.

"Dad had some pretty big feet. It may take me a long time to fill his shoes...if ever. I'm just taking it one day at a time."

"Well, you're doing a great job; I'm proud of you and Dad would be, too."

"Thanks, man."

"Are you coming to Baltimore for Memorial Day?"

"Naw…I'm supposed to help Lisa's mom move that weekend, but I'll see you the week after that because y'all are coming for Chanelle's graduation party, right?"

"You know it. Sheila and I are going to drive up that morning. How are Lisa and Chanelle doing?"

"Man, Chanelle is getting way out of line. Would you believe that she skipped curfew Saturday night and was brought home drunk by the police?"

"My goodness…"

"I went over yesterday after church and got on her. She didn't really say much to me, but apparently she's been getting real smart with Lisa. Since she is supposed to be looking for a summer job, I'm going to talk to her about some temporary positions available at the center. I figured it would give the two of us a chance to spend some time together since she'd be working primarily with me. Lisa was cool with the idea. I'm waiting for Chanelle to be in a better mood before I bring it up to her. She's on punishment for a while and I'm standing behind Lisa one-hundred percent."

"Sounds like things are going pretty good between you and Lisa."

"I wish…She doesn't hold long conversations with me. I'm surprised she shared the things she did. She was at her wits' end this weekend because her mother gave her some grief about punishing Chanelle. I'm glad that I'm here to give her some support. I only wish…never mind."

"You might as well say it now."

"I wish she would consider giving us another try."

"Give it some time."

"Man, I've been up here for four months and yesterday was only the third time I've set foot in Lisa's house. She's not trying to be around me."

"Keep standing in faith, bruh. We know God made a way for you to move to Ohio. You've done your part; now leave the rest up to Him."

"Seeing my girls after all this time makes me want my family back even more. I miss them, but now isn't the time to approach Lisa about reconciling. It's been five years since the divorce and she hates me as much now as she did then."

"I'm sure she doesn't hate you…strongly dislike, maybe." He tried to lighten the mood. "Seriously though, she doesn't hate you, she hates what you did. There is a difference."

"I hate what I did, too," he said, solemnly.

"Look, man, don't go getting all depressed on me. Before you left you were on cloud nine saying how you felt God was about to fix everything you'd messed up. What happened to all that faith?"

"It's still there…for the most part. I wish I could get a little glimpse of Lisa showing interest."

"Faith is the substance of things hoped for and the evidence of things not seen. You have to believe before you see; otherwise it's not faith."

"Yeah, I know…Listen, man, thanks for calling, but I'm going to get off this phone and call it a night."

"Yeah, I better get going as well. I'm leaving tomorrow after-noon to go preach a three-day revival in Missouri and I still have some things to get together."

"All right. Take it easy and have a safe trip."

CHAPTER 7

A Whole 'Nother Story

By Thursday morning, Callie had finally worked up the nerve to do it. She was going to take Bryan's advice and tell Lisa all that had recently come to light. The turning point came yesterday during her weekly session with Dr. Samuels, her therapist, who had suggested that she still attend Chanelle's graduation party next month. Dr. Samuels encouraged her to continue moving forward with life rather than allowing her circumstances to become an automatic death sentence. Unlike Bryan, Dr. Samuels didn't think full disclosure was necessary, but he said if Callie was ready, it wouldn't hurt to have the support of additional loved ones. Callie didn't know if she'd necessarily use the word "ready," but with such a heavy burden on her heart she had to do something.

Callie had yet to return any calls she'd received from church members concerned that they hadn't seen or heard from her in a while. Though she appreciated their sentiments, she wasn't ready to face them. No Bible-reading, tongue-speaking, Holy Ghost-filled, running-all-around-the-church, fire-baptized Christian was going to get her out of this one, so she didn't see a need to get her church family involved. No matter how many times she and

Lisa bumped heads, they were sisters—by blood. That had to count for something.

Callie decided to call her sister immediately instead of waiting until the evening as she had originally planned. With so much anxiety building up inside of her, she didn't think there'd be any peace until she got this over with. Plus, given any extra amount of time, she was sure to find a way to talk herself out of it. Though it was only a little after four in the morning California time, Ohio's time was three hours ahead and Callie knew her sister would be up. Ready or not, she was going to make the call.

"You're up awfully early!" Lisa wasted no time answering her cell.

"Yeah...I couldn't sleep much. Do you have a minute? I'd like to talk to you about something."

"Yeah, go ahead. I'm just on my way to work. I hope you're not calling about the graduation party. I know by now I should have all the details together, but I don't."

"That wasn't exactly the reason why I was calling."

"Good, because I still have so much to do. I haven't been motivated lately. Both Chanelle and Mama are driving me crazy. Chanelle is on lockdown until graduation because she was brought home drunk by the police Saturday night. Then, earlier this week, Mama and I got into it because she doesn't agree with the way I handled the situation. Now she's mad at me, too."

"I'm sorry you're having such a hard time. What I—"

"Girl, I feel like I'm about to lose my mind. Mama always has something to say every time I discipline Chanelle. It gets on my nerves. Neither of them has said more than three words to me since Monday night."

"Well, Mama's moving out soon. I'm sure things will get a lot easier for you then."

"I hope so…Even then that will only solve one of my problems. Chanelle is a whole 'nother story. No matter what I do, her behavior doesn't seem to be getting any better. I took away her cell phone thinking that might do it, but I broke down and gave it back to her last night. Not that she really deserved it. Odds are she's going to make some unauthorized calls. I guess it was my way of calling a truce because I'm tired of being perceived as the mean one all the time."

"I've told you before what her problem is. She's acting out because of the divorce. As I've suggested many times, you should let her talk with a therapist." Callie found herself getting irritated. She called to unload her burdens. It wasn't supposed be the other way around. This conversation was so typical of Lisa. Her problems and life situations always seemed much more significant than anyone else's.

"Chanelle's not crazy; she's rebellious. If she wants to discuss something, I'm here. And anyhow, RJ has been in town now for a few months. At least Chanelle gets to see and talk to him more now than she has in years. There's nothing I can or want to do about divorcing RJ. She doesn't need therapy. She's simply going to have to get over it."

"There may be feelings that she's uncomfortable sharing with you. Children don't just get over divorce. It's not like there weren't any traumatic events that took place. Chanelle was there the night you and RJ got arrested; duh…I'm sure that's still branded in her mind."

"It's branded in mine, too," Lisa replied in a dignified manner.

"If it's still affecting you—an adult—consider the effect it's having on Chanelle. You're apparently too self-absorbed to realize that."

Callie heard the deep sigh her sister took on the other end. She took a couple of needed deep breaths herself because she was beyond fed up with this ridiculous conversation and really wanted to reach through the phone and grab Lisa by the neck.

Finally, Lisa said, "Let's drop this because it's leading nowhere but into an argument. My point is simply that the past is the past. Chanelle doesn't need counseling. RJ's in Columbus now and we're making the best of our situation. Besides him trying to find ways to be around me unnecessarily, things have been fairly good. If I had to choose between living with him and living with Mama, I'd almost be tempted to choose him. At least he doesn't—"

When Callie realized that she and Lisa had been disconnected, she was almost relieved. She made a mental note to tell Bryan—and Dr. Samuels—that their advice stunk! Lisa was obviously too engulfed in her own world to be prepared for the bombshell Callie had to deliver. This was a sign that Callie needed to keep her mouth shut.

"I'm sorry; my cell phone dropped the call when I pulled into the parking garage," Lisa explained when she called back several minutes later. "I didn't want you to think I'd purposely hung up on you."

"That's fine." Callie could not have cared less one way or the other.

"Well, I'm just getting to my office, so I better get to work... Oh, what did you want to talk to me about?"

"Nothing big; I'm not going to make it to Chanelle's graduation party."

"*Why!*"

"I'm teaching a three-week seminar."

"And? The party is on a Saturday."

"So is the class."

"Since when did you start being mandated to teach on the

weekends? To my knowledge, you've never had to do that before."

"Yeah…well sometimes things change."

"Whatever…Everyone was expecting you. Mama and Chanelle will be disappointed. You can be the one to tell them you're bailing out." Lisa made no attempt to camouflage her attitude.

"Fine! It's not like I can really count on you for anything anyway." They were disconnected again, this time courtesy of Callie.

CHAPTER 8
Super Holy

Unlike last Saturday when she'd taken it easy, Lisa had been on the go since waking up this morning. She went to the grocery store, dry cleaners, post office and then rode with Olivia to Indiana and spent the day at Metamora. Metamora was a historic town built in the 1800s about three hours from Columbus. It made a nice getaway spot, being rich in history, antiques, gift shops and more. There was also a canal that ran through the center of town and an old train ride, both of which Lisa always enjoyed. Her mother and Chanelle had been invited to come. Considering the tension between them, Lisa's feelings weren't hurt when her mother, who really didn't care for Olivia anyway, declined, and when Chanelle chose to help RJ get things together at the center.

As usual, whenever they spent time together, Lisa and Olivia enjoyed themselves tremendously. They ate more junk food than should have been allowed by law and, at times, laughed so much that they cried. It was a little after eight when Liv dropped her off at home. Now, an hour later, she was sprawled on the couch going over the list of people who had RSVP'd for Chanelle's graduation party a few weeks away. She twirled the one invitation in her hand that she'd been hesitant to mail, wondering whether or not she should invite her father.

When Lisa first began planning the party, she had initially determined that her father would not be welcomed. Not only was she concerned about how her mother would feel since she had left him, but Lisa also didn't care to see him herself. However, her mother encouraged her to keep in mind that the party was to honor Chanelle's accomplishments and that they both needed to set their personal feelings aside.

"Mama, are you sure you won't mind if Daddy comes?" Lisa had inquired.

"Chile, I ain't studin' your father. It doesn't make me any difference one way or the other. You know he likes to showboat. If, for no other reason, I'd say invite him so Chanelle can get a couple of hundred out of him."

No matter how Lisa felt about her father, he was crazy about his only granddaughter and prior to last summer, Chanelle was head over heels for her "Papa," too. It wasn't until she rode with Lisa in the middle of the night to the University of Maryland Hospital in Baltimore that Chanelle had began to show any signs of withdrawal from him. Her face no longer lit up whenever his name was brought into a conversation. It was also the night that Lisa realized how much she hated her father after seeing the extent of physical damage done to her mother.

Hattie had been admitted with severe injuries. Lisa's father had always been abusive, leaving a bruise here or a mark there, but hospitalization had never been necessary and Chanelle had always been spared from knowing the truth, thanks to the bogus stories Lisa or her mother would make up to explain why Hattie was "visiting" them for a few days. Considering that Lisa only lived about fifteen minutes away from her mother at the time, she was certain that their stories sounded quite peculiar.

Nevertheless, Chanelle never displayed any signs that she didn't believe their tales. But last summer, when Lisa raced across the Interstate from Columbus to Baltimore, she used very decorative words to let Chanelle know that her grandfather was, and had always been, a monster. Even now, if Lisa pondered that night too long, animosity would ooze through her pores. Despite her personal feelings, Lisa decided she would send her father's invitation first thing Monday morning for the sake of doing the right thing. With any luck, he wouldn't show.

To Lisa's knowledge, Callie had yet to call and tell their mother and Chanelle that she wouldn't make it. The two of them hadn't spoken since Thursday. Right or wrong, Lisa hadn't lost sleep over their spat. Callie had better make that call because if either their mother or Chanelle asked her why Callie backed out of the trip, she planned to say that Callie simply didn't want to come because that's exactly what it sounded like to her!

A little later, Lisa welcomed the interruption from Eric when he called to see how her day went and to say—for the umpteenth time—how he was looking forward to having dinner with her family on Monday. They met yesterday for lunch and Eric was beaming with excitement, but Lisa still wasn't crazy about the idea of him coming over. There was never a window of opportunity for her to cancel, so she was going along with the plan, praying that all would go well.

As if on cue, the second she hung up the phone with Eric, her mother came in singing, *"What a mighty God we serve..."*

"Hey, Mama. What's got you in such good spirits?"

"Girl, I'll tell you in a minute. First, I need to say something."

Lisa sat up straight on the couch to make room for her mother. "Is everything okay?"

"Yes, honey, everything is fine, except for the fact that I owe you an apology. I'm sorry for barely speaking to you this whole week. I know better than that. My behavior was uncalled for. I want you to understand, I may have had my own opinions of what you should do with Chanelle, but I was never really mad at you for grounding her. I was thinking about how soon it's going to be before I move. I guess I was getting a little scared and taking it out on you."

"Scared about what, Mama?"

"I've lived in Baltimore all my life. I made a big deal about you asking me to move here with you, but the truth is: I needed to make this move. I've wanted to get away from your father for a long time; I just never had the courage to do it. I was emotionally dependent on him. No matter how much he was out runnin' the streets, he still handled business at home. I went straight from living with my parents to living with him and then here with you. I've never been on my own before. Part of me is scared. I wonder if I'll be able to make it by myself."

Lisa, filled with sympathy, said, "If you don't want to move out, you don't have to."

Her mother chuckled lightly. "You're only saying that because I already gave those people my deposit."

Lisa felt that she'd been sincere, but psychologically, could there be some truth to her mother's accusations?

"I do want to get my own place. I'm just saying that it will be an adjustment for me, but maybe it's time for me to move into this next phase of my life. I am concerned about the city's crime rate, though. Every time I look at the news there's always something negative going on."

"But it wasn't any different in Baltimore. In fact, crime was worse there."

"I know, but Baltimore was my home. I knew which neighborhoods were safe and which ones to avoid. I'm still learning this city. I'm glad that my place isn't too far from here."

"Are you sure you're ready for this?"

"Yes, I'm sure. Thanks, Lisa."

"For what?"

"For putting up with me this past week. I should've told you what was going on in my head instead of copping an attitude."

"It's okay. I understand. Speaking of attitudes, I've had a change of my own...I am going to send Daddy an invitation to Chanelle's graduation party."

"Good for you, baby. That's the mature thing to do. Don't worry about me. I'll be all right. Will you?"

Lisa gave a reassuring nod as her mother leaned over for a hug. "By the way, do you have any plans Monday evening?"

"No. Why, what's up?"

"I have a friend coming over for dinner that would like to meet you. He's a minister at my church."

"*He...*" Lisa pretended not to notice her mother's suspicious look. "Does Chanelle know him?"

"Yes and no. She knows him from church, but she doesn't know we're friends."

"Things must be pretty serious between you and this fellah if you're bringing him home, huh?"

"Not as serious as you may think. We're taking things slow."

"Now you know I'm still partial toward RJ, but I realize that I can't make the two of you get back together, so if things work out between you and this minister guy I'll be happy for you."

"Thanks, Mama." Lisa didn't understand why RJ's name was even brought into the conversation. She was irked by the adoration her mother still had for him as if she had forgotten everything he'd put Lisa through. "Are you going to tell me what you were so cheerful about coming in the house?"

Her face lit up and she reached down in her purse and handed Lisa a hundred-dollar bill.

"What's this for?"

"I know you don't need the money, but I thought I'd bless you since I got blessed. Girl, I won a thousand dollars on a scratch-off today."

"Thanks, but no thanks." Lisa gave the money back. "I don't consider winning the lottery a blessing."

"Have it your way. I should've known you'd get all super holy on me." Her mother puckered her lips and shoved the money back in her pocketbook. "You're crazy for turning down free money. I'm going to pay my tithes on today's winnings and I betcha Pastor Burlington won't give me that back."

"Maybe not, but if he realized where it came from, I'm certain you'd find yourself being the main topic of one of his gambling sermons," Lisa teased.

"Gambling ain't really no sin; especially when you pay tithes on the winnings."

"What scripture you find that in?" She smirked.

"I'm just saying...it's because I've been so faithful in tithing that I win good money. I'm helping the church."

"All good money isn't necessarily God money. That's like a dope dealer saying it's okay to sell drugs as long as he pays tithes."

"No, it isn't. Gambling is a victimless activity, selling drugs isn't."

Lisa rolled her eyes, figuring that after over four decades of her mother "walking with the Lord," she ought not to be making excuses to play the lottery. "Victimless, huh? Tell that to the people who have thousands of dollars in debt thinking they'll hit it big one day."

Her mother began to chuckle. "You know...we could go on about this all night."

Lisa laughed, too. "You're right. How about we just agree to disagree for now..." She knew this wouldn't be the last time they'd discuss this topic. They'd bumped heads about the lottery thing more times than Lisa could count.

"I was going to give Chanelle some money, too. Are you going to have a problem with that?"

"No, go ahead. Just don't tell her where it came from. She's not here, though. She's still with RJ."

"I figured she'd be back by now."

"He didn't have a set time to bring her home. I told him I'd be gone most of the day. Since it's getting late, I guess I could call and tell him I'm here."

"Well, I'm about to go upstairs and go to bed. I'll give Chanelle the money in the morning. Good night…"

"The same to you. Hey…"

"What?" Her mother paused on the bottom step.

"Thanks for asking me before giving the money to Chanelle."

"Girl, I'm tired. I don't feel like arguing any more than you do."

Lisa couldn't help but laugh. If her mother being tired was the only reason they didn't get into it about Chanelle tonight, then thank goodness for fatigue! She quickly dialed RJ's cell. "It's me… I'm calling to let you know I'm home."

"I'm glad you made it safely. Did you have fun?"

"Yeah, we had a great time."

"This um…friend of yours, did he have any trouble finding the place?"

"Not that it's any of your business, but my friend was actually a *she*; and no, she didn't have any problems getting to Metamora. It's not the first time we've been."

RJ sounded somewhat relieved. "Since you seem to be a regular tourist, maybe one day we can ride down there…the two of us and Chanelle, of course. It's been a long time since we've done anything as a family."

The nerve he had to suggest family time made Lisa sick to her stomach. "You have yourself to thank for that. Anyhow, I just wanted to tell you that I'm back. What time are you bringing Chanelle home?"

"Um, baby—"

"You mean, *Lisa*."

He sighed in defeat. "Whatever...I dropped Chanelle off hours ago. She should be there."

"What!" Just as Lisa was digesting RJ's statement, Chanelle walked through the front door. "I have to go. She's here now." Lisa hung up the phone and turned toward her daughter like a lioness ready to attack its prey. "Where have you been?"

CHAPTER 9
W.W.O.D?

After talking to—rather going off on—Chanelle, Lisa found out that she'd snuck out with Kyle once more. This time he had picked her up and they went out to a movie, so Lisa was told. Chanelle's plan was to pretend that she had still been with R.J. Apparently, she had been banking on the lack of communication between her parents and was downright stunned when Lisa confronted her. To Lisa's surprise, instead of copping an attitude, Chanelle had been more cooperative about getting busted for being out with Kyle this time than she had been previously. Any order Lisa barked was immediately fulfilled without question or hesitation. The girl probably knew she was treading on thin ice. Had Lisa not already spent a lot of money planning this graduation party, she would have been tempted to cancel it to prove a point.

"Girl, I don't know what I'm going to do about Chanelle," Lisa confessed to Olivia who had dropped by her office Monday afternoon after coming from her weekly board meeting. "Punishing her is not working. She's graduating in a few weeks and will turn eighteen in August. And on top of that, she'll be living on campus when school starts. Nothing I say or do fazes her because she realizes she'll be moving out soon. I have no idea how to keep her from this boy."

Liv sat across from Lisa's desk as calm as still, blue waters. She'd been listening to Lisa vent for at least forty minutes now and as irritated as Liv was about Chanelle sneaking out with Kyle again, she had yet to break a sweat. Olivia's ability to stay composed under pressure was one of the things Lisa loved about her best friend. Dressed in a pastel green short-sleeved silk shirt, cream dress pants and a pair of open-toe Manolos, Liv was beautiful. At age forty-nine, she didn't look a day over thirty. Her caramel brown skin was wrinkle- and surgery-free.

After patiently listening to Lisa's woes, Liv finally spoke up and said, "You're going to have to take a more drastic approach if you want to keep the little bum out of her life."

"Girl, I'm open to any and all suggestions. Short of ordering a hit, I'm not sure what to do."

"A hit can be arranged if need be." Olivia smiled mischievously, producing a chuckle from Lisa.

"Listen to us talking crazy. This thing with Kyle really has me stressed out if I can start joking about killing folks." Lisa ignored her work phone when it rang and seconds later the familiar number danced across her cell phone. "That's Eric." She sighed. He was calling about their plans that evening. Lisa had informed Chanelle about their expected guest yesterday after church. Though both her mother and daughter were okay with him coming, Lisa still had reservations because she'd never brought a guy home before. "I hate to do this at such short notice, but I'm going to cancel dinner tonight. I'm too stressed."

"Don't do that; canceling your date will not solve this issue with Chanelle and Kyle, but I know something that will. You should speak with Kyle's mother."

"And say what?"

"Anything you want. Just be sure that when you leave, the ghetto chick understands that she better find some way to keep her son away from your daughter or else."

"I don't know about that, Liv; it sounds too much like a threat."

"If no one else hears you threaten her, it didn't happen." She winked. "Seriously, either talk to her or allow this entire thing to keep eating away at you."

Lisa toyed with the idea in her head. "It'll be like pulling teeth to get the number from Chanelle. I guess I could sneak and get it out of her cell phone. I'll give his mom a call later this week."

"Forget about calling. You remember where he lives, don't you?"

Lisa nodded affirmatively. The night the police officer took her to get her car, he'd pointed out the house where Chanelle had been picked up. The picture of the Section-8 complex was branded in her mind like pornographic images on a computer's hard drive.

"Then go talk to her. And don't wait until later this week. Do it as soon as you get off of work so you can get it over with. Shoot, girl, leave now."

"I can't possibly go today. I need to get home because Eric's coming over tonight; and leaving now is not an option. With Megan out of the office, I'm pretty much holding down the fort on my own."

"Yeah, and it's really in danger of falling, right? That's why we've been sitting here talking for an hour and the fort is still intact. Girl, it's only three o'clock. You have plenty of time to go confront the chick and get home in time for dinner."

"What if she's not home? Most people work during the day, you know?"

"What if she is? You'll never know until you knock on the door. What's the real reason you're hesitant to talk to her?"

"I don't know; I want to think more about what to say. I'm worried that interfering may escalate Chanelle's interest in him."

"Not if you're persuasive enough, it won't. Girl, remember... Kyle's ghetto mama doesn't have anything on you. I really shouldn't be calling her names when I don't know her, but real mothers don't allow their teenage sons to have parties where underage kids get drunk. Kids will be kids, but no matter what they do, we must look out for their best interests. Justin has not been perfect. The bottom line is that when he was in trouble, there was nothing Isaac and I didn't do to help him. A mother will do anything to protect her child. Chanelle hangin' with this thug is trouble. Now, do whatever you have to do to keep her safe."

Olivia's pep talk had encouraged Lisa quite a bit. Leaving work about a quarter after three, she took a deep breath and knocked on the screen door. The neighborhood was infested with trashy streets and boarded homes. The environment wasn't completely foreign to Lisa. She and RJ used to venture into high-risk areas such as this in Baltimore during their evangelistic missions. Truth-be-told, this neighborhood seemed mild compared to some of their ministry spots. Still, how anyone could live under such conditions was a mystery. Lisa used to be sympathetic to these kinds of people until the night she was arrested and accused of being one of them.

Still standing at the door, Lisa knocked harder this time. She hated coming over unannounced, but Liv was right—she had to nip this in the bud face-to-face. Considering the circumstances, the element of surprise was best.

Suddenly the door opened, and to Lisa's surprise, a young heavyset white woman with dusty blonde hair and several tattoos appeared, holding an infant baby girl on her hip. "Can I help you?" she asked suspiciously.

"Is this the home of Kyle Lewis? I need to speak with his mother."

"I'm Kyle's mother. Who are you?"

"*You're* Kyle's mother?" Lisa couldn't believe that she'd heard the lady correctly. She looked too young to have a seventeen-year-old son.

"That's what I said; who are you?"

"Um…I'm Lisa Hampton."

"*Hampton* as in Chanelle Hampton?"

"Yes. I'm her mother."

"Oh, wow." She smiled brightly, opening the screen door latch. "Please forgive my rudeness. Most people who come by here aren't dressed as nicely as you are, so I didn't know what to think. My first thought was that maybe you were a social worker or something. Anyhow, I'm sorry. Please, come in! Excuse the mess. We need to be out of here by the end of the month and, as you can see, I have tons of things to pack still."

"Don't worry about it," Lisa said politely, but the filthy carpet, cluttered boxes, and dusty furniture were enough to make anyone feel uneasy. The smell of smoked cigarettes didn't help either.

"I'm Stacie. It's so nice to meet you." She extended her hand and Lisa faked a smile to shake it. "Let me move some of these clothes out the way so you can sit down." When Stacie set the baby on the floor so she could free her hands to make room on the couch, Lisa shuddered. The dingy carpet wasn't fit for a cockroach—though she'd bet there was a cluster of them living there. "The least I can do is make you feel at home while you're here."

Stacie could try all she wanted to make Lisa feel "at home," but it wasn't going to happen! As soon as Lisa's bottom was introduced to the sofa, it screamed for relief from the uncomfortable springs. "I'm sorry for dropping by like this; I wanted to speak with you about Chanelle and Kyle."

"No—No!" Stacie said to the baby girl who began pulling more junk out of the boxes. "Excuse me for just a second.... Jameela!" she yelled. "Come get Nia. I have company."

"Company" was a funny word for her to use. Lisa felt too uncomfortable in this pigsty to be considered as such.

"Sorry to interrupt you like that. I should've known better than to think she would stay out of things." A young, biracial girl came into the room and got the baby. She didn't bother making eye contact or acknowledging Lisa, which further proved Olivia's point that this woman was ghetto. A decent mother would raise her children to be respectful and to speak to adults, especially when in the comfort of their own home. "It's such a pleasure to meet you. I've been telling Chanelle for months now that we should get together. She's been such a positive influence on Kyle. I can tell she comes from a real good home."

That little liar told me she met Kyle a few weeks ago! Lisa thought to herself.

"I love your daughter like she's one of my own."

"Umhmm...Lately Chanelle has been doing some things I don't approve of."

"If you're referring to the party, I'm so sorry she got caught up with that. I hope she didn't get in too much trouble. I'd told Kyle he could have a few friends over. He grew up in this neighborhood, so it's going to be hard for him leaving his friends and all. I didn't think things would get out of control like they did."

"Since when does allowing your teenage son to have a party where there will be alcohol be considered keeping things under control? What parent would do such a thing?"

"I didn't allow Kyle to have alcohol," she said defensively. "Like I said, I told him he could have a few friends over. I had no idea things would go as far as they did and I'm very sorry Chanelle was here."

Stacie's sincerity didn't dissuade Lisa's anger. "And were you the one supervising this party?"

"There was no one supervising the party because there wasn't supposed to be a party. I was at work. I work third shift."

"So you were going to allow your teenage son to be alone with my teenage daughter while you were at work?"

"Normally I don't work weekends, but since we're getting ready to move, every penny counts. Kyle is usually very responsible. I leave him here all the time with the kids. This is the first and only time he's disappointed me."

Lisa was unable to prevent curiosity from getting the best of her. "All of what kids? How many children do you have?"

"Five; four boys and a girl. Kyle's my oldest."

"You mean two girls?" Lisa was willing to bet there were at least four different baby daddies in the mix. Olivia was *so* right! This chick was beyond ghetto and definitely not the kind of person she wanted her daughter socializing with.

"No, I said what I meant. I know how many children I have."

"What about the baby?"

"Who, Nia? That's my granddaughter."

Lisa was sure her expression gave away her shock. "Chanelle has never told me much about Kyle, and now I understand why. I strongly disapprove of her dating anyone with children. My daughter has a lot going for her and I don't want her taking on adult responsibilities that she's not able to handle."

"I understand your concern, but Kyle doesn't have any kids. Nia is Jameela's daughter."

Lisa fought hard to keep her jaw from dropping to the floor. "You mean that little girl who came down the stairs?"

"Forgive me if I seem rude, but what does my daughter's child have to do with the party last weekend?"

Just then the front door opened. "Hey, what's u—" A young, slender, bi-racial boy came in dribbling a basketball. His sentence was left dangling once he looked at Lisa.

"Kyle, where have you been? You got out of school an hour ago and I told you to come straight home."

Lisa eyed him up and down. His pants rested well below his hips and she could clearly see that he was wearing white boxer shorts. His cornrows peeked from underneath his doo-rag. What in the world did Chanelle see in him?

"My bad....stopped over Stick's for a minute to shoot some hoops."

Stacie sucked her teeth. "Do you know Lisa, Chanelle's mother?"

"Um...hi!" He avoided any real eye contact.

"Hello," Lisa forced herself to say.

"Uh...Stacie, I forgot my bag at Stick's. I'll be back in a few."

"Okay, but don't stay gone too long. We need your help around here."

"Ahiight." He scooted out the door just as fast as he'd come in.

"Do all of your kids call you by your first name?" Lisa asked in disbelief.

"Yeah, why?"

"Let me get to the point of why I'm here."

The words "please do" seemed to be painted all over Stacie's expression.

"I'm sure your son is a very decent young man...It'll be best for him to stay away from Chanelle. She starts college in the fall and needs to focus more on preparing for school and less on boys. She doesn't need to be entangled in any relationship right now."

"Why don't you just come out and say what's really on your mind?"

"Truth is....Chanelle already has a boyfriend. As a matter of fact, she's dating Justin Scott, the starting running back for Ohio State." She couldn't blame that lie on Olivia's advice. She'd blurted it out all on her own. She'd pray and ask Jesus to forgive her in a minute. Right now the lie seemed a necessary evil.

"It's funny that you don't mind her dating this Justin dude, but she can't date Kyle. You know...I've been trying to be cool and all because you're Chanelle's mom, but I get what you're saying. You don't think Kyle is good enough for Chanelle, do you?"

"No, that's not what I'm saying at all!" That was an ever bigger lie than the first one she had told! "It's just that Chanelle's behavior has gotten progressively worse recently, and her coming home drunk was the final straw." Somehow the tables had turned and Lisa found herself on the defensive.

"Let's get one thing straight," Stacie said with more swerve in her neck than Lisa had ever seen from a white girl. Finding herself even uneasier, she fiddled with her necklace. "My son did not make Chanelle get drunk."

"I'm not saying he did. All I'm trying to say is that—"

"I heard you loud and clear. No need to explain yourself again. I'll tell Kyle that he needs to stay away from Chanelle. Now, if you'll excuse me, I have a lot of stuff to do yet, and I'd greatly appreciate it if you'd get up out of here." Her eyes glared with fire and Lisa could tell that she'd practiced great restraint not to swear at her.

"Stacie, wait—"

"Good-bye!"

Without further hesitation, Lisa got up and walked out. Her mission to permanently remove Kyle from Chanelle's life had been accomplished, but she felt horrible. W.W.O.D— what would Olivia do right now? Lisa wondered if she should go back in and apologize. Liv would most likely tell Lisa to "shake it off" and keep moving. Despite the nudging guilt of having hurt Stacie's feelings, Lisa did exactly that. Besides, she didn't have time for drama. She had a guest coming for dinner.

CHAPTER 10
A Step Further

Lisa called and updated Liv immediately upon leaving Stacie's house, disclosing everything except that their children were now supposedly dating. Despite the twinge of guilt she had previously felt, by the time Lisa got home she was feeling much better. It was a little shy of five when she walked in and found a note from her mother on the dry-erase board: *Went to pay on my furniture. Chanelle's with me. We'll be back well before your minister friend gets here. Love, Mama.*

Lisa quickly jumped in the shower before preparing dinner. She began getting more excited about this evening and now appreciated Eric's insistence. At thirty-eight, it was ludicrous that she had been sneaking around with him like they were engaged in some type of forbidden affair. It was about time things were out and in the open.

Her mother and daughter got home around six. Chanelle came in and kissed her on the cheek and then ran upstairs to finish her homework. About an hour later, the ringing doorbell announced Eric's arrival. It was as if Eric was peeking through the kitchen window and waited until the oven timer went off because he and the homemade lasagna were in sync; and the freshly made salad was crisp and ready. Lisa hurried to greet him, yelling to her mother and daughter to come down.

"Mmm...something smells good..." he said, stepping into the house and gently kissing her cheek, stirring up a surprise tingling sensation within her.

"I brought something." He handed her a plastic grocery bag. "Since you're providing dinner, I figured the least I could do was bring dessert."

"Thank you. I was so focused on the meal that I didn't even think about anything sweet." She opened the bag and saw a red velvet cake and a box of peanut brittle. "Um...thanks."

"What's wrong?" He obviously noticed her hesitation.

"I can eat the cake, but FYI, I'm allergic to peanuts. If I eat the peanut brittle, I'll get a serious case of hives that'll send me into a tailspin."

"Oh gosh, I'm so sorry!"

"There's nothing for you to be sorry about. You didn't know. Besides, I'm sure my mother and daughter will eat it."

"Eat what?" Her mother strolled into the living room. Lisa explained the situation while she reached out to shake Eric's hand.

"Mama, this is my friend, Eric; Eric meet my mother, Hattie Davis."

"Hi, Minister, nice to meet you."

"Please...call me Eric. Nice to meet you as well."

"Mama, is Chanelle on her way down?"

"When I poked my head in her room to make sure she'd heard you, she was on her cell phone. She should be down in a minute."

Technically still on punishment, Chanelle was only supposed to use her cell phone for emergency calls, but Lisa had stopped giving her grief about it. Within seconds of her mother speaking, Chanelle descended into the living room.

"Hi, Chanelle." Eric smiled and extended his hand. "I've seen you at church many times, but I don't think we've ever been formally introduced. I'm—"

"I know who you are," she said rudely, smacking her lips and trudging into the kitchen.

Had Chanelle waited to see the fierce look her mother gave her, she probably would've dropped dead from its intensity. Even Lisa's mother seemed surprised by Chanelle's reaction. Lisa turned to Eric to apologize, but without her even saying a word, he said, "It's okay. Give her time to warm up to me."

Unfortunately, Chanelle remained cold and distant during dinner. Lisa wondered if perhaps Chanelle wasn't as receptive of her relationship with Eric as she had thought. Even still, Lisa could not take the brash responses, unnecessary sighing, and eye rolling any longer. "Chanelle, may I have a word with you in the living room?"

"For what? Am I embarrassing you?"

"Yes, you are."

"Good. Now you know how it feels. At least I'm not gonna go to his mama behind your back and tell lies about you. I just spoke to Kyle. Stacie told him everything you said."

Lisa burned with anger. "First of all, I don't care what her children call her, but when you're in my presence, you will put a 'miss' in front of her name."

Chanelle rolled her eyes. "You're so old-fashioned."

"Yeah, well, you ought to be thankful for that; otherwise you could end up pregnant and with a baby like Kyle's sister."

"Just because Jameela has a baby doesn't mean that Miss Stacie is a bad mother. I don't know why you think you're so much better than her."

Eric and Lisa's mother looked liked clueless spectators. Lisa didn't want this banter to continue in front of Eric, but she couldn't stop Chanelle from pulling her in. "No one said that I was better than her. I just know that it's wise to watch the type of company you keep rather than hanging around with any and everyone. And for the record, young lady, I don't have to explain anything to you. In case you've forgotten, *I'm* the mother, *you're* the child. You're not supposed to be talking to Kyle anyhow. Stacie had no business telling her child the details of our adult conversation. I did what I needed to in order to protect you."

"Protect me from what?" Chanelle screamed.

Lisa stood up from the table and glared at her daughter. "That's enough! We're not going to discuss this right now."

"You act like Kyle is some type of criminal or something."

"One day when you have kids of your own, you'll understand what it means to only want what's the best for them."

"Yeah, well, I'll be real and give people chances. I won't write them off the list just because they don't live in the suburbs and make millions of dollars. You act all high and mighty and get on me because I lied to you, but you're no better. You obviously didn't have a problem lying today. I can't wait 'til I move out of this house! You're such a hypocrite!" Before Lisa could fully comprehend the fierceness of Chanelle's words, her daughter had spun out of the kitchen and up the stairs.

Lisa stormed after her, but then stood at the bottom of the stairs powerless. Both her mother and Eric were right behind her. Part of her wanted to go knock the snot out of Chanelle, but it wasn't necessarily for being disrespectful as much as it was for embarrassing her in front of her guest.

"I'll go talk to her," Lisa's mother said calmly. "Eric, in case I don't make it back down, it was a pleasure meeting you."

Feeling in despair, Lisa walked to the sofa and collapsed. "I'm so sorry about this." Tears colored her voice. "Having you come over tonight was a bad idea. I should've known that there would be too much tension in this house."

"It's okay, Lisa." He came and sat next to her and gently grabbed her hand. "I'm here if you want to talk about it."

"There is so much drama going on, I wouldn't know where to start."

"How about with what just happened?"

Lisa explained the whole situation that began last weekend with Chanelle coming home drunk, sneaking out again this past weekend, and the visit she made to Kyle's mother's this afternoon after work. Lisa wasn't sure if it was her level of comfort or level of discouragement that prompted her to confide in Eric, but she left no stone unturned in telling her story, disclosing even her own little white lie about saying Chanelle and Justin were dating.

"Lisa, I have to be honest with you…it sounds like you're so busy trying to handle this thing yourself that God hasn't been able to work because you've been in His way."

Had such a comment come from her mother, Lisa would've instinctively taken offense. But, she could tell from the soft look in Eric's eyes that he didn't mean any harm. The way he caressed her hand confirmed his gentle nature. "Do you think I was wrong by going to his house?"

"Not necessarily….I think some of the things you said were wrong—and manipulative. As a mother, you have a right to tell Chanelle that she can't see that boy. You even had a right to share your concerns with his mother, but you have an obligation to turn Chanelle over to God. I can guarantee that if you continuously tell her that you don't like him, it'll draw her closer to him. Stop telling her how much you dislike him. She clearly knows by now. Start praying about the relationship and trust that God will either open her eyes or give you a different view of things."

Eric was doing alright until he said that last part. "I can't see myself changing my mind about this boy," Lisa snarled.

"Maybe he's simply a product of his environment. People don't have the same opportunities in life. You can't expect him or his mother to have the same morals and values that you have if they've never been exposed to them."

"Whatever the case may be, he's a bad influence on Chanelle."

"Maybe he is. I don't know because I've never met him. What I do know is that Chanelle did have a choice. She didn't have to drink. The problem is not necessarily Kyle. You can sabotage this thing she has with him all you want, but there will be more bad influences that come into her life. If Chanelle doesn't exercise the wisdom she has to make good choices then this is just the tip of the iceberg."

Lisa was forced to admit to herself that Eric had a good point.

"And this Justin character you're trying to hook her up with. Is this the Scotts' son?"

"Yes...It's more wishful thinking than anything else. Olivia's my best friend and I know Justin comes from a good home."

"You can't handpick who Chanelle's going to be with."

"I realize that," Lisa said in defeat. She was starting to wonder if she was imitating her mother, who made no secret how much she still loved Lisa's ex. Lisa cringed at the thought that she made Chanelle feel the same way her mother made her feel every time Hattie brought up RJ's name.

"The Scotts are good people."

"I agree."

"They do so much for the church and the community. To be as wealthy as they are, they are so humble."

"Liv told me that she and Isaac have had issues with Justin. You can never tell. She and Isaac are so close with him. I can't see that type of thing ever happening with Chanelle and me."

"Be careful that you don't speak continual discord into existence. You know the Bible says that there is power of life and death in our tongues."

Lisa smiled. "Yes, sir."

"I don't mean to pry, but how is Chanelle's relationship with her father?"

"As far as I know, things have been great between them. I told you before that he moved here a couple of months ago to head the rehabilitation center that Hope Ministries Church built. Chanelle will be working with him this summer. At first I wasn't crazy about RJ living here, but it's going to work out great for Chanelle. She does need a stable relationship with him. At least the stigma of being his wife and daughter didn't follow us here."

"What do you mean by stigma? Are you ever going to tell me what happened between the two of you?"

Lisa froze in her response and started fiddling with her necklace. Besides Olivia, she hadn't told anyone in Ohio what more than half the residents of Baltimore already knew.

"Something tells me that whatever happened, it was serious enough to still be a sore subject. Does it have anything to do with this?" He reached out and grabbed her necklace charm.

She nodded affirmatively.

"When a woman is referred to as a First Lady, it usually means her husband is in a prominent position. I don't think RJ was any type of politician, so I'm assuming that, in your case, First Lady meant the pastor's wife."

An uncomfortable, warm sensation fell on Lisa and she wondered how she'd let the conversation venture so far into her previous marriage.

"Am I'm right? Was RJ a pastor?"

Again, she nodded in agreement.

"Whatever happened..." Eric would not stop pressing. "... know that it has no bearing on how I feel about you. Just please tell me now if you still have feelings for him so I'll know where things stand."

"No, I don't have feelings for RJ! What would make you think that?"

"I don't know. I guess because you continue to wear the necklace. I'm assuming it's pretty special to you. Is it something he gave you?"

"No. It was a gift the church gave me one year when we celebrated RJ's pastoral anniversary. The necklace does have sentimental value. Not because it reminds me of RJ, but because it reminds me of a time in my life when I felt appreciated, respected and valued; a time that RJ unfairly stripped me of." Before she could stop herself, Lisa began telling Eric about the horrible things that had taken place in her marriage. She didn't realize how much hostility she still held toward her ex until she started reliving the experience. "I moved here to get away from the scandal."

"You have nothing to be ashamed about and I pray that God delivers you from the emotional bondage of everything that has happened to you. You're a beautiful person, Lisa. You don't need this necklace to remind you that you're someone important. From the moment I saw you, I realized there was something special about you and I prayed that God would grant me the opportunity to get to know you better. I am blessed that He granted my petition and if it's okay with you, I would like to go on record stating that I am interested in taking this relationship a step further. Are you okay with that?"

"I'm not sure exactly what you mean…"

Eric got up from the sofa and onto his knee. Immediately, Lisa's heart began palpitating. Could this be what she thought? When Eric pulled a small box from his back pocket, she was no longer uncertain about his motives. "This may seem sort of sudden and I know you're going through some things, but I believe God has put us together for such a time as this. Will you marry me so we can be one in flesh before God?"

"For such a time as this" was a direct quote taken from the book of Esther when her cousin, Mordecai, was trying to encourage her to speak to the king on behalf of all the Jews. It wasn't exactly the wording Lisa would have chosen, but it still brought an overwhelming sensation of joy. "I would be honored to." She fluttered from his approving smile.

Eric flipped open the box and slid a beautiful diamond solitaire onto her finger, causing tears to sprout from her eyes. For the very first time since they'd been "dating" he caressed her lips briefly with his warm, soft ones. The kiss produced a few sparks, but not necessarily fireworks because it was so short.

They spent the rest of the evening in awe, talking and laughing about different things. Neither her mother nor Chanelle came down the remainder of the night. Eric graciously helped Lisa put away the food, load the dishwasher and sample the red velvet cake he had brought for dessert, but the peanut brittle was left untouched.

Eric mentioned that he looked forward to meeting more of Lisa's family members at Chanelle's graduation party. He wasn't intimidated by the fact that RJ would be there at all. Lisa confided in him how upset she had been because her sister wasn't coming. After finding out that Callie's husband had committed suicide last fall, he encouraged Lisa to take it easy on Callie and not to expect too much from her. "It's rough, in general, anytime someone close to us dies. It took my mother years to get over my father's death, and he died from a heart attack. I'm sure it's especially rough on your sister because her husband took his own life."

"I know she had a hard time at first and was seeing a counselor, but she seemed to be doing fine until recently."

"So you say. My guess would be that for whatever reason, she's not really over his death yet. Maybe something has happened to remind her of him...an anniversary, a birthday, anything. She might be dealing with depression. Sometimes depressed people do and say things that don't make sense. Just be patient with her and keep praying for her. I'll pray for her, too."

"You're so right." Lisa felt bad about how she had reacted toward her sister during their last conversation and made up her mind to call Callie the next day. "I'm so glad God has brought you into my life. Your spirit of wisdom and discernment are a blessing."

It was way past eleven o'clock and Eric said he should get going. Before leaving, he said a very encouraging and strengthening prayer about everything they had talked about that evening. "I love you, sweetheart," he said before brushing her lips with a kiss.

Lisa desired a longer encounter, but she allowed him to leave without protest. She shut the door and leaned back as she gazed at her engagement ring with adoration. Any man who could witness such a turbulent explosion, listen to all the junk Lisa had gone through, and *still* want to marry her, was worth keeping!

CHAPTER 11
Something's Not Quite Right

Lisa was so elated about Eric's proposal that she galloped up the stairs two at a time, bumping into her daughter in the hallway as Chanelle came from the bathroom. The rage Lisa had previously felt toward Chanelle remained dormant, thanks to her feelings of euphoria, but Lisa refused to let her daughter's behavior slide by without saying something. "I don't appreciate the little stunt you pulled tonight. These temper tantrums of yours must stop if you know what's good for you."

Chanelle leaned against the wall, folding her arms seemingly unbothered by the subtle threat. "I didn't have a tantrum. I'm tired of you acting like I'm some ten-year-old child. Goodness, I'll be eighteen soon."

"I was going to buy you a car this summer, even after you skipped curfew, because as a mother, I didn't want my baby to have to take the city bus any time you wanted to leave campus. However, since you see fit to remind me that you're almost grown, I'm going to treat you as such. For starters, you can buy your own car this summer and buy your own insurance because that's what grown folk do."

Chanelle squirmed. "What I mean is—"

"No, save your breath." Lisa used her hand to simulate a stop sign. "I heard you loud and clear. By the way, you're no longer on punishment. You may be grown and all, but remember that as long as you abide under *my* roof, you will respect me. As for this issue with Kyle, I'll admit I shouldn't have told Stacie that you were dating Justin. For that, I was wrong and I repent. So, if you want to continue seeing Kyle, go right ahead. I'm not going to interfere anymore because grown folks are allowed to date whomever they please." Lisa smirked as Eric's advice of "staying out of God's way" replayed in her mind.

Suddenly Chanelle's pinched her eyes together into a scowl. "Gee, thanks, but Kyle doesn't want to have anything else to do with me now, thanks to you." She went into her room, loudly slamming the door.

Under different circumstances, Lisa most likely would've said something to Chanelle about slamming a door that *she* paid for, but all she could think was "Hallelujah!" to Kyle not wanting to communicate with her daughter any longer. Maybe this was God's way of working things out!

Once inside her room, Lisa bounced on her bed and gawked again at her sparkling new diamond. Eric's proposal had come unexpectedly. She hadn't realized that he liked her *that* much. She was eager to tell Liv about the proposal. It was ten until midnight. Lisa knew Isaac was still out of town, so she had no qualms about calling their house this late.

Lisa woke Olivia up, but Liv didn't care. She wanted to know everything that happened and Lisa spared no details, including her daughter's embarrassing performance. The two of them talked for nearly an hour until Lisa's mother peeked inside her room.

"Is everything okay? What's all the noise about?"

"Yes, Mama, everything is fine. Sorry for being so loud. Liv,

I'll call you tomorrow. I'm gonna tell Mama now since she's up."

"Tell me what?" Her mother stood in the doorway with curiosity reigning through her eyes.

"Eric proposed to me tonight." She waved her diamond in the air.

"Oh, wow...congratulations." Her enthusiasm seemed forced. "Does Chanelle know?"

"Not yet. I'll tell her tomorrow."

"Umph...just the other day you said y'all were taking things slow. This is sort of sudden, don't you think?"

"No, I don't," she lied. "It may seem sudden to you because you just met Eric tonight. But, God placed Eric and me together for such a time as this." As soon as Lisa said the words, she immediately realized that she hadn't sounded as eloquent as she had hoped. The smirk on her mother's face confirmed her thoughts.

"Alrighty then, Mordecai...You and Minister Erin—"

"*Eric!*"

"Whatever...the two of y'all can go 'head and save the Jews together. I'm going back to bed."

"Mama, wait...what do you think of Eric?" Lisa wasn't sure why she felt the need to have her mother's approval, knowing full well of her mom's bias toward RJ.

"I think he's nice. Anything else is irrelevant because if you're happy, then I'm happy for you."

"C'mon, Mama. You can tell me what you really think. You don't have problems doing so any other time without my asking, so don't hold your tongue now."

"Okay, I'll be completely honest with you," she said as though she'd been waiting for the invitation. "I get this feeling that something's not quite right about him."

"Puh-leeze!" Lisa bubbled with laughter. Like her mother really knew how to pick a good man. Where was all her wisdom when she and Lisa's father married? As far as Lisa was concerned, everything was right about Eric. So what if the engagement was quick? She believed in her heart that he was the one. "That's the same thing you said about Marvin when Callie got engaged. I don't know why I asked. You'd say that about anyone except for RJ."

Hattie shrugged her shoulders. "It wasn't any secret how I felt about Marvin. I mean...I love Bryan like he was my blood, but his daddy...don't get me started. The man's dead, so I'm not going to talk ill of him. You're probably right, though, about me being biased. I still love me some RJ."

"Tell me something I don't know."

"He's a good guy that made some bad choices. Anyway, you asked what I thought about Eric and I've said my piece, so good night."

When her mother left the room, Lisa once again stared at her ring with admiration. As if it had become a noose around her neck, Lisa quickly unclasped the First Lady from around her. She would soon begin a brand new life with Eric. It was time to officially bury her past, so she retired the necklace deep inside her jewelry box.

Lisa did share the news with Chanelle the next morning who showed just as much excitement as someone on the way to the dentist's office for a root canal. Lisa didn't pay her any mind, knowing that her daughter was still sour about her own relationship with Kyle. After having her morning coffee, she left for work as usual.

Lisa spent the first couple of hours at work showing off her engagement ring to co-workers. Her assistant, Megan, was especially elated and, like Olivia, wanted to know everything that had taken place. Lisa gave her the abridged version, which went straight from dinner to the proposal, skipping all the drama in between. The remainder of her day soared by as she toggled between "I'm so happy for you" and "I love you" emails and phone calls from Olivia and Eric, respectively. It wasn't until she was on her way home that she realized there was one important person she hadn't yet shared her news with—her sister! Immediately, she tried calling Callie at her office, hoping to catch her between classes.

"Department of Humanities, how can I direct your call?" a woman answered.

This was weird. Lisa was sure she had dialed Callie's direct number. "Callie Jamison, please?"

"I'm sorry...Dr. Jamison is on sabbatical right now, but I can transfer your call to Dr. Darryl Peters. He's taken over her classes for the remainder of the quarter."

"What do you mean, she's on sabbatical? When did this happen?"

"Ma'am, if you'll hold one second, I'm going to trans—"

Lisa didn't stick on the line long enough for the woman to finish. She hung up and quickly called her sister at home. "Bryan?"

"Yeah..."

"This is Lisa. What's going on with Callie? I called the school and they said she was on sabbatical. Is everything all right?"

"Um....Hold on, here she is..."

It was a matter of seconds before Callie's voice sounded on the other end. "Hey, Lisa." Her voice, an octave lower than normal, was filled with gloom.

"Hey, are you all right? The school told me you're on sabbatical."

"Yeah...that's correct."

"What happened? I thought you had to teach some kind of lecture series this summer?"

"Oh, that...I changed my mind," she said unconvincingly. "I'm going to LA with Bryan and Tyra for a while. You know, Tyra's due the end of next month. I'm going to help her out with the baby for a few months."

"What about Chanelle's graduation party?"

"I still won't be coming. Like I said…I'm going to be in LA."

Lisa wasn't buying it. "Funny, you never mentioned any of this before."

"Sorry…I didn't think I needed to lay out my itinerary for you. What's up? What did you call for, anyway?"

Feeling dejected, Lisa had the mind to be just as rude with her response. *"She might be dealing with depression,"* Eric's voice rang loudly through her head. Lisa took a deep breath. "I wanted to tell you that I'm engaged."

"Good for you…listen, I have to go right now. We have a six-hour drive ahead of us and I need to finish getting my stuff together. I'll give you a call later."

Before Lisa could say anything else, the line went dead.

CHAPTER 12
Nothing, Honey

When Olivia suggested that everyone hang out at her house on Memorial Day, Lisa jumped at the opportunity. Memorial Day came the Monday prior to the graduation party Lisa was planning for Chanelle, so she hadn't even entertained the idea of cooking out, considering she'd be playing hostess in a few short days.

The "everyone" Olivia referred to was Lisa, her mother, Chanelle, and Eric. But only she and Chanelle were available. Eric had driven a couple hours north of Columbus to Sandusky, Ohio to visit with his mother. Technically, Lisa's mother could have come and it didn't surprise Lisa one bit when her mother declined the invitation. She'd never been fond of Olivia. Her mother didn't like anyone except for RJ, who had helped her move into her own apartment over the weekend. Thanks to him and the crew he assembled, Lisa didn't have to do much except transport a few boxes in her car. She secretly got a kick out of the double take her ex-husband did when he saw the rock on her finger, but pretended not to notice. Lisa didn't stick around long enough for RJ to ask her any questions. She knew whatever he didn't get a chance to ask her, he had most likely asked her mother, and Lisa was certain her mother had been sure to share her warped theory of Eric with him.

Lisa pulled up to the two-story brick home and sat in the driveway for a minute. In Baltimore, she and RJ once shared a beautiful home such as this. It wasn't quite as extravagant as the Scotts' residence, but it was definitely high-class. Sure she had a nice "middle-class," place now, but it was nothing compared to the house she owned in Baltimore; the one that was foreclosed on thanks to RJ.

While other guests were inside the Scott home taking advantage of all the amenities such as a pool table, game room and theater-like screen, Lisa sat alone on the deck, which, by itself, seemed bigger than her entire property. As the cool, tangy punch trickled down her throat, she recalled the first time Olivia had ever invited her over to this gated community. It was only days after they had been trapped together in the elevator. Lisa walked inside the foyer and was riveted by the two-story front window and crystal chandelier, which looked like it belonged in an art gallery. Lisa had only seen houses like this in the movies. As a matter of fact, she didn't know houses like this existed outside of Hollywood; and if they did she'd never known a black person to own one. The Scotts had really made their mark in not only Columbus, but other major cities as well with Isaac's law firms bringing in revenue from many big-name clients.

At first, Lisa was a little star-struck by Isaac's notoriety and grateful to have such an esteemed couple take her under their wings. Lisa loved being invited—via Olivia and Isaac—to events like The Governor's Ball or receiving V.I.P. tickets to the Mayor's Luncheon. She secretly hoped that the launching of Eric's ministry would grant them a spot on the A-lists throughout the country. There was no doubt in her mind that Eric would become as well-known as T.D. Jakes and Creflo Dollar. First Ladies Serita Jakes and Taffy Dollar had to marvel at their husbands' success. What wife wouldn't enjoy worldwide televised ministries and being treated like royalty by the congregation? RJ had had the potential to make all her dreams of being a First Lady come true. If only he hadn't fallen from grace...

"Excuse me, Ma'am, there are guests inside. Don't you think it's rather rude for you to sit out here being antisocial?" Lisa hadn't even noticed that Isaac had come from the great room.

"Oh, shut up." She nudged him gently as he sat his incredibly tall frame in the chair next to her. Stretching well over six feet, Isaac was unable to scoot his chair comfortably underneath the table. "You're the host, I'm not, so why are you outside?"

"To be honest, after getting in from New York late last night, I really wanted a nice quiet evening, but Liv had already set this up."

"Is that your cue that Chanelle and I should have stayed home?"

He scrunched his thick eyebrows to the middle of his head, playfully giving her a scolding look. "Now you know you and Chanelle are like family. More so than some blood-related folks inside. It's most of them other folk that I'm ready to kick out my house—the relatives that don't call unless they need money or have caught a case and are looking for an attorney, pro bono, of course. We definitely don't mind helping people, but I hate the feeling of being used."

"Unfortunately, that's the nature of some people. It's okay to say no at times."

"Liv's way better at that than I am. When Justin goes into the NFL we're going to have many more long lost cousins emerge."

"Keep talking and I'm going to be one of them," Lisa joked, forcing Isaac to chuckle slightly.

"Considering that you handpicked Justin to be Chanelle's boyfriend, claiming to be a cousin will be just a little incestuous. Such practice is shunned by today's society. That's why Liv and I keep tight-lipped about the fact that we're half brother and sister."

"I might have to sell that headline to the tabloids. How much you think I can get for it?"

"I'll give you a dollar right now if you promise not to say anything."

Lisa laughed. "You really have a few loose screws somewhere, don't you?"

"Maybe one or two…Seriously though, have you noticed how chummy Chanelle and Justin have been today? They've virtually been side-by-side since everyone got here. When Olivia sent Justin to the store to get some more ice, guess who went with him?"

Lisa smiled, approvingly. "I know. I'm pretending not to notice because if I do, Chanelle will swear I had something to do with this. I'm staying out the way and allowing nature to take its course. I'm just glad she's not seeing that other boy anymore."

"Yeah, Liv told me all about that."

"Shoot, that's enough to celebrate in and of itself."

"Speaking of celebration, have you and Eric set a wedding date?"

"Not officially. I've been so consumed with Chanelle's graduation party these last two weeks that Eric and I haven't really talked about it much. We would like to get married by the end of the year, though."

"Liv is so excited about the engagement party."

Lisa's eyes grew bigger. "What party?"

The smile on Isaac's face deflated like a balloon pricked with a needle. "Uh-oh. I have a feeling I need to invoke my Fifth Amendment rights about now."

"It's too late, you've already spilled the beans. So, Liv's throwing me an engagement party?" Lisa stirred with excitement at the thought.

"Yes, but you better promise me that you won't breathe a word of it to her. I didn't realize that it was a surprise! Olivia will be ticked if she knew I told you. It could make my nights at home very lonesome these next few weeks, if you know what I mean." Isaac winked.

Lisa laughed. "Don't worry; I won't say anything. I'd hate for a brotha's bedroom ministry to be affected."

Olivia opened the great room door and poked her head out. "What are y'all out here talking about?"

Isaac shot a quick look of warning Lisa's way before replying, "Oh, nothing, honey."

Callie stood in the hall outside Bryan's office, listening to the intense debate between him and his wife.

"Have you forgotten that we have guests outside? I can't believe you would bring me inside the house to talk about something this ridiculous!" she overheard Bryan say.

"It's not ridiculous!" Tyra protested. "I don't want her here anymore."

She pressed her ear so hard to the door that it began to throb.

"So, it's like that? Mom is going through a very difficult crisis and all you can do is play into your own fears."

"I'd rather be safe than sorry. This is serious, Bryan."

"We've already told her that she could stay as long as she wants....now you want to go back on your word."

"I think the situation justifies doing so. Maybe she can stay at a hotel or something, but we can't have her here."

As painful as it was to listen to, Callie couldn't break away. She stretched her neck, absorbing every word.

"For goodness sake, Tyra, she's not some vagabond I picked up off the street. She's my mother!"

"Technically, she isn't!"

Tyra's rebuttal plunged a hole into Callie's heart. She clutched her chest, wishing she could keep it from hurting, as the tears sprung down her face. Bryan was the only child she could claim since she could never have any of her own.

"What has gotten into you?" Bryan shouted. "Don't you ever make a statement like that again! Callie is the only mother I've ever known and I will not allow you or anyone else to take that away from me!"

"I'm sor—"

"Save it, Tyra! I don't want to hear another word about my mother leaving. Know this…if she goes, so do I."

Callie bolted quietly across the hardwood floor and had barely made it to her room by the time she heard Bryan stomp down the hall. She buried her face in the silk-linen pillowcase and sulked for at least an hour before Bryan came in.

"Hey, what are you doing cooped up in here? Aren't you coming out?"

"Maybe later. I have a headache." Callie lay spread across the full-sized bed, pretending to watch some made-for-TV movie.

"Something's bothering you. I can tell." He walked inside, blocking her view of the television. "What's wrong?

"Nothing…"

"Mom, seriously…tell me what's wrong because I'm going to stand here until you do."

"I want to go home."

"Home? Why? Has anyone said anything to you to make you feel uncomfortable?

By "anyone" Callie was certain he meant Tyra. "No…"

"Then why are you in such a hurry to go back? You've only been here two weeks. We've talked about you staying for several months."

"I realize that I have to face this situation on my own. I need to stop using you as a crutch eventually; why not start now?"

"Remember when I was growing up and you would say 'Bryan, I can tell you're keeping something from me. I'm going to keep digging until I get the truth. It's in your best interest to just come out and tell me?'"

Callie snickered, amused by his overly dramatic imitation of her voice. "What does that have to do with anything?"

"I'm not buying your story, Mom. Either way, I'm going to find out what's going on with you, so you might as well save me a bunch of time and spit it out."

Callie sighed, knowing Bryan would not let up. "I overheard you and Tyra arguing earlier."

Bryan turned pale and dropped his head as he slumped next to her on the bed. "How much did you hear?"

"Enough to know that my being here is causing problems in your marriage."

"But, Tyra is acting stupid. She heard some urban legend from her cousin's boyfriend and now all of a sudden she's freaked out."

"Even so, she's still your wife. As much as I love you and appreciate everything you've done and want to do for me, I always want you to make your marriage a priority. You can't do anything to save me. You guys are about to have your first child. The last thing that baby needs is to come home to chaos."

"I'm the head of this household; I'm just going to put my foot down and call it a day."

"No. Things are already awkward enough between her and me," Callie explained, now able to make sense of the weird vibes she had been getting from Tyra since her arrival. "Forcing your hand will only make things worse."

"But, I don't want you to leave," he whined. "I'll talk to Tyra again…give her a little time; I'm sure she'll come around. I don't think you should go back home. You don't need to be by yourself. I love you too much to let you go through this on your own."

Callie reached over to him. "I love you, too, baby, but I can't stay here. I won't stay here without Tyra's consent."

Bryan was quiet for a few moments before speaking up. "I understand if you don't feel comfortable staying here, but I'm not sending you back home."

"You don't have a choice. Your wife is about to give birth very soon."

"I know that. I think you should go to Lisa's. I'm sure she'd be glad if you made it for Chanelle's graduation party since she thinks you're no longer coming."

"No!" Callie shook her head emphatically. "It's way too expensive to get a plane ticket at such late notice."

"I'll get you to Ohio. You don't have to worry about that."

"You're about to have a baby. Don't waste your money on me," she argued.

Bryan looked unconvinced. "It's here or Lisa's. Those are your only two options."

Callie began to get irritated. "I do have another option. I can go home like I said I wanted to do," she snarled.

"Tough. It's not going to happen. Like it or not, you need to be around family right now. I saw you, Mom. You were having a meltdown. Being alone is the last thing you need right now. I'm sure your therapist would agree. Isn't that one of the reasons why you're here?"

Callie gritted her teeth, hating the fact he was right. It annoyed her even more that he used his courtroom voice as though he had been interrogating her on the witness stand. "I'll go, but I'm not ready to tell Lisa anything."

"No one said you had to."

CHAPTER 13
With All Due Respect

Anxiously, Lisa checked her watch every few seconds, wondering what in the world was taking so long! According to the schedule monitor, Callie's flight had landed twenty minutes ago!

"Don't worry; she'll be here in a minute," Eric softly assured, rubbing her tense shoulders as she roamed from face to face hoping to spot her sister.

"I wish she'd hurry. Guests will start arriving within the next hour or so and I would like to be there to greet them."

"If you're not, it won't be a big deal. Your mom and Olivia have everything under control."

Lisa rolled her eyes without Eric seeing her. He was too diplomatic-minded right now for her to get her point across to him, so she didn't bother trying. She wished that Callie had gotten a flight that arrived earlier instead of one that arrived mid-Saturday afternoon—the *day* of Chanelle's party. And a little advance notice would've been nice, too. It wasn't until late yesterday evening that Lisa found out her sister was even coming at all.

"I'm going to need you to pick me up at the airport at two thirty-seven tomorrow." Callie had immediately barked her demand without the courtesy of saying "hello" first. "I'm coming to Chanelle's graduation party."

"Thanks for telling me at the last minute. It's not like I don't have stuff to do tomorrow."

"Sorry," she said with no ounce of sincerity. "I just decided to come. Are you going to pick me up or what?"

"Yes."

Eric had been with Lisa when she'd received the call and she bent his ear venting about Callie's attitude. He said a quick prayer about the situation and encouraged Lisa to "be patient" with her sister who was "likely still dealing with depression." Depressed or not, Lisa's patience with Callie was wearing thin. It worked in Callie's favor that Eric had accompanied her to the airport. With him around, Lisa would have a better chance of holding her tongue.

"Hey…" Callie walked up to them as they stood in baggage claim. It took Lisa a few seconds to fully recognize her sister because Callie's once beautiful, dark, vibrant complexion looked pale. Though still rather thick in the waist and hips, she had lost a significant amount of weight, detectable by her loose clothing. Lisa welcomed her sister with a hug and introduced her and Eric to one another.

"It's so nice to meet you," Eric was quick to speak.

Callie's smile seemed unnatural. Her once plump cheeks were now deflated and drooped like those of a puppy. She sounded cheerful when she said to Eric, "Nice to meet you as well," but the dark circles tattooed under her eyes overshadowed any joy projected through her voice.

"How was your flight?" Lisa asked.

"It was fine. I slept most of the way."

"I'm surprised you came up with Tyra so close to delivering."

"Yeah, well, turns out she's not going to need my help when the baby gets here after all. Her mother and sister have her covered. Since I already have the time off, I figured I'd come and visit you guys for a while. If that's all right…"

Callie's explanation didn't quite add up. *"Sometimes depressed people do and say things that don't make sense,"* Eric had advised her the night he'd proposed. Seeing Callie in person confirmed that Eric had been right. Sympathy replaced all the irritability that had consumed Lisa minutes earlier. "You're welcome to stay as long as you want. Now, let's get to the house and get you settled in before the party starts."

A smiled crossed Lisa's face as she watched her daughter interact with her friends and other guests. Chanelle seemed so carefree and loving. It was hard to believe that this was the same child who had been causing her so much grief. Lisa was especially surprised to see how tight she and Justin were becoming. Every time Chanelle was spotted, Justin was glued to her side along with Chanelle's best friend, Gericka. Though the two hadn't publicly come out and stated that they were interested in each other, anyone could see that there was a definite attraction between them. Under different circumstances Lisa might be concerned about her daughter taking interest in an older boy. Justin was, after all, about to be a junior in college, but Lisa knew him very well and if Chanelle wanted to date him, it was all right with her. Besides, technically, there was only a two-and-a-half-year age difference between them.

If the number of attendees measured success, this graduation party was off the charts. Lisa's backyard was decorated with guests of many different shapes and sizes who poured in from all over the city and beyond, including friends and relatives from Baltimore. Lisa was particularly glad to see RJ's younger brother, David, and his wife, Sheila. They were Chanelle's godparents, but they had no children of their own. David would always hold a special place in Lisa's heart. Though they hadn't spoken much since she'd been in Ohio, Lisa would never forget all that David had done for her after RJ's actions had scandalized her name seven years ago.

It was the most horrific time in Lisa's life and had David not been one of her most avid supporters, Lisa was uncertain of what would have become of her and Chanelle. David and Sheila provided Lisa and Chanelle a place to stay when their home was foreclosed. Lisa could've stayed with her parents, but having experienced the turbulence of their marriage all her life, she didn't want to expose Chanelle to it on a daily basis. Not only did they provide her with shelter, but David and Sheila gave Lisa several thousand dollars to help her out when she moved to Columbus. She would always be indebted to them for their love and generosity.

As guests poured in, they congratulated Lisa in addition to Chanelle because of her recent engagement. This was the first time that people outside of church and work had become aware of her relationship with Eric. Unfortunately, Lisa's father had slithered up from Maryland after all. "Thanks for inviting me, Skeeter." He smiled, calling her the nickname he'd assigned to her as a child—a name she had far outgrown! Had it not been for his deep voice and bald head, Lisa could have sworn that she was looking into the face of her sister. Callie was the spitting image of their father, Raymond Davis. Both were tall with dark skin and big-boned features.

"I invited you for Chanelle's sake."

"I'm just glad you thought of me at all. Thank you."

"Yeah, well, thank the Lord because I only did what I thought was right." Lisa walked away quickly, not wanting to carry on any further. Inviting him had been the right thing. Chanelle seemed ecstatic to see him. Unlike Lisa, she didn't appear to be holding on to any resentment from their midnight drive last summer. Honestly, Lisa wasn't as bothered by her father's presence as she thought she would be. The one thing Lisa really didn't like were the conversations that took place between her parents. She'd witnessed, on more than one occasion, her parents conversing with each other. At one point, Lisa pulled her mother aside and questioned her about these chat sessions, and her mother assured her that she was only being "cordial" to him because this day was for Chanelle and not the time to hash out her personal feelings.

Lisa had to admit her father was making attempts to talk to everyone, not just her mother. Even Callie engaged in what seemed like an extended conversation with him. That was surprising; Callie had been everything but a social butterfly with the other guests. But then again, Callie had remained close to him despite all that happened. Though she had clearly expressed disdain for their father's actions, Callie never treated him any differently as far as Lisa was aware.

Lisa was in the kitchen refilling the hors d'oeuvre tray when Olivia walked in behind her. "Girl, how does it feel to have two men eyeing you?" she asked over the blaring music.

Lisa smiled. "Whatever…"

"Quit pretending like you haven't noticed. RJ looks like he's going to jump out of his skin every time he sees you and Eric together. Girl, I'm scared that the brotha is going to—" Olivia's sentence was left hanging, broken when RJ walked through the back door. Looking as if she'd gotten busted stealing cookies from the jar, Liv quickly picked up the half-filled tray and excused herself.

"I'm glad I finally got you alone. There's something I've been wanting to give you." Pulling out his wallet, RJ presented her with a check written for seven hundred dollars. Lisa could tell that he had been working out. The shirt he was wearing seemed to cling to every muscle on his chest.

"What's this for?"

"It may not cover all of the expenses for Chanelle's party, but I wanted to at least give you something on it."

"Thanks." Lisa folded the check in her hand. Her purse was upstairs in her bedroom and the pink sundress she had on didn't have any pockets. She really didn't need RJ's money to help pay for anything. Part of her felt bad for taking it; he was just getting back on his feet. Yet, there was a part of Lisa that remained unsympathetic. It had been a total of seven years since RJ first turned her entire world upside down and five years since their divorce. She hadn't received a single dime of child support from him in all these years, so this money was well overdue and much less than she deserved.

"The party is great. Everyone seems to be enjoying themselves and you look *really* nice." He flashed a smile that used to spark a tingling in her lower extremities but now had a null effect.

"Thanks," Lisa repeated blandly.

"So...the word is that you're getting married." He looked as if she owed him some kind of explanation.

"Yep, hopefully before the end of this year."

"I'm taking a big risk, but I have to say this." He closed the gap between them to a few inches. "I still love you, Lisa. If there's any part of you that feels the same for me, please consider postponing your engagement and giving us another try. I messed up—"

"That's an understatement," she spat, stepping back, hoping to create more space, but wedging the edge of the counter in her back instead, allowing RJ to zero in. Nervous, Lisa instinctively reached for her First Lady necklace, but it wasn't there.

"Baby, I know...I totally screwed things up with us, but you're making a mistake by marrying this guy. Do you really know him?"

"I'm sure much better than I knew you. I didn't really know you after all, did I? Thanks for the offer to reconcile, but I'm willing to take my chances with Eric." She tried to gently push him aside, but RJ grabbed hold of her arm.

"You're making a mistake," he said emphatically. "Something about this man seems odd."

Lisa laughed sarcastically, jerking free from his grip. "Gee, I wonder who planted that idea in your head. The next time you and Mama have a panel discussion about my fiancé, please remember that I couldn't care less what either of you think. Chanelle is okay with it and her opinion is the only one that matters to me."

"Sweetheart, is everything okay?" Eric couldn't have come in at a more perfect time. He walked over to where she and RJ were standing, territorially putting his arm around her waist, forcing RJ to step back.

"Yes, honey, I'm fine. We were clearing up a misunderstanding."

"Hello, I'm Minister Eric Freeman. And you are...?" he asked as if he didn't already know. Lisa fought hard to keep a prideful "ahah!" smile from spreading on her face as lines of tension formed in RJ's forehead.

"I'm Robert Hampton."

"Oh, so *you're* RJ. It's nice to meet you. Lisa has told me a lot about you."

"Wish I could say the same...Anyhow, Lisa, how about we finish our discussion another time?"

"I don't think that'll be necessary."

"I think it is. There's a lot more that needs to be said."

"Maybe you should drop whatever the two of you were talking about," Eric broke through. "She's apparently not interested in conversing with you."

"Look, man, with all due respect, you need to stay out of it. I don't need your permission to speak with my wife!" yelled RJ.

"Don't you mean *ex-wife*? In case you haven't been informed, *I* am the man in Lisa's life." Holding her even tighter, Eric's voice was stern and steady.

If Lisa was a betting woman, she'd put money on the fact that RJ's muscular physique could probably crush Eric's slender one, but what Eric lacked in physical strength, he made up for spiritually. Lisa felt like she'd been taken back to biblical times and was witnessing David confront Goliath because like David, skinny li'l Eric was fearless against the muscular giant. RJ looked at her, then Eric, and then back at her.

"So, it's like that?"

There was a desperation in his voice that begged for mercy, but instead, she answered him coldly. "Yeah…it is."

RJ kicked the back screen door open and stamped out.

"Do you want to talk about whatever it was that just happened?"

"Yes, but not right now." She gave him a quick peck on the lips. "Let's get back out to the party."

Without pushing any further, Eric nodded understandingly. Hand-in-hand they walked out the same door that RJ had burst through moments earlier.

CHAPTER 14
A Living Legend

"We're getting ready to put the movie in. Would you care to join us?" Tyra poked her head into Bryan's study.

"No thanks…" His eyes remained glued to the paperwork on his desk.

"In case you haven't noticed, we have company. It's sort of rude for you not to interact with them at all. The least you can do is come say hello."

His jaws tensed and he looked up at her. For someone who had recently given birth, Tyra still looked hot with her short, bob-like haircut and the camouflage tank top that showed just enough cleavage to pique his interest. She had been fortunate enough to gain minimal weight during the pregnancy and so she looked very good for someone who recently had a baby. Even if there weren't doctor's orders to refrain from intercourse for several weeks, he would have done so on his own accord because of his anger toward her. "In case *you* haven't noticed, I'm working, so you and your guests will have to watch the movie without me."

Tyra grunted, slamming the door on her way out.

Truthfully, he didn't have to work. Sure he had some briefs to polish up, but they really could wait. He was still upset about how

Tyra had handled the situation with his mother and wasn't feeling very hospitable. Callie had been in Ohio for the last couple of weeks and hadn't been able to lay eyes on her granddaughter in person because of Tyra's stupidity. And now Tyra had the nerve to tell him he was being rude because he refused to entertain *her* family. "Women…" Bryan muttered to himself.

The tension between him and Tyra had been so thick lately that not even Naomi's cute little baby smile could cut through it. If anything, Bryan was glad that the new little bundle of joy took up so much of their attention. With her needs in high demand, less time was devoted to the ever-increasing wedge growing between him and his wife.

Tyra had irrationally built a case solely on myths, refusing to read or even listen to the facts. How in the world was he supposed to remain happily married when he was starting to feel like he didn't really know the woman he slept next to at night? The Tyra he'd fell in love with would've never been so cruel.

In an act of frustration with his mother's situation and his recently strained marriage, Bryan threw his pen down and tilted back in his leather executive chair. With his hands cupped behind his head, he looked up toward Heaven and said, "God, why do you let bad things happen to good people?" What happened to his mother wasn't fair. Callie was such a good person. In many ways she had been his guardian angel. If it weren't for her, who would've sewn the holes he got in his pants; embarrassed him by screaming *"That's my baby!"* overly loud whenever he scored a touchdown or made a tackle in high school; or sent him care packages in college? Thinking about the many things Callie had done caused a smile to form across his face as a tear gathered in the corner pockets of his eyes. *"Real men don't cry!"* His father's voice echoed through his head. "And how would you know?" He angrily spewed out loud, though no one was around to hear or answer him.

For the first time since he could remember, Bryan allowed the tears to fall. Perhaps it was because he now realized that he couldn't healthily go on without such a release, or maybe it was to spite his father. Whatever the case, what started as a slow, steady drop quickly turned into a continuous flow and he soon found himself curled over his desk, sobbing uncontrollably. Like Job had once done, Bryan cursed the day he was born. That day his biological mother had lost her life as he made his grand entrance into the world. And now, the only mother he'd ever known had given up hers the day she decided to help make his better.

Bryan was unsure of how long he lay across his desk. It had to be quite a while, at least twenty minutes or so; his computer had gone into sleep mode. He had to admit, it felt good letting his bottled-up emotions loose. He sat up, taking several deep breaths as he looked at the tear-stained paperwork on his desk that would have to be redone. He'd deal with that later; right now he pushed the briefs aside and grabbed his Bible, looking for words of encouragement.

Callie heard the blaring sound of her cell phone as she came from the bathroom. "Hey, Bry, what's up?"

"I just wanted to call and say hi. Were you busy?"

"No; I'm the only one here. I wasn't doing anything. Chanelle is with RJ and Lisa went out to dinner with her fiancé."

"Oh…" His voice seemed to trail off into space.

"Bryan, are you okay? You don't sound like yourself."

"I'm fine. How did your appointment with Dr. Lancer go the other day?"

"It was okay; pretty much the same routine I go through with Dr. Samuels." Per the referral of her therapist in Sacramento, Callie had hooked up with Dr. Lancer, a local psychiatrist who was a friend of Dr. Samuels. "Part of me feels like this whole counseling thing is a waste of time. Talking about everything won't change anything."

"Don't give up, Mom. I can identify with your feelings of frustration. I was upset earlier and I asked God why He allowed this to happen."

"Did He give you an answer?"

"Not necessarily..."

"Figures...," she uttered without Bryan's knowledge.

"But, I read a few Psalms and then I began reading through the twelfth chapter of 2 Corinthians where Paul talked about praying three times for God to remove a thorn in his flesh, but God only said, 'My grace is sufficient for thee.'"

"No offense, but I'm sure my thorn is a lot more life-threatening than Paul's ever was."

"The point I'm making is that as confusing and painful as this whole thing is, you have to lean on God. He allowed it to happen and He will see you through. Don't lose faith in Him."

"I'd be lying if I didn't admit to you that I am struggling with my faith. You said something so true. God *allowed* this to happen. Quite frankly, that ticks me off. I feel like I'm reaping something I didn't sow. With all that's happened, it's going to take me a while to be able to trust God again." She started to add the words "if ever" at the end, but thought against it.

"God can handle your feelings. It's understandable that you're angry. I am, too. This just isn't fair! But, God is able to do the impossible. I don't know what He has planned, but He does have something."

"Bryan, baby, I realize you mean well, but if I'm going to sit and listen to this, I might as well have accepted the offer to have dinner with Lisa and her dorky fiancé."

"I'll respect your wishes for now, but I'm going to keep praying."

"One of us has to. I don't have anything nice to say, so I'm not saying anything at all," she tried to sound as if she was joking, but she wasn't.

"The Lord hasn't forsaken you. Whenever you're ready to talk, He'll be there and so will I. Anyhow…what is it that you don't like about Lisa's fiancé?"

"I never said I didn't like him."

"You called him dorky. Last time I checked, that wasn't a compliment."

"Mama is the one who doesn't like him. He gets on my nerves. Lisa is supposed to be going out of town with him to see his mother for the Fourth of July. I'm afraid she might ask me to come also, but I'm going to go with RJ and Chanelle to Baltimore."

"That'll be nice. Hopefully you'll get a chance to spend some time with your father and other relatives."

"Daddy is…never mind. My purpose for going to Baltimore is more to avoid hanging with Lisa and her boyfriend more than anything else."

"Why does he get on your nerves so much?"

"He can't engage in a conversation without quoting at least a half-dozen scriptures. Sometimes it seems as if he's going to break out in a sermon at any given moment. For instance, Mama was telling us that one of her friends broke both of her hipbones recently. This crazy man suggests that Mama remind her friend about how 2 Timothy 2:12 says that 'If we suffer, we shall also reign with him,'" Callie began, cracking up. "I mean c'mon, the woman is in serious pain. I'm sure right now she'd much prefer morphine over hearing someone tell her that she needs to suffer with Christ."

Bryan laughed as well. "Don't be too hard on him. He's probably trying to impress you guys. I know I did and said some dumb things in front of Tyra's family when we were dating. I really liked Tyra and I didn't want anyone to dislike me. I wasn't kissing their behinds or anything, but I was always on my best behavior. Maybe he wants to make a good impression."

"If you say so. Eric seems like a really nice guy, but it's hard to talk to him about anything other than the Bible. When he asked if I wanted to join them for dinner tonight, I hurried up and said I wasn't hungry. He probably heard my stomach growling, though." Callie laughed again.

"That's a sound I haven't heard in a while."

"What?"

"Your laugh. It's refreshing."

Suddenly Callie was brought back to the real world and the momentary joyfulness she felt recapping that event to Bryan quickly dissipated. "Well, there hasn't been much to laugh about these days."

"Sounds like the trip to Ohio has done you some good."

"It's been okay. Things have gone better than I thought they would go between Lisa and me. We've bumped heads over a few minor things, but nothing major. For us, that's saying a lot because we're like oil and water. Lisa acts very uppity, but she's not so bad when compared to her friend, Olivia. The lady doesn't come across snooty, but she carries herself in such a way that it's like she rules the world. I guess I might be the same way if Isaac Scott was my husband."

"You mean Isaac Scott as in *the* most influential and successful attorney ever known to man?"

"Yep..."

"Wow! That man owns law firms all over the country. Attorneys bust their butts trying to get on with one of his offices. He's like a living legend."

"Yeah...I've pretty much gathered that. Anyhow, enough about Lisa and her rich friends; how's Naomi? By the way, Lisa and Mama said to tell you 'thanks' for the pictures that you sent of Naomi."

"Let them know they're welcomed. Naomi is doing great. She's finally sleeping more than just a couple of hours at night. I hope she doesn't expect to be held all night tonight. Ty's mom and sister are here and I'm willing to bet they haven't put her down since they arrived."

"Boy, I didn't know you had company. What in the world are you doing on the phone?"

Callie heard Bryan suck his teeth. "After the way Tyra treated you, I'm not trying to spend time with her family."

"Bryan, don't let me come between you and Tyra."

"But she was wrong, Mom."

"I understand that, but Tyra is your wife. You were preaching to me earlier and all the while you're sitting up here acting stubborn. You're so busy quoting scriptures about the thorn in my flesh that you should have been reading 1 Peter 3:9 about not rendering evil for evil. Two wrongs don't make a right, you know?"

He chuckled. "It's funny how we can get into the Bible and find a Word for other people's behavior, but not our own, huh? I'm still mad at Ty and I seriously don't know how long it will last. I feel like she totally disregarded your feelings, my feelings, and plain old common sense."

"It's okay for you to be mad. Take it one day at a time. But also socialize with your wife's family because it's the right thing to do, despite your being upset. As a wise man once told me that 'God can handle your feelings.'"

"Yeah, well, he meant to encourage you, not to be corrected by you."

"Tough...stuff happens sometimes. Now that wise man needs to get off the phone, be nice to his wife and enjoy his company."

"If you say so...I love you, Mom."

"I love you, too, baby."

CHAPTER 15
Already Been Tested

"Over there is the mall," Eric announced, cruising his Taurus on Route 250 in Sandusky as they headed to his mother's house. "This whole strip has been built up quite a bit. All those establishments we passed along the way weren't there when I was growing up. This area continues to be developed; I'm sure it's largely due to Cedar Point."

"Umph…," Lisa grunted. Her stomach knotted in anxiety about meeting Eric's mother. Initially, Lisa was excited when Eric asked if she would accompany him today and had looked forward to meeting her future mother-in-law. But, during the two-hour-plus ride from Columbus, Eric had made her nervous with all of his instructions about the dos and don'ts of being in his mother's presence. *Do* call her Mrs. Henry Freeman because she always wants to reverence her late husband. *Don't* walk into her house until invited in. Even if she holds the door open, wait until she officially gives the "okay" because otherwise she thinks it's rude. *Do* be sure to remove your shoes before stepping into the living room because it's the most sacred room in her house. *Don't* ever bring up her husband's name unless she begins the conversation because, as his widow, she wants to properly honor his memory.

The complete list of "do and don'ts" totaled at least ten, all of which gave Lisa a headache. Eric may have thought he was prepping her, but what he really did was alarm her. She wished she had been privy to this information prior to agreeing to come today because she would have suddenly become affected with a stomach virus.

"What's wrong, sweetheart?" Eric must've noticed her distress.

"I'm starting to have second thoughts about coming today."

"Relax…Mother can be a little picky at times, but she's super excited about meeting you."

From where Lisa came, people normally referred to their mothers simply as "mama" or some version similar. Saying "mother" was a little strange to her, but then again, everyone had their quirks. If she thought long enough, Lisa bet she could come up with something she said or did that Eric would find peculiar.

"She's going to love you just like I do," he continued.

"I hope so…"

Eric reached over and patted her knee for reassurance. "She will, honey. You'll see. If you and Mother feel up to it later, I want to take you all to the Cedar Point pier this evening so we can see the fireworks." He smiled. "We're going to have a great time."

Lisa breathed deeply, trying to calm her nerves, as they pulled up the gravel driveway to the small tan house decorated with yellow shutters. This was it…the moment she, rather he, had been waiting for.

"Hello, Precious!" A tiny old lady answered the door. She was a cute little thing. In many ways she favored the late Coretta Scott King, except Mrs. Freeman was much more petite. Her silver hair was tightly pulled back into a bun that seemed like it had been a permanent fixture to her head.

"Mother, how are you?" He bent and embraced her lovingly.

His averagely tall frame seemed to smother her teeny, fragile one. Mrs. Freeman scanned Lisa from head to toe. Had Eric not been casually dressed, Lisa would have felt out of place in her short-sleeved shirt and gauchos; his mother had on a blue polka dot dress with a shawl. Why in the world did she have on a shawl when it was at least ninety-something degrees outside! Lisa looked away shyly for fear of her thoughts being read through her eyes.

"Mother, this is my fiancée, Lisa."

"Hi, Mrs. Free… Mrs. Henry Freeman. It's so nice to meet you."

"I only shake the hands of strangers. Any woman marrying my Precious is not a stranger, so you have to give me a hug." Lisa obediently wrapped her arms around her skeletal body, feeling a little at ease because of the warm welcome. "I'm glad you were able to come, dear."

Eric walked in and his mother held the door for Lisa, but she didn't budge until she heard Mrs. Freeman say, "Dear, won't you please come in?" She smiled ever so brightly, apparently pleased that Eric had relayed the rules and that Lisa had followed them.

Things were off to a better start than Lisa had anticipated. It was obvious Mrs. Freeman had some very weird idiosyncrasies, but she seemed nice. She led them through the tiny foyer into the living room where Lisa immediately took off her shoes, following Eric's lead.

Eric had told her that the living room was sacred, but to Lisa it looked more like a shrine of some kind with pictures galore on the walls of Eric and a man Lisa assumed was his father. She took a seat next to him on the plastic-covered sofa while his mother sat in an adjacent chair.

It didn't take long for Lisa to become bored as the conversation turned into what seemed like an extensively long Bible Study. Mrs.

Freeman started it, asking Eric if he'd read his Word that day. Of course he had and she asked him to expound upon what he'd read. Eric was a dynamic teacher and Lisa even became enlightened about a few things. She just didn't realize that his mother would not only ask what he'd read that morning, but the previous mornings as well. Lisa loved the Lord and all, but her idea of spending the Fourth of July did not include spending an entire afternoon talking about how it was Israel's fault that they had to spend forty years in wilderness because they continued to disobey God. Mrs. Freeman, on the other hand, enjoyed every bit of it and even when Eric tried to change topics to something non-biblical, she turned it right back around.

Lisa would have appreciated it if there had been a television in the room to keep her attention, but instead of a television, there was a tape player going that churned out dreary-sounding spirituals. It must've been one of those automatic tape players that never stopped, but continuously switched from side A to B because Lisa swore that she'd already heard the last couple of songs already. She was starting to get nauseous. Maybe she was delirious from the thousands of images on the walls of Eric and his father.

Lisa wondered if the blinds had been glued shut; there wasn't an ounce of sunlight peeking into the room. The small, rattling box fan did nothing except circulate hot air. Both Eric and his mother were visibly sweating, but neither seemed to mind. Silently, Lisa screamed for someone to turn on the air conditioning, open a window, or something!

"I'm getting hungry, Mother," Eric said after several hours of nonstop talking. Lisa had been nodding, smiling and fighting every temptation in her mind to doze off. "I'm sure Lisa is, too. Why don't I run up to the store and get some stuff so I can start the grill?" Lisa was relieved and saw this as her chance to get some air until Eric said, "You don't mind staying and keeping Mother company while I run out, do you? It'll give the two of you a chance to get to know each other better."

Lisa looked over to see Mrs. Freeman smiling softly. She could have punched Eric in his upper lip for asking a loaded question, giving her only one way to answer. "Sure, I'll stay. May I get a cold glass of water or something? It may just be me, but I'm feeling a bit stuffy."

"I'm a little hot, too," Eric co-signed. "Mother, would you mind if I turned on the air conditioner?"

"No, Precious, go right ahead. I'll get you both some ice water."

"Don't worry about me; I'm about to leave, but Lisa may still want some."

"Yes, thank you. That'll be nice," Lisa replied, hoping that she hadn't broken any golden rule with her request.

When Eric left, Mrs. Freeman brought her glass of water back in the living room and broke the ice by asking, "Have you ever been to Sandusky before?"

"No, ma'am; this is my first time."

"Precious told me that you have a daughter. I was hoping to meet her as well. Why didn't she come with you?"

Why do you call your son "Precious," she wanted to ask, but answered accordingly after she taking a quick drink. "She and her father went to Baltimore to spend the holiday with his brother."

"I guess I'll have to meet her another time. How are your mother and your sister? Precious tells me that you have a sister visiting from California."

"Yes, ma'am. Both of them are doing well. My mother is with some friends in Columbus and my sister went to Maryland with my daughter and ex-husband." Precious had better not been telling his mother all of her business. Lisa said her mother and sister were doing "well," but truth was, she sensed something weird going on with both of them. Their mother didn't come around as much as she had been when Callie first arrived. And Callie's insisting to borrow Lisa's car every Tuesday so she could run some errands was more than a little crazy. How in the world could Callie have errands in a city she didn't even live in?

"He tells me that you know Isaac Scott and his wife."

"Um hmm…Olivia's my best friend." Lisa noted how strange she had been acting as well, but knew it was because of the "surprise" engagement party Liv was throwing for her and Eric on the second Saturday of this month. Lisa knew that was the day because Olivia had asked her and Eric if they would be free that evening under the pretense that Isaac's law firm was having a banquet. Maybe Olivia had gotten her mother and sister in cahoots with her and that's why they've been acting so strange also.

"It's a blessing to have friends. Bishop Henry was my best friend. He passed on to glory when Precious was a young man. Precious is destined to follow in his father's footsteps, you know? I was barren, but the Lord opened my womb and blessed me with Precious after Bishop Henry and I were married for twenty-seven years. Precious is anointed and I hope he doesn't allow anyone to keep him from God's path of righteousness."

The smile that had been plastered on Mrs. Freeman's face was now edged into a scowl. Lisa was immediately put on guard by the sudden change in her personality. The ice water Mrs. Freeman had brought her did wonders to cool Lisa's body temperature, but she now swore not to take another drink, afraid that some little microcosms of saliva might be floating in the glass. "Mrs. Freeman, I can assure you that I will support Eric in whatever path God has him on. I would hate to see him go astray."

"How dare you dishonor my husband's memory!" She pounded her fist on the little coffee table with so much force that one of the picture frames fell over. "It's Mrs. *Henry* Freeman!"

"I apologize," Lisa said more out of disbelief than regret, wanting to laugh. She didn't realize how angry Eric's mother would become over something so minor.

"Please don't let it happen again. I will forever honor my husband's memory." The beads of sweat around her forehead had already dried thanks to the AC, but she fanned herself anyhow. "It seems like you already have a great influence on my Precious. If it weren't for you, he wouldn't have turned on the air conditioner. I'm on a fixed income."

"I'm sorry, ma'am, but I was starting to boil. If it will ease your mind, I'd be happy to give you some money on your gas and electric bill this month."

"No, that's fine. The Lord will make a way; He always does."

If she was certain that the Lord would take care of her, Lisa wanted to ask her what the point was of even bringing up the air conditioner! She wished Eric would hurry and came back.

"I do like you, you know?"

"I'm not really getting that impression." At this point Lisa wasn't sure how important gaining her favor was any longer.

"I'm concerned about Precious. You see, when Bishop Henry and I married, I was pure. I would like Precious to marry a woman who's pure as well, but it's too late for you. Your goods have already been tested." She smiled warmly as though she had given a compliment.

Out of respect for Eric, Lisa took a deep sigh in order to swallow the words that she really wanted to say to this old bat. "Mrs. Henry Freeman, yes, I've been married before. Please forgive me because I'm not trying to sound rude. I'm just amazed at how you can feel so free to speak on a situation you know absolutely nothing about."

"I do know that my Precious may be committing adultery if he marries you. I assume you are a woman of the Word, so you should know that, in Matthew 5:32, Jesus states that anyone who marries a divorced woman commits adultery."

"I assure you that my reasons for getting divorced were biblical, but I'm not going to discuss them with you. Eric knows all about what happened between my ex-husband and me. Perhaps if you knew, you wouldn't be so quick to judge. Eric's happy. It's obvious that you care about him very much. It seems to me like you'd be happy for him as well."

The wrinkles in his mother's face looked as if they had sunk deeper. She was clearly upset and Lisa held her breath when Eric finally walked back into the living room jubilantly and asked, "How did things go?"

To Lisa's surprise, Mrs. Freeman's Hyde personality exited and Dr. Jekyll returned. "Oh, Precious. Thank you for bringing Lisa with you. She's so delightful."

Eric snuck Lisa an "I-told-you-everything-would-be-fine" wink.

Lisa stared at him, hoping he could read her expression. *If only you knew…*

CHAPTER 16
As Luck Would Have It

Whenever Eric's back was turned, Mrs. Freeman continued to sneak sharp glances toward Lisa throughout the day. Lisa went to great lengths to avoid being left alone with her. When Eric went to the restroom she followed him and stood outside the door under the pretense of having to go as well. She even managed to talk him out of his plan to take them to see the fireworks by saying she had a headache. It wasn't a total lie. Instead of the Bible, Mrs. Freeman began to talk nonstop about Precious and Bishop Henry, and it really did cause Lisa's head to hurt. It was as if she worshipped the ground they walked on.

Before leaving, Eric mentioned to his mother that he and Lisa would probably come back to Sandusky Labor Day weekend. Little did he know that he'd be making that trip alone! If Lisa had her way she wouldn't see Mrs. Henry Freeman again until the wedding. With any luck, her fragile behind would croak by then. "Lord forgive me for feeling that way," Lisa quietly uttered, knowing her thoughts were wrong.

"Thanks for coming up here with me, sweetheart. Mother really enjoyed our company," Eric said as they were heading back.

"You mean she really enjoyed *your* company. I certainly didn't get any warm fuzzies from her."

Eric looked astonished. "What are you talking about?"

Though Lisa hadn't planned to fill him in on the conversation that had taken place while he was at the store, she did anyhow, preemptively—in case his mother decided to put a twisted spin on things. "I don't think she wants us to get married, or at least she doesn't want you to marry me," she exhaled, telling him of all the words that had been exchanged between her and his mother.

"Honey, I'm so sorry. I definitely apologize for Mother's behavior. It may seem like she doesn't like you, but trust me…I've known her all my life. After forty-three years I know when she doesn't care much for someone. Mother likes you. I'm sure her behavior was fueled by fear. She's very old and lonely and probably afraid that I won't come see her as often once we marry. Still, that's no excuse for the things she said to you. I'm especially appalled that she brought up that scripture in Matthew. She ought to know that I wouldn't do anything that's contrary to God's Word. The Lord has brought us together and Mother is going to have to accept that. I'm going to have a talk with her."

"Please don't. I'm sure that'll only make her feel worse. Let's give her some time to get used to me."

Eric seemed pleased with the suggestion. "I guess you're right. If she says something like that again, let me know and I'll ask God to give me the right words to put Mother in her place. How dare her she try and hold you accountable for your past? She knows the Bible as well as I do and in Luke 6: 37, Jesus specifically says 'Judge not, and ye shall not be judged…' I pray Mother repents for her behavior today."

Lisa smiled victoriously, appreciating the fact that, despite his mother's efforts, Eric wasn't a mama's boy after all. She admired his willingness to stand up to his mother, but she didn't fully buy Eric's explanation of her bipolar behavior. Lisa kept her sentiments quiet, though, and leaned back on the headrest and dozed off until her cell phone rang.

"Hi, Mama." Lisa faintly heard Chanelle through what sounded like an atomic bomb in the background.

"What's all that noise?"

"Sorry…we're at the Inner Harbor watching the fireworks. I ca…" Her voice faded out.

"Baby, speak up, I can barely hear you."

"I said I called because I ran into Miss Emma. She wanted me to call you so she could say hi."

Figuring the message could have simply been relayed to Chanelle instead of having her call, Lisa said, "It's too noisy to hold a conversation; just tell her—"

"Lisa?" sang the familiar, yet unmissed, voice of her former neighbor.

"Hi, Emma, how are you?"

"Girl, I about flipped my top when I saw Chanelle. She's gotten so grown up. She looks just like you. RJ told me that he recently moved to Ohio."

"Um hmm…"

"Do I detect a rekindled romance blooming? It must be nice to have him up there with you guys. With the both of y'all in a new city, you can get a fresh start and not have to be reminded of… well, you know."

"Emma, I appreciate your wanting to speak and all, but there's too much noise in the background for us to really talk. Will you put Chanelle back on the phone, please?"

"Yeah and I'll be sure to get your number from her so we can catch up later."

"Oh, that's not necessary." Lisa tried her best to sound polite, but from the deflated sound of Emma's voice responding "Okay," she hadn't been successful. When Chanelle got back on the line, Lisa gave her daughter clear instructions. "Under no circumstances do you give that woman my telephone number. I do not want to be bothered with her."

"I understand…"

"Where's your dad and Callie?"

"Daddy's right here, but Aunt Callie went with Uncle David to get something to drink. She has her cell phone with her; you can call her if you want."

"No, that's okay. I'll see her tomorrow when y'all get back. Tell your father I said to drive safely. I love you."

"Love you, too."

"Is Chanelle enjoying her visit in Baltimore?" Eric asked when Lisa had hung up.

"Sounds like she's doing all right. Of all the people she could have run into, as luck would have it, she ran into one of our former neighbors, Mrs. Kravitz."

"Honey, can you refrain from using the word luck? It's not biblical, you know? Things happen because of Divine providence…luck has nothing to do with it."

"Calm your nerves, Eric. It was just a figure of speech," she said intolerantly.

"I know, but as Christians we can't be careless with the words we choose."

"Never mind I even said anything. I had no idea it would spark a theological debate! I got a good healthy dose of the Word at your mama's, so I'm good for today," she said nastily. They were thirty miles from Columbus and Lisa vowed not to say another thing to him the rest of the way.

Eric started to laugh.

"What's so funny?"

"Do you realize this is our first quarrel? I take full responsibility, too. I realize that you were bothered by my mother; I should have been more sensitive to your feelings instead of making a federal case out of one little word. I feel the devil trying to come between us, so will you accept my apology, sweetheart?"

Lisa's heart melted. This moment reminded her of why she had fallen in love with Eric. His apology was an example of Proverbs 15:1, which states that a soft answer turns away wrath. With him responding so gently to her sarcasm, she couldn't stay upset with him. "Of course, I forgive you." She smiled at him adoringly. "And I'm sorry as well."

"Okay, now finish telling me about Mrs. Kravitz. Boy, that name really sounds familiar to me for some reason."

"It's the name of the nosey neighbor character from that old television show, *Bewitched*. Her real name is Emma, but RJ and I nicknamed her Mrs. Kravitz for obvious reasons. One time, when our daughter was about six or so, Chanelle answered the phone and said 'Mommy, it's for you.' I asked her who it was and I almost had a heart attack when she said 'Mrs. Kravitz.'" Lisa began laughing. "Oh my goodness…it was so embarrassing because I know Emma heard her. I got on the phone and played it off like I didn't have a clue who it was. RJ was in the background dying laughing."

"Shame on both you and RJ for making fun of that woman. As a man of the cloth, RJ definitely should've been aware that Ephesians 5:4 speaks against jesting," he said sternly. "Considering everything you told me about him, this doesn't surprise me."

At first, Lisa thought Eric was really scolding her and she was about to get indignant with him again, but his soft gaze caused her to believe otherwise and she chuckled. "Right or wrong, Emma lived up to that name. Even now, she couldn't resist bringing up old stuff."

"Well, let's pray that she learns to mind her own business. If I know anything, it's that God can handle even the smallest details of our lives. Whatever concerns us concerns Him. I tell you…I continuously praise Him about how well Chanelle is doing now."

"I know that's right. It's hard to believe that Chanelle is the same child who gave me grief a couple of months ago. I'm so proud of her now."

"And you should be. She is well on the right path. I'm proud of you for sticking to your word. Most parents would've caved in and bought her a car, even though they'd already stated they wouldn't. She's learning responsibility."

"Well, don't go congratulating me too soon because I'm not sure I would have been able to handle my baby being stranded on campus without a vehicle. I most likely would've allowed her to suffer during the summer and then caved in this fall. Thanks to Olivia and Isaac, I don't have to give in. Did I tell you that they gave her ten thousand dollars for graduation?"

"No! Are you serious? I guess if anyone can afford to give away that much money they certainly can."

"Yeah, tell me about it. In total, Chanelle raked in a little over twelve thousand. She has more than enough to buy her own car. Justin has taken her out car shopping a couple of times, but she put all the money in the bank and she's going to wait until it's closer to the start of school before she buys anything. She doesn't need it now anyhow. If I don't take her to work, RJ's picking her up. On the weekends she's usually out with Gericka or Justin."

"Justin has been a good influence on her, hasn't he?"

"Oh yes! It wasn't until she stopped seeing that other boy that her behavior began to change. Sometimes Justin even goes down to the center while she's working and volunteers. He claims that he wants to do community service, but Liv and I both know it's because he wants to be around Chanelle."

"I'm so glad things are working out. I can tell a huge weight has been lifted off your shoulders."

Lisa couldn't agree more. "Amen to that!" Now that things with Chanelle had settled down significantly, Lisa was looking forward to concentrating solely on planning her wedding. Though his mama seemed a little off, it didn't change how she felt about Eric. He was the perfect man of God for her and she could not imagine living the rest of her life without him.

CHAPTER 17
Quite the Charmer

It was the second Saturday in July. RJ's chest burned with fire from a combination of hurt, anger and even the jealously he'd been tortured with ever since learning of Lisa's engagement. He recalled the day he had first caught wind of the news nearly two months ago. He had been helping Lisa's mother move into her own apartment and got a glimpse of the ring when the sunlight hit it just right, causing a spectrum of color to catch his eye. Immediately, RJ felt sick, like an invisible hand had twisted every organ ~~he had~~ in his body. Wishing…hoping…even praying that the sparkling diamond wasn't what he thought it was, but his worst fears were confirmed when Hattie informed him of Lisa's engagement.

That night RJ cried on his ex-mother-in-law's shoulder like a wounded child needing comfort. "God, did I hear you wrong?" he had wailed! He had been so sure that God had promised to bring him and Lisa back together. RJ had always thought Lisa would come back to Baltimore, but when Pastor Burlington called him about the director position at the center, RJ knew it was the confirmation he needed and set forth with one mission: to reclaim his family. Tonight, his conviction grew feeble. At seven o'clock, the love of his life was celebrating her engagement to another man.

RJ was hoping Callie would share some insight about her sister's engagement while they were driving to and from Baltimore, but she rode silently, seemingly preoccupied with matters on her own mind. It was Lisa's mother who told him about the surprise engagement party. She had said ~~stated~~ that she really didn't want to go because she hadn't yet been sold on Lisa's fiancé, but wanted to support her daughter. RJ knew that another reason Hattie had been steering clear of Lisa was because of the news she had not yet shared with her or Chanelle; only he and Callie knew Hattie's secret.

RJ felt like a three-legged monkey for taking Hattie's concerns about Lisa's fiancé and running with them, feeling bold enough to confront Lisa at Chanelle's graduation party. Later, he realized that he'd bought into his ex-mother-in-law's suspicions about Eric for his own selfish reasons. He didn't know enough about Eric not to like him, but he didn't want to like him. RJ would be uncomfortable with anyone Lisa chose to marry because *he* was supposed to be her husband.

Tears dashed from his eyes as he clutched a picture of him and Lisa in his hand. The picture was at least ten years old, taken one night after their pastoral anniversary celebration. Lisa hadn't changed a bit. She was fine then and she was even finer now. The only difference between then and now is that RJ hadn't witnessed her beautiful smile, such as the one she wore in that picture, for quite some time. Sometimes he wished he could have kept up the façade just to make Lisa happy. Now someone else was putting a smile on her face!

"I can't take it, Lord!" he cried. Though RJ loved his job at the center, once Lisa married this man, he planned to move back to

Maryland. There was no way he could sit and watch her start a new life with anyone other than himself! It seemed like all his prayers to restore his family had been in vain.

"I wonder how long this banquet is going to last?" Eric asked as they headed downtown to the Hyatt Regency. Dressed as like two teenagers going to prom, Eric was in a tuxedo and Lisa wore an elegant coral spaghetti strap gown.

"I don't know…"

"I hope it doesn't last all night. I'm not really in the mood to sit with a group of uptight attorneys who'll bore me to death with a bunch of legal jargon I don't understand. Isaac isn't like that, but I can't attest for the rest of the people that work for him. I don't know why in the world we were invited to attend or why you even wanted to. Neither of us knows anything about law."

"Honey, relax. I'm sure it'll be more fun than you imagine."

"We'll see about that," Eric grunted.

Lisa giggled silently, wanting so badly to tell Eric that the boring banquet was actually an engagement party in their honor, but she didn't want to ruin the surprise for him.

When they walked into the ballroom at the downtown hotel, both were astonished by the number of guests and how beautifully decorated the place was. Though Lisa had technically known about the "surprise" party, she was still speechless by the lengths that Olivia and Isaac had gone. This gala far outdid any event where balloons and streamers filled the place. This ballroom was adorned with crystal, silk linen tablecloths and a live Jazz band. Eric's face lit up like fireworks and Lisa was overcome with emotions that even the foreknowledge of this party hadn't prepared her for.

"This is the reason why I've been acting so crazy lately," Olivia admitted after embracing the couple. "I was so scared that somehow you would find out and the surprise would be ruined."

"Liv didn't think everyone would be able to keep this a secret." Isaac winked and smiled.

Olivia gently nudged him in the side. "Oh hush. Anyhow, Lisa, I hope you like what we've done."

"Are you kidding? I love it!"

"Thank you so much," Eric chimed in.

Well wishes began to pour in from guests, who also seemed impressed by the caliber of the event. Besides her mother and sister, Lisa's assistant, Megan, was one of the first to come up and speak.

"It's so nice to finally meet you. Lisa is a great person. Consider yourself one lucky man," she kidded.

"*Lucky?*" Eric cautioned.

"I'm sure what Megan is really saying is that every day of our marriage you better count your blessings, mister, and thank God for giving you such as wonderful wife," Lisa playfully interjected to avoid the possibility of Eric embarrassing her by rebuking Megan for her vernacular.

"I definitely will do that." He smiled.

"I can't believe so many people from the office are here," she said to Megan.

"It doesn't surprise me. When two of the company's most influential board members send personal invitations to nearly every employee, people are going to respond."

Lisa and Eric both laughed. "I guess I didn't look at it that way," said Lisa.

"Even Mr. Criton is here and you know he usually never attends employee social events."

That was true. Neil Criton was Brentson's Chief Executive Officer and was probably the board's third most influential member, inferior only to the Scotts. He was a nice man, but kept work relationships at the office. He never really seemed interested in getting to know anyone on a more personal basis. Lisa was surprised and honored that he had attended.

The engagement party was phenomenal! The evening was filled with loads of food, fun and fellowship. Lisa wasn't extremely bothered by the lack of enthusiasm shown by her mother and sister. She had expected as much since neither of them has really done any cartwheels about her engagement. Callie had been acting weird ever since her arrival to Columbus, but her mother's behavior was a little more unusual and didn't really begin until a few days after Chanelle's graduation party. Initially, Lisa assumed it was because her mother was in on the planning of tonight's celebration, but seeing how the odd behavior continued, she wondered if something else was going on. She'd made a mental note to confront her mother at a later time. What really seemed peculiar to Lisa was how quiet and withdrawn Chanelle had been the entire night. Lisa walked over to where Justin and Chanelle were sitting. Along the way, she thanked several guests for coming. When she finally reached her daughter, she asked, "Honey, is everything okay?"

Chanelle seemed to hesitate at first, but then answered, "Yes."

"Are you sure? You don't look like yourself."

"She's tired," Justin spoke up. "We both are. Mom had us running around all day to get stuff together for tonight."

Lisa could believe it. Justin had picked Chanelle up around nine this morning under the pretense of his parents needing help with the "banquet." Lisa was tickled to death that her soon-to-be eighteen-year-old daughter had gotten out of bed on a Saturday morning before noon. Saturdays were pretty much the only day Chanelle slept in during the summer since she worked at the center during the week, and of course they had church on Sundays. Lisa was honored that Chanelle had drudged out of bed early to help get things together for her engagement party. Lisa took her daughter's actions as a sign of support.

"Honey, you do look exhausted. Mama's car is still in the shop; she rode with Callie in my car. If you want, I'll ask Eric if he'll mind them riding back with us; then you can take my car and go home."

"Don't worry about it, Miss Lisa. I can take her home," Justin offered. "Matter of fact, I'm a little worn out myself because of football conditioning. You won't mind if I sneak out a little early as well, will you?"

"Not at all. You two are the youngest here. If you weren't tired, you're probably bored, huh, hanging out with all us old fogies?"

"I don't know about everyone else, but you and Mom are definitely no old fogies. You two are the most beautiful older women I've ever seen," he said playfully.

Lisa looked at Chanelle. "Isn't he quite the charmer?"

Chanelle grinned weakly.

"Go'on and get my baby out of here so I don't have to argue with her too much about getting up and going to church tomorrow. I'll let Liv know you're going home," she said to Justin.

Lisa accidentally bumped into Eric while walking and scanning the room for Olivia. "Please watch where you're going...my fiancée loves me and wouldn't appreciate you mauling me over like that."

"What else wouldn't she appreciate?" toyed Lisa.

"If I did this..." Eric leaned over and gave Lisa a brief, stomach-tickling kiss. She hadn't expected such a bold move from him, but she was definitely looking forward to more sparkling moments like this.

"In case y'all didn't know, this is the engagement party, *not* the honeymoon," teased Olivia.

"I was just looking for you," said Lisa. "Justin and Chanelle left. He's dropping her off and heading home since somebody worked them into exhaustion all day."

"Whatever!" Olivia playfully rolled her eyes. "Knowing Justin, he left because he thought he might have to help clean up."

"Lisa and I will stay and help," Eric offered.

"Nonsense; you two are the guests of honor. Plus, I'm not even staying. Isaac's in charge of the clean-up crew. Check with him. He may have hired some people to take care of it."

It was after ten and most people had already started clearing out. Lisa's mother and sister were among those saying their final good-byes before leaving.

"Callie, call me if you have any trouble finding your way back to the house after you drop off Mama."

"I should be fine."

"This was a lovely party," her mother said to Olivia.

"It sure was," echoed Lisa, surprised at how polite her mother was being. Olivia wasn't exactly one of her top-ten most liked people. It wasn't like Olivia had ever done anything to Hattie. Olivia had always treated her kindly and with respect. Lisa assumed her mother was just funny-acting. At times, Lisa probably didn't make Hattie's list, but no doubt RJ reigned at number one.

"Thanks. I wanted to do something to show Lisa how much her friendship means to me."

"Well, we have to go," Callie interrupted rather rudely. "I'll see you at the house."

"I hope she doesn't get lost," Lisa said after they had walked away.

"She should be fine. She managed to pick your mother up and make it here okay," noted Olivia.

"I know, but it was broad daylight then. It's dark now."

"Honey, I'll tell you what. Why don't you hurry and catch them and just ride home with them. The party's pretty much over now anyhow. I want to stick around and see if Isaac has enough hands," Eric suggested.

"Are you sure? I'd hate to end our night so abruptly."

"It's not abrupt. I'll call you when I get home."

"Okay." She gave him a quick peck. "Liv, I'll talk to you later. Thanks, again!" she said, sprinting as fast as she could in her high heels, hoping she hadn't missed them.

CHAPTER 18
So Dramatic

Fortunately for Lisa, her mother and sister made a pit stop to the ladies room before heading out and she caught up with them in the lobby.

"Hey, Eric may stay to help clean up, so I'm going to ride with you guys."

Lisa noticed the awkward expression her mother gave, but she didn't comment on it.

Once they got to the car, Callie handed over the keys to Lisa and sat in the back. The ride to her mother's apartment was eerily silent. Lisa tried to spark up a conversation by making comments here and there, but neither her mother nor sister took the bait. After several failed attempts, Lisa finally said, "Mama, you haven't been yourself lately. Is everything okay?"

"Yes, I'm just a li'l tired."

"So, you really enjoyed the party?"

"Of course, why wouldn't I have?"

"I don't know...It's no secret that you aren't overly fond of Liv." When Hattie first came to Columbus, she used to always refer to Olivia as Oleta. Though her mother was prone to mess up names every now and again, Lisa was certain that she did it with Olivia on purpose just to be ornery—very few people in the United States had not heard of Isaac and Olivia Scott.

"I have my opinions about her. I don't think she's all that she's cracked up to be, but I will still give credit where credit is due. Olivia and her husband did a wonderful job. It was nice of them to honor you and Eric."

Lisa witnessed her sister pucker her lips in the rearview mirror when their mother stated her opinion about Olivia. For some reason it really irked her that Callie seemed to adopt her mother's feelings. Lisa tolerated her mother's views, but Callie ought not dare utter one negative word about Olivia. Yeah, blood was supposed to be thicker than water, but exceptions were made. Even in the Bible, Jonathan's loyalty was to his friend, David, rather than to his father, Saul.

Lisa felt that her relationship with Olivia was very similar to that of Jonathan's and David's. Lisa used to always think that maybe she and Callie weren't close because of the nine-year age difference between them, but Olivia was much closer to Callie's age than hers. In fact, Olivia was eleven years older than Lisa, and yet they'd bonded like their hearts had been knitted together since birth. There wasn't anything that the two women wouldn't do to protect each other. Callie best keep her mouth shut about Liv or she'd find herself on the first available flight back to California.

Lisa pulled into the parking space in front of her mother's apartment door, but when her mother started to get out the car, Lisa clutched her arm. "Shut the door," she ordered.

"For what?"

"I think I just saw someone in your apartment."

She shook her head. "Good night, Lisa."

"No, Mama, I'm serious. I could've sworn I saw some kind of shadow."

"Girl, go home and get some rest. Everything's all right. I'll talk to you later this week."

She tried to leave, but Lisa still held on to her. "I think we should call the police, just to be safe. I may be tired, but I'm not crazy. I know I saw a shadow."

"Lisa, she said everything's fine. Just let her go," Callie muttered.

Something about the whole scene didn't feel right. Lisa found it quite peculiar that her mother, who had been concerned about crime rates in the city, wasn't the least bit alarmed about the possibility of an intruder. She released her mother's arm and said, "Good night." She watched her mother closely. "I'll be right back," she said to Callie. When Hattie unlocked the front door, before she could shut it good, Lisa was standing in the entryway. To her left, posted on her mother's couch like he belonged there, was someone who had become a stranger to her. He looked real comfortable dressed in a white t-shirt and boxer shorts with his feet planted on the coffee table, watching TV, and eating chips.

Her adrenaline raced to its peak as she whispered under her breath, *"Dad?"* She glared toward the couch where the villain sat.

He stood up with a weak smile. "Hi, Skeeter."

"Don't you dare Skeeter me! You have some nerve showing your face around here. Get in the car and go back to Baltimore, now!" she shouted.

Callie ran from Lisa's car and grabbed her gently. "Come on, let's go."

Lisa jerked away. "I'm not going anywhere until he does." She glared at her father.

"I'm afraid that's not going to happen, Skeeter."

"My name is Lisa! Lisa, Lisa, Lisa!" She ranted like a small child with a tantrum.

"Baby, I think it'll be best if you go home and get some rest. We'll talk about all of this later," her mother suggested.

"Let's go," Callie repeated.

"Mama, I'm sorry if my attitude or whatever made you want to move out. I know you're scared of being on your own, but you don't have to live with this man. Come on, you can come back home with me."

"Lisa, I want to try and work things out with your father."

"What is it going to take, Mama? Will he have to kill you before you finally understand that he doesn't mean you any good?"

"Skee—I mean, Lisa," her father interjected, "I understand why you feel this way, but you have to believe me...I've changed."

"Oh puh-leeze! I'd be a freakin' millionaire if I had a penny for every time I've heard you say that."

"I know...but I mean it this time."

"C'mon, Mama, you can't be buying this, can you? The man hospitalized you!"

"Can we take this inside, please?" her mother requested, obviously embarrassed by the attention Lisa's drama was drawing. Her neighbor had turned on outside lights and was peeking out the window.

"No! I'm not going in there, not with him inside." She turned around and stormed to her car. Callie was saying something to her parents and Lisa impatiently waited all of thirty seconds or less for her sister to join her before barreling down on the horn.

"You need to quit acting so dramatic," Callie scorned once Lisa sped away.

"Whatever! I don't see why you're not as concerned about Mama's safety as I am."

"I am concerned about her safety. That doesn't stop me from loving my father. When he was here for Chanelle's graduation he confided a lot in me. I believe he's changed and so does Mama. If she wants to give him another chance then she has the right to do so."

"Please don't tell me you're really buying this 'I've changed' routine. You are, aren't you? *Unbelievable!*" She looked at her sister with disgust and pressed the pedal down even further.

CHAPTER 19
Temporary Insanity

"Hey, Lisa, how quickly can you get here?" one of her cousins had called and asked.

"I don't know. Why, what's up?"

"Can you just come quickly, please?" Her cousin's voice was saturated with fear.

"What's going on? You're scaring me."

"It's Aunt Hattie...she's in the hospital."

"What happened?"

"We really don't know, but she's bleeding internally. She has several cracked ribs, a broken collarbone, a fractured wrist, and the left side of her face is completely swollen. She can't even see out of her left eye."

"Did Daddy do this?" Lisa yelled.

"That's what we suspect, but she hasn't said one way or the other. One of the neighbors heard them arguing and called the police. By the time they got there your dad was gone so they've put a warrant out for him."

"I'm on my way..." Lisa hung up the phone.

That was the last of many calls she'd gotten about her father's physical abuse. That night was the first time her mother admitted that she had had enough and agreed to move to Columbus with Lisa and Chanelle. Perhaps it was being hospitalized that had been the last straw. Whatever it had been, Lisa had been so proud of her mother for gathering up the courage to finally leave him. Now, just a year later, her mother was welcoming that monster back into her life! And Callie's stupid behind was in support of their reunion.

Lisa refused to say another word to her sister during the remaining ride from her mother's house to hers. As a matter of fact, she didn't want to speak with *anyone* and willfully ignored both Olivia's and Eric's phone calls. Lisa had developed a migraine so intense that she took two of the strongest over-the-counter meds that she could find and went straight to bed. The odds of her drifting off to sleep were not in her favor because she tossed and turned like a ship in the middle of a raging sea, her mind refusing to be at peace.

"Mama?" Chanelle crept up to her bedside and called out to her softly.

"What?" she moaned.

"Can I use your car and go over to Gericka's?"

"No, Chanelle. It's too late for you to be going over anyone's house."

"Then will you let me go get her and bring her back over here?"

"No…"

"Mama, *please*…"

"No! Besides, you're not supposed to be driving my car anyhow."

"You offered to let me drive it from the hotel."

"I was making an exception because you didn't seem to feel good. You hanging out with Gericka is not an emergency. She's more than welcome to stay over another night."

"But Ma—"

"I said no and that's it. End of discussion! Now leave me alone," she barked.

Chanelle sighed and turned to walk out of the room, mumbling something under her breath.

It took a few seconds for her daughter's response to register, but once it became clear Lisa shot up. Her seventeen-year-old daughter had just called her a "B." Lisa could only assume that it was temporary insanity that would've made her daughter believe she could say something like that and live. Before Chanelle could make it to the doorway, Lisa jumped out of bed like a jackrabbit and, within seconds, had Chanelle and her micro braids pinned to the floor.

"Get off of me!" Chanelle struggled to break free.

Lord have mercy...Lisa thought as she realized her hands grappled her daughter's neck. The light from the hall poured into the room and Lisa expected to see a look of remorse on her daughter's face, but instead Chanelle glared at her as if to say, "Yeah, I said it and I'm not taking it back." The teenager began fighting like a pit bull that had been trained to attack and Lisa accepted the challenge. Blow for blow, thump for thump, mother and daughter went at each other with full force.

"Stop it!" Callie yelled, turning on Lisa's bedroom light and pulling them apart just as Lisa detached a handful of braids from her daughter's scalp.

The light magnified the horrid scene. Chanelle stared at her mother with hatred. Her pajamas were torn and blood seeped from her busted lip. Besides a few minor scratches, Lisa was physically unscathed, but emotionally she was bleeding for dear life. Who was this child standing before her? How did this Jerry Springer-type drama unfold in her house?

"What is going on with you two?"

Chanelle was first to speak. "Look what she did to me!" she yelled. "I'm callin' the police."

"You better make sure they take you with them because if they leave you here, they'll be coming back for your body!"

"Whatever. You don't scare me. If the police come I bet you'll be the one leaving. I won't be eighteen for a few more weeks, so technically, I am still a minor. You can go to jail for this."

"Once you got bold enough to call me out of my name, you took the risk of a grown woman and I beat you as such."

Tit for tat, they exchanged verbal attacks and threats. Lisa reached to get another hold on Chanelle, but Callie blocked her efforts. "I'm not putting up with your smart mouth. Get out now!" she ordered.

"Lisa, think about what you're saying," her sister urged.

"I know full well what I'm saying. If she's grown enough to talk to me like that, then she's grown enough to be on the streets."

"Fine with me. I can't stand living with you anyway!" Chanelle spewed and stormed off.

"I understand you're mad, but—" Callie attempted to speak.

"Earlier you bragged on minding your own business, so do it now!" Lisa finally released the fistful of hair and plopped down on her bed.

"Where is Chanelle going to go?"

"I don't know and I don't care. If you're so worried about her, then you can go with her."

Callie shook her head disappointedly and walked out.

Minutes later Chanelle walked back in Lisa's room, fully dressed and carrying a duffel bag. "My money is in the bank and I don't have any cash on me. Since you want me out so bad tonight you can at least give me some money to catch a cab."

She stood with her hand out like Lisa owed her something. If she weren't so angry, she might have laughed at her daughter's audacity. "You got some nerve coming in here asking me for money after you have acted a fool. You got about three seconds to get out of my face before I jump on your behind again."

Chanelle stared at her angrily. "I hate you!" she yelled before running out the room.

The words stung Lisa like a wasp. She and Chanelle had bumped heads on plenty of occasions, but nothing ever like this. She had never disrespected Lisa the way she'd done so tonight. Her chest felt so heavy, she bawled, hoping to release the tension, but the pain did not cease. She picked up the phone and dialed Eric.

CHAPTER 20
High Maintenance

RJ raced across the freeway trying to make it to Lisa's house to get Chanelle. He couldn't believe what had happened. Part of him felt responsible. If he had not faltered in his duties as the head of the household, this night would have never happened. Things were definitely out of order. So what if Lisa was engaged to be married to what's-his-face; it didn't change the fact that Lisa was his *first* and that Chanelle was *his* daughter. He had been playing it cool, allowing Lisa to call all the shots as not to ruffle her feathers, but not any more. From now on, he was taking a more active role and it would start tonight!

RJ pulled in Lisa's driveway behind a black Taurus about a quarter to one. He wanted to throw a few blows himself when Lisa's fiancé answered the door like he was the man of the house.

"Well, hello, there," he said smugly. "If you're looking for Lisa, she's in the back."

"Where's Chanelle?"

"We don't know. She took off. I came because Lisa needed me."

"Yeah, well, I'm here because they *both* need me," he scoffed on his way to the kitchen.

Lisa sat at the table groping the sides of her head. She looked a mess. Her hair flew in all directions and the puffiness under her bloodshot eyes made it appear as if she hadn't slept in years. Not expecting to see him, she asked, "What are you doing here?"

"I'm surprised that you didn't call me."

She looked at him as if to say "For what?" and that alone was enough to irk RJ, but when her fiancé came in the kitchen and stood behind her and massaged her shoulders, RJ couldn't hold his tongue.

"I don't see why you called him and not me. I'm Chanelle's father. This dude shouldn't even be involved in the situation."

"Excuse me, sir, but this dude has a name, and I'd suggest you lower your voice if you wish to speak with my lady."

"Man, I don't give a care what your name is. And I'd suggest you learn when to speak and when not to. You marrying Lisa is one thing, but for her not to call me when she has a brawl with our daughter is another. The only people this truly affects are Lisa and me, so your best bet would be to stay out of it."

Eric didn't challenge RJ this time, but Lisa had no problem speaking up.

"Get to the point of why you're here. Did Chanelle call you to come get her so she could share your guest room at Pastor Burlington's house? If so, she's already gone and I don't know where she went."

"No, Chanelle didn't call him, I did." Callie appeared in the kitchen door. "Before you start going off, let me say that I called him because I'd rather Chanelle leave with her father than for that child to be out there wandering the streets."

"*Child?*" Lisa hissed.

"Don't you think you should at least call the police?" suggested a more controlled RJ this time.

"That *child* will be eighteen shortly and has over ten thousand dollars in her bank account. I'm sure she'll survive."

"C'mon, Lisa, be for real."

"I am. When Chanelle decides she wants to talk to me with some respect, then I'll spend my time worrying about her. Maybe if she'd called you out of your name, you'd understand how I feel." Eric continued rubbing her shoulders silently.

"Lisa, I'm not saying that you don't have a right to be angry—"

"RJ, it's not worth trying to talk any sense into her," interrupted Callie. "Lisa was already in a funky mood when we came home because she found out about Mama and Daddy."

"Oh ," said RJ.

"So you knew about them, too? It figures. You know what? I don't feel like talking to either one of you any longer. RJ, you can get out of my house and Callie, you need to stay out of matters that don't concern you. Chanelle is my daughter and there was no reason for you to call him."

"She's my daughter, too!" screamed RJ.

Lisa laughed wickedly. "You sure didn't act like you had a family in Baltimore, so don't act like you have one now!"

"Oh, so you want to throw Baltimore up in my face. Well—"

"It's time for you to go," demanded Eric. "I allowed you to say your peace. Lisa's already told you once to leave. She's not going to have to say it again."

RJ really wanted to punch Eric in his mouth! "I'm leaving, but only because I'm going to try and find my daughter. Don't you ever forget that though you may be marrying Lisa, when it comes to Chanelle, *I* have the final say so." He pounded his fist on the table to emphasize his point. "Callie, call me anytime I'm needed." He brushed past her, through the living room and out the door.

RJ cased the neighborhood and surrounding areas for over an hour with no sign of his daughter anywhere. When fear began to grip him, RJ started praying that God's angels would surround, watch over and protect Chanelle from any harm or danger.

All of his messages to her cell phone had gone unanswered. RJ pulled into the gas station several miles from Lisa's house at the corner of Brice and Livingston and showed the attendant a picture of Chanelle, hoping the man had seen her. "No, sir," the guy answered. After leaving his number for the attendant to call if Chanelle was spotted, RJ jumped back in his vehicle and continued his search.

Eric stayed with Lisa until about three in the morning, comforting and praying for her. All of Eric's praying hadn't done a thing to pacify her rage against Callie and RJ. As soon as Eric left, Lisa marched up the stairs and burst into Callie's room.

"How dare you!"

"What's your problem now?" Callie sat up and turned on the light, fully alert.

"You had no business calling RJ over here."

"Don't tell me what I should not have done. Like RJ said, Chanelle is his daughter, too. He had a right to know."

"RJ bounces back in town and is trying to play the loving, concerned father, but you and I both know it hasn't always been that way."

"Oh, Lisa, suck it up!" She got out of bed and stood face-to-face with her sister. "RJ hurt you...Big deal! Unlike that jerk you're about to marry, RJ's human. And like it or not, humans make mistakes!"

"*Mistakes?* How does pretending to be on a mission to rid the streets of Baltimore from drugs while secretly using the church's money to buy crack for himself classify as a mistake? Not to mention that he repeatedly had an affair with one of the women we were supposed to be helping?"

"Boohoo, RJ cheated on you. Have you ever considered the possibility that you drove him to both the drugs and the other woman by being so high-maintenance? You were more in love with the idea of being a preacher's wife than you were with him."

"How can you stand here and be so callous! That man would have me sitting in the car while he supposedly went in to pray for people and he'd be inside snorting crack and screwing one of them!"

As Lisa spoke, the feelings of betrayal and hurt that she thought she'd gotten over began resurfacing. Initially, she had been a part of the mission to save drug-addicted souls and would accompany him inside the residences, but after he went alone a few times, he had forbidden her to go inside ever again, claiming that it was "too dangerous." Her new responsibility had been to "watch and pray" from the outside. Lisa wondered how many times she had foolishly sat in the car thinking her husband was busy about the Lord's work, but the only thing he was busy doing was getting his freak on.

Had RJ just done his dirt without dragging her in the midst of it, maybe Lisa wouldn't have been so angry. Not likely, but maybe. He had smeared her name just as much as he had his own. Unbeknownst to either of them, the police had been staking out the place he frequented. One night, he, Lisa, and Chanelle were on their way to Bible study when RJ suddenly announced that he wanted to stop and invite one of the drug addicts. Lisa remembered thinking how odd this last-minute invitation seemed and how unusual it was that he was taking Chanelle into the neighborhood as well. During previous trips, they'd always obtained a sitter for her. Being the good "Pastor's wife," Lisa went along with the plan. It wasn't long afterwards when the apartment and their car were swarmed with police officers and RJ was literally brought out with his pants down. Having seen her many times before, the police had thought Lisa was somehow involved with drugs as well.

It was so embarrassing. Their pictures were plastered all over the news and in the papers. Lisa was eventually cleared of all charges, but the stigma never escaped her. Whispers from her neighbors…skeptical looks from the other parents at Chanelle's school…most people had already convicted her. What was even worse was that she had nothing. She'd depended on RJ for everything and little did she know that, in addition to the church's money, he'd also smoked away their savings. It was RJ's brother, David, who gave her a lump sum of money to start over. It was by the grace of God that she landed such a high position at Brenston. God had brought her through that horrible time. How dare her sister make light of it!

"Chanelle was more accurate in her description of you than you think. You really are a bi—" Lisa drew back to slap Callie, but her sister caught her hand prior to impact. "Watch, it! I am not Chanelle. I'm a lot heavier and I hit a lot harder."

"I can't believe you would say something like that."

"Poor Lisa… Everyone's being so mean to her. RJ cheated on her and her daughter and sister called her a bad name. Her life is so messed up," she mocked. "Try walking in my shoes for a while. Try being gang-raped at the age of fifteen, causing so much internal damage that it ruined any possibility of you ever having kids. Try marrying a man and, after twenty-four years, he commits suicide. Try finding out that the son of a gun killed himself because he didn't have the guts to tell you that he was HIV-positive and now so are you! You think you have problems, Lisa? I'd trade lives with you in a minute. You feel like you're going to die, but I've already been given a death sentence!" she screamed.

Her sister's confession forced all traces of anger from Lisa's body. Compassion flooded her veins. "Oh, Callie," she cried. "I'm so sorry; I didn't know."

"And you didn't care to know either. I tried calling you to talk, but as usual, you're so consumed with your own life that you don't care about mine."

"That's not true," she pleaded. "I care about you very much! I love you."

"No, you love people with titles and money." Callie's eyes burned with fire. "Those are the only people worthy of your attention."

Realizing now was not the time to defend her honor, Lisa said to her sister, "I'm sorry I wasn't there when you needed me, but I'm here now. If you want to talk about this tonight, we can. I know you are hurting, but I promise you that no matter what it feels like God has not forsaken you. The Bible says—"

"Don't you dare get all sanctified on me now," Callie hissed. "Go back to your room and sulk over your own problems like you always do. I can deal with mine." Callie pushed Lisa out of the room with so much force that she almost fell to the ground.

Lisa heard her sister lock the door. "Cal, please talk to me. Don't shut me out. I want to help you."

Callie gave no response. Lisa waited outside her door, hoping for an invitation back in. When Callie remained silent, Lisa went to her room and collapsed on her knees and began praying.

CHAPTER 21

Familiar Territory

Lisa prayed and cried, cried and prayed for hours about her sister's revelation of being HIV-positive. She couldn't even begin to wrap her mind around the pain that Callie had to be feeling. She was drenched with guilt. Callie had been with her for two months and, instead of taking the time to really find out what was going on with her, Lisa had written her sister's behavior off as depression. Odds were that Callie was depressed. Who wouldn't be, under such circumstances? Still, Lisa wished she had made more of an effort to show Callie how much she cared about her well-being.

It was well into the early morning when Lisa finally drifted off to sleep. She'd been awake long enough to witness the sunrise. The shrilling sound of her phone woke her up Sunday afternoon. "Hey Liv," she said as if medicated with Novocain.

"What's going on? I saw Eric at church and he said you'd had a rough night. He said that I should call you."

"Girl, if you only knew." Lisa gave her friend a very quick recap of the situation with her parents and the fight with her daughter. "Chanelle is more than welcome to come back home if she's willing to apologize and act like she has some sense from now on, but I'm not about to chase her down. Chanelle knows how to get in touch with me if she wants to. I love my daughter with all my heart, but I refuse to let her run things around here. If she wants to be grown, she needs to be out there on her own."

"I'm so sorry to hear all of this happened last night. I wonder what was going on with Chanelle. She seemed fine yesterday. She and Justin ran back and forth between the hotel and the house every time I needed something else for the party. Do you think she somehow found out about your dad being here?"

"It's possible, but I doubt she would be as mad as I am about it. She was happy to see him at the graduation party. Chanelle started trippin' because she didn't get her way. It all seems so crazy."

"No wonder Eric was concerned about you."

"Girl, he doesn't even know the drama that unfolded after he left."

"There's *more?*"

"Yeah, Callie and I got into it."

"Well, she had no business calling RJ."

"I know, but I'm really not even mad at her about that anymore. I found out about some things going on with her and I really need to speak with her further."

"Is she okay?"

"Honestly, I don't think so." Lisa's phone beeped. "Liv, let me answer this call. I'll talk to you later," she said and clicked over.

"Why didn't you tell me that Chanelle has gone missing?"

"Mama, you act like she's been kidnapped."

"Well, RJ has been looking for her all night and he still hasn't found her."

"Apparently she doesn't want to be found."

"I don't see why you won't call the police."

"There's no reason to. She hasn't been abducted. She left on her own free will. I'm not wasting their time or mine."

"I would've never done you like this."

"And I would've never been crazy enough to call you out of your name. Bye, Mama…I'm not in the mood to talk to you about this. I need to talk to Callie."

"You done ran her off just like you did Chanelle," her mother accused.

"What are you talking about?"

"Callie has gone back home."

"No, she hasn't!" Lisa ran into the guest room to disprove her mother's theory. She flung the door open and found the room empty with no trace that Callie had ever occupied it. Lisa was gripped with disbelief. "When did she leave and why didn't she say anything to me?"

"RJ said he dropped her off at the airport sometime this morning. You gon' tell me what you did to her?"

"Why are you assuming that I did something? I didn't do anything to her."

"Well, she sure left in a hurry and no one knows why. At least we know she's going home, though. No one knows where Chanelle is and everyone is worried about her, but you."

Lisa wanted to retaliate and tell her mother that she needed to worry about not getting her behind beat again, but she held her tongue from being disrespectful and instead said, "Mama, I have to go." She hung up and called RJ. "You got your nerve, coming to my house to get my sister and not saying anything to me."

"Lisa, shut up! I've been up all night long and you want to call me talking stupid. You didn't have the decency to call me about my daughter and now you want me to explain why I didn't say anything to you when I picked up your sister. I don't have time for this."

Lisa couldn't believe the harsh way RJ spoke to her and she was even more astonished when he hung up. She was the one who normally indulged in such privileges. Cautiously, she called back and, with a softer tone, asked, "Did Callie at least tell you why she was leaving?"

"No," he answered roughly.

Lisa sighed. "I'm really worried about her. She revealed some things about Marvin's death last night and I was hoping to talk to her this morning."

"Well, I can't help you; she's gone. Now if you don't mind, I'm about to go."

"RJ..." Lisa swallowed her pride. She wasn't used to him getting angry with her and she realized that she'd really messed up. "I'm sorry that I didn't call you last night." She hoped to appease his anger, though not really certain why she cared. "The whole thing happened so quickly. First, I was upset about Mama and Daddy and then, the next thing I know, Chanelle was calling me out of my name because I refused to let her go pick up her friend. Maybe I did overreact. I don't know, but I do know she crossed the line. And for that, I'm allowing her to deal with the consequences of her actions. It's not that I don't care..." Her throat tightened, forcing her to stop speaking.

"I know, and you're right; Chanelle was wrong. I don't blame you for being upset with her. As parents, sometimes we have to apply tough love. Just don't be mad at me because I want to help her. Lisa, I let both you and Chanelle down before. It's too late for me to make things up to you, but it's not too late for me to be there for my baby girl. Promise me that if you hear from her, you'll let me know."

"I promise," she swore.

Lisa took the next few days off of work to clear her mind. By Thursday, she hadn't heard from either her sister or Chanelle. Callie had called RJ and their mother to say she'd made it home safely, but she had yet to return any of Lisa's pleading messages. Lisa honestly didn't know which person worried her more: Callie or Chanelle. Being her daughter, Chanelle definitely pulled on her heartstrings, but Callie had a tight grip as well.

Lisa hadn't shared Callie's secret with anyone, not even Eric or Olivia. She did ask them to pray for her, though. At least she knew where Callie was; Chanelle's whereabouts were yet to be determined. She hadn't even showed up for her shifts at the center. Lisa wasn't sure how long she'd be able to hold on to this "tough love." It seemed to be harder on her than it was on Chanelle.

Her parents had come by earlier in the day to check on her. Seeing the two of them together was still a sore sight but in light of the events that unfolded after their reconciliation was uncovered, Lisa tried not to focus too much on them. Though it was clear that her father was bending over backward to show her that he had changed, Lisa wasn't convinced and continued praying for her mother's safety. Her parents' marital trouble was the last thing she needed to deal with right now.

Not expecting company, Lisa ran to the door the minute the bell rang. Flashbacks of the night Chanelle came home drunk haunted her as she recalled the gut-wrenching feeling she had when she saw the police lights twirling through the window. That night all the anger she'd built up about Chanelle missing curfew had been temporarily pushed aside as concern for her daughter's safety took its place. Likewise, the more time passed with Chanelle missing in action, the less concerned she was about being right and the more she wanted to find her baby.

"I'm sorry…I know I should've called first." RJ stood at the door.

"That's okay; come in."

"I won't stay long. I came by to let you know that I heard from Chanelle."

Hope poured into Lisa's spirit. "Is she okay?"

"As far as I can tell. I didn't talk to her on the phone. She sent me a text message."

"What did she say?"

"Nothing much; just that she was fine and didn't want to talk to anyone."

"How can you be sure it's her? What if something happened and someone took her phone? Anyone could have sent that message."

"I think it was her."

"The only way to be sure is to send her a message asking a question that only she would know. Give me your phone," she ordered. RJ obliged and Lisa typed: What's the last name of your mother's sister?

A few minutes later a correct response came back.

Lisa immediately tried calling Chanelle from RJ's cell phone. No answer.

"Where are you?" she texted.

"I'm fine."

"It's Mom. Dad's here; please come home."

"Tell Dad I'll talk to him later. Don't want to talk to you."

Those words pierced Lisa's heart. She tried sending other messages and no longer received replies.

"Well, I'm glad to know she's okay," she said defeatedly.

When RJ pulled her close to his chest, she didn't resist. "When she contacts me again, I'll try and convince her to call you." He bent down and kissed her forehead and Lisa surprised herself when she didn't withdraw. She took in every whiff of his cologne as she listened to his heartbeat. There was a familiarity about being in RJ's arms that felt good, scarily good. Wondering what Eric would think if he walked in and saw this, Lisa quickly put space between them. "Um...thanks for stopping by."

"I love you," RJ blurted.

Lisa stood speechless. She could tell by the sincerity of his eyes that he meant every word. She cared for RJ as her child's father and her ex-husband, but she *loved* Eric.

"It's okay; I don't expect you to say anything. I just want you to know that I love you. Pardon me if I'm overstepping my bounds due to your situation and all, but I couldn't hold it in any longer. Anyhow, I'll let you know when I hear from Chanelle again."

He left Lisa paralyzed in speech and walked out.

CHAPTER 22
A Bit On Edge

L isa sat at her desk, trying to work, despite her mind being millions of miles away. Over six weeks had passed and Chanelle still had not contacted her. The joy Lisa felt the night of her engagement party had been replaced by the memories of having a fistfight with her daughter. Liv had emailed her tons of pictures from the day of the party and Lisa would often stare at them, wondering why Chanelle seemed to have such a dramatic shift in her mood.

Lisa's emotions swung back and forth from angry to hurt. She was hurt because her daughter had made contact with RJ and her mother, but not her. She was angry because, technically, Chanelle had been in the wrong, so as far as Lisa was concerned, her daughter really had no right to be mad. Chanelle was legally an adult now so maybe this whole disappearing act was a stunt to prove her independence. Lisa refused to leave any more messages for her. Chanelle was obviously on some type of power play. Having all that money in her account probably increased her feelings of autonomy. Lisa was sure her unruly daughter would be back once her finances were depleted. It was only a matter of time.

Lisa was less reluctant to call her sister. "Callie, please call me back," she pleaded with her sister's answering machine one afternoon while sitting at work. "I haven't said anything to Mama about what you told me, or anyone else. I want to talk to you, please. I'm worried about you, Cal. I love you!" She hung up in despair. She'd left messages for her sister on nearly a daily basis, sometimes multiple times, yet Callie never called back.

"This is Lisa," she answered when her work phone rang.

"How's my lovely lady doing?"

"I'm all right, Eric. I was just thinking about Callie."

"I know; that's why I want to take you out tonight. We haven't gone anywhere since the engagement party."

"Baby, I haven't been in the mood. I don't feel like going anywhere tonight."

"Come on, sweetheart. You've been down in the dumps too long. Let's get out and have some fun. I can't believe that you've allowed your sister's departure to affect you like this. What's the deal with her anyway? You never really said."

Up to this point, Lisa had shared pretty much everything about her life with Eric, but she couldn't bring herself to tell him, or Olivia, about Callie's illness. It seemed so personal and she didn't want to betray her sister's trust, though technically it had been revealed out of anger rather than confidence. "It's too complicated to explain. The bottom line is that we were right in assuming that she was still having trouble dealing with her husband's suicide. I can't help but to worry about her."

"If you're worrying then you're not praying. Remember Paul's instructions in 1 Peter 5:7? 'Casting all your care upon him; for he careth for you.'"

Lisa rolled her eyes. Sometimes she wished she could talk to him about her feelings without always being rebuked. "Yes, I'm very familiar with that scripture. Excuse me for not being instantly deep and having real feelings. It's hard not to worry about the people you care most about. Obviously you're worried about me to some extent or else you wouldn't be pressing me to go out tonight."

"I'm concerned about your well-being, but I'm not sitting around moping like you are about your sister."

"Eric, I'm already stressed out enough; talking to you isn't making it any better."

"I'm sorry, sweetheart. I love and care about you so much, I just...never mind. We haven't hung out for over a month. The devil is trying to mess with me. I'm dealing with a selfish spirit right now. I really miss spending time with you, like we used to before all this drama unfolded. I'm sorry for getting on your back. I love you and want the best for you. I thought maybe going out would get your mind off of things; at least temporarily."

"I love you, too." Her irritation with him softened. It made her feel good that, even when he was on her nerves, Eric always had her best interest at heart. "You're probably right. It may do me some good to get out."

"So, then, we're on for this evening?"

"Yes, we're on."

Lisa hung up the phone appreciating the wonderful man whom God had blessed her with. They had yet to officially set a wedding date. With all the other stuff on Lisa's mind, she hadn't been able to devote as much attention to planning her wedding as she'd liked. Hopefully they could still tie the knot before this year came to an end, which wasn't far away.

"Knock knock," Olivia announced her arrival.

"Hey, what brings you by?"

Olivia seemed a bit on edge. "I came by to see if you have heard from Chanelle at all today."

"No, I haven't, why? Is there something you know that I don't?" Olivia took a seat. "She called Justin this morning."

"She did! What did she say? Did you talk to her?"

"No. She didn't call the house. She called his cell phone. He's back on campus now."

"What did she say?" pressed Lisa.

"From what I understand, nothing much. She didn't want Justin worrying about her so she called to let him know she's okay."

Lisa's anger resurfaced. "See how screwed up her priorities are. I mean, I'm glad she called Justin. He's been such a good influence on her; maybe he can talk some sense into her head. I'm angry that she hasn't called me. She hasn't even called Mama or RJ. She's sent them a few text messages, but that's it. Did she say where she was staying?"

"No. Do you think she's over at that one girl's house?"

"Who, Gericka? I doubt it. It's possible that she may have spent a night or two over there, but Chanelle has been gone for a while. I'm sure Gericka's parents would have called me by now."

"And you're sure Chanelle hasn't tried to contact you this morning?"

"Yes, I'm sure. She hasn't contacted me at all. You know, I'm worried about her, but on the other hand, it ticks me off that she's being this stubborn because I wouldn't let her use my car to pick up her friend. Do you think that there may be something else going on with her?"

"Like what?"

"I don't know; that's what I'm trying to figure out. Maybe she's going through some late adolescent crisis. She's supposed to start school soon. Maybe that's got her a little nervous. You think?"

Olivia shrugged her shoulders. "Who knows? Chanelle has given you trouble before. It's hard to tap into the mind of a teenager.

You probably need to do something to get your mind off of her."

"You sound like Eric. He was just getting on my case about worrying too much. He's taking me out tonight."

"Good…Well, listen, I'll let you get back to work. I wanted to touch base with you about Chanelle. Call me later, okay?" She left just as unexpectedly as she had arrived.

CHAPTER 23
Bottom Dollar

As expected, Eric showed up promptly, holding a batch of long-stemmed roses. "Thank you," she beamed.

"I was hoping these would get me out of the dog house."

"You were never in there." Lisa smiled lovingly as he leaned down for a kiss. "Let me grab my purse and I'll be ready."

"You're wearing *that*…?"

"Yeah. Why?" Lisa eyed his attire. Eric had on a pair of khaki shorts with a white polo shirt. She thought the yellow sundress she was wearing was a nice fit with his apparel.

"Nothing. You look nice…"

Nice? She didn't spend an hour primping merely to look *nice*. "What's wrong?"

"It's just…you look a little too worldly. Maybe it's the earrings. They're awfully long, don't you think?"

Lisa laughed. "You're probably right. Truth is, I raided Chanelle's jewelry box." She quickly pulled the three-inch shimmering stems from her ears.

She started to go back upstairs to get some other ones, but Eric said, "Honey, you don't need any at all. You look gorgeous," so she laid them on the coffee table and they left.

Eric took her to dinner at a restaurant up North, which happened to have a local Jazz band playing that night. Eric didn't seem too crazy about the music and Lisa assumed it was because this band had a more contemporary style than the band Olivia had booked for their engagement party. Eric was more on the conservative side. Lisa didn't mind the music. It provided the mental getaway she had been in need of. "Thanks, Eric. I'm so glad you convinced me to come out. This has been good for me. You always seem to know exactly what I need."

"That's my job. As your future husband, I have to look after you. I take my role as your spiritual covering very seriously."

"You amaze me. I'm looking forward to becoming your wife."

"And me as well. The other day Mother asked me if we had set a date."

Lisa wished he hadn't interrupted their evening by bringing up that nut! "Really? That surprises me."

He chuckled. "I realize she gave you a hard time when you all first met, but she's just as excited as I am."

If she didn't have the willpower to keep her lips glued shut, Lisa could have really said something sarcastic in response.

"What do you think about getting married New Year's Eve? It'll be a great way to end one year and bring in the next," he gleamed.

"That'll be a great idea."

Eric and Lisa continued talking about their wedding while holding hands and gazing into each other's eyes. They each ordered a slice of double-layer chocolate fudge cake for dessert. Eric's came topped with crushed nuts, but of course, due to Lisa's peanut allergies, she had to order hers without.

The night had been very peaceful and Lisa was happy to have the mental diversion. She got through the entire evening without bringing up any of her family drama.

"Baby, will you excuse me for a moment?" Eric grimaced in pain.

"Sure. Are you okay?"

"I will be. Let's just say that the chocolate cake is already starting to run through me, if you know what I mean."

Lisa laughed. It was more information than she wanted to know, but she found it amusing that they were able to disclose such intimate details to one another; and was glad that she wasn't in a similar position.

She began to drink the rest of her half and half, a drink extremely popular in Baltimore comprised of half lemonade and half iced tea. When she moved to Columbus, Lisa was shocked that not many people had heard of the drink. It was a common thing where she was from and had only recently been popularized here. Previously, whenever she went out, she had to custom order it and give her server specific instructions on how to make it. The half and half she was drinking didn't quite have that Baltimorian taste, but it would do. Once she had polished off her drink, instead of sitting at the table waiting for Eric to finish his business, she decided to join the rest of the crowd on the dance floor as the smooth Jazz selection played.

As she swayed to the music she found herself getting a little envious of the other couples and wished Eric would hurry and join her. He didn't seem like much of a dancer, but she'd planned on getting him out that night. She closed her eyes and her body flowed slowly with the rhythm. It was relaxing and song after song she danced away every burden on her mind. Lisa imagined herself free as a bird. No limitations...no bondage...no—

"What do you think you're doing?" Her tranquility came to an abrupt end by the sound of Eric's fuming voice yelling loudly in her ear.

She looked up and saw fire in his eyes. "What?"

"Let's go. We have to get out of here. This was a bad idea." He grabbed her arm, dragging her away.

She jerked free from his grip. "I don't want to go anywhere. I'm having a good time. What's wrong with you?"

"We'll discuss this in the car." He threw some money on the table and walked out. Lisa had no choice but to follow him if she wanted a ride back home.

"What was that all about?"

Eric remained silent as he peeled out of the parking lot, likely leaving skid marks. "I cannot believe you would disgrace me like that!" He stared straight ahead, gripping the steering wheel so tight Lisa swore he would get calluses.

"What did I do?"

"I go to the restroom for twenty minutes and come back to find you sashaying on the dance floor."

"You can't be serious?"

"Oh, you bet your bottom dollar, I'm serious. God has anointed me as His chosen vessel. My last name is Freeman, for goodness sake. I'm a *free* man and you must walk in a way that represents my deliverance from the bondage of this world. No wife of mine has any business out there pop, lock and dropping it like it's hot!"

"I have not yet become your wife! Besides that, I wasn't doing anything. You act like I was all up on somebody dancing provocatively or something."

"You were dancing with the Devil!"

She laughed in disbelief. "What?"

"Yeah, Satan had his arms wrapped all around you while you were out there shaking your behind. That was the Devil's music and you were his dance partner."

Lisa had never witnessed such fury from Eric in the entire five months they'd been together. He'd always been so kind, loving and patient. "Where are you taking me?" She wondered when he exited at Miller-Kelton instead of continuing east on I-70.

"We need to go someplace quiet to talk."

"No, what you need to do is take me home. I don't want to talk to you."

He ignored her and drove to the nearest park anyhow.

Lisa scanned their environment, examining any and all vehicles passing by.

"What are you looking for?" he snarled, turning off the engine.

"I don't know. I'm thinking this has to be some kind of practical joke. I keep hoping to spot some type of hidden camera crew or something. Am I getting *Punk'd*?"

"No, Lisa! I can't believe you're taking this so lightly!"

"And I can't believe you're really upset because I was dancing by myself to Jazz music, at a restaurant that *you* took me to."

"I'm sorry." His demeanor suddenly changed. "You're right. I am responsible for tonight because I chose the restaurant. Had I known that the band would have been there I would have taken you somewhere else."

"I don't want to hear your apologies. It's not going to work this time. Take me home."

"I will. Baby, just hear me out first, please. I prayed every day that God would send me a Godly woman and until I met you, no one had measured up. You are the Eve to my Adam. You're the—"

"Get to the point!"

"I don't know what happened tonight. I feel the Devil is trying to come between us."

"Naw, you're not going to blame this one on the Devil. This was all you, bruh."

He sighed. "Regardless, we still have to hang in there and be strong. I admitted to you earlier that I was dealing with a selfish spirit—"

"More like a stupid one if you ask me."

"Will you please cut out all the sarcasm?"

"No, Eric, tonight you've really worked my nerves. I was enjoying myself and you managed to stress me out all over again. I should have gone with my gut and stayed home."

"I know how we can solve this real quick; let's pray together."

"Nope. I don't want to pray with you; I want to go home."

"A couple that prays together stays together. It's important to have daily devotions and prayer time with God."

"I know…I have done my devotions today. As a matter of fact, I have devotion and prayer time each morning before I leave for work. If I need to do more tonight, I'll do it on my own. Right now, I want you to take me home!"

"How long did you pray?"

"Huh?"

"This morning, in your private time…how long did you pray?"

"I don't know…I guess about fifteen or twenty minutes. Why? What does the length of my prayers have to do with anything?"

"A lot. We need to be on the same page. Starting tomorrow morning, I'm going to call you at four so we can spend time with the Lord together over the phone."

Lisa was dumbfounded. Where were the practical joke cameras when she needed them? "Either I'm excessively irritated or you're overly insane…"

"No, Lisa, I'm serious. Look at what happened to us tonight. I'm not going to blame it all on your not praying the required time. Truthfully, I probably cheated God about three minutes or so this morning. Usually I get down on my knees and pray for an hour and thirty-three minutes each morning. After I pray, I saturate myself in the Word for another hour and thirty-three minutes before I officially begin my day."

Lisa was very curious about why he timed his prayers so meticulously, but dared not to ask. Instead, she replied, "It's nice to know you have that much time on your hands every morning, but I don't."

"Well, I suggest you change that. When you become my wife we will definitely be doing our devotion and prayer time together—exactly an hour and thirty-three minutes for each."

Now she couldn't help herself, she had to know. "Why are so you specific about the timeframe?"

"Because…" He looked shocked, as if she should already know. "Jesus was thirty-three when He was crucified, signaling that He had completed His mission. In order for our devotion and prayer times to be complete, they must end at thirty-three."

Lisa swallowed hard not to laugh. "After tonight, I no longer want to be your wife. No offense, but you're crazy. I now have a better appreciation for the fact that God did not give me a spirit of fear, but one of power, love and a *sound* mind, which is much more than I can say for you."

"Are you trying to quote 2 Timothy 1:7? If so, know that it doesn't say 'God did not.' It says God *hath* not…" he emphasized passionately. "If you're going to quote the Bible, do it correctly!" He flipped the switch and got angry once again. "I don't know how you were brought up, but Mother raised me never to change the Word of God."

Lisa laughed, sarcastically. "Oh, so your mama has something to do with this? That doesn't surprise me. She's not the brightest apple in the bunch. For the last time, take…me…home! "

Lisa leaned her head back on the headrest and closed her eyes. Hearing Eric fumble for a few seconds, she expected him to start the car and pull off. Instead, he'd poured anointing oil on his hand and the next thing she knew he'd placed his greasy palm on her forehead and began shouting: "Satan, I rebuke you in the Name of Jesus. Come out of her. Lisa Hampton, I command you by the power invested in me through the Holy Spirit to come forth!"

No longer mad, she was livid. Lisa slapped his hand off her so quick. "Get off of me, you nut!"

Eric continued screaming for her to "come forth" as if he was Jesus calling Lazarus from the grave. She got out of the car; her forehead dripped with oil. Immediately she tried to call Olivia for a ride, but got her voicemail. She dialed her mother's number and tensed when her father answered.

"Can I speak to Mama, please?" Lisa was not yet fully supportive of the two of them living together. Though she had come a long way, him answering the phone was something that she still wasn't ready for.

"Hey, Skeeter; one second please."

"Hello?"

"Mama, I need you to come get me..."

CHAPTER 24
True Colors

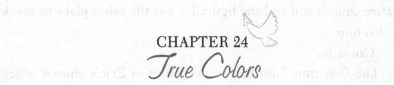

L isa waited patiently for her mother as Eric eerily continued sitting in his car, yelling and rebuking the spirit of Satan to release and let her go. She prayed that her mother had accurately written down the directions she had given. About fifteen minutes later, Lisa recognized her father's gold Cutlass coming her way. She slid in the back seat as Eric continued his séance.

Safely secured in her father's car, Lisa was now more amused by Eric's behavior than she was mad at him. She rolled with laughter as she told her parents about the night's events. "See, I knew that man was crazy," her mother bragged. "I tried to tell you the night y'all got engaged. I said, 'something's not quite right about him,' but noooah, you said I was just saying that because he wasn't RJ."

The sound of her mother's "I-told-you-so" tone got under Lisa's skin a little, but part of her wondered if her mother had more of a spirit of discernment than she had given her credit for. It was she who had said the exact same thing about Marvin, Callie's late husband. Callie's latest revelation proved their mother to be right as well.

Lisa didn't go to Bible study that week so as to avoid running into Eric. His voice messages to see if she had been "clothed and in her right mind" had gone unanswered. By Sunday morning, she knew she had to face him. After service, she knocked on his office door. There were many people lingering after church still and she figured it was the safest place to speak with him.

"Come in."

The first time Lisa had stepped foot in Eric's church office was earlier this year when she followed him back after one of the anniversary meetings to get some papers from him. Back then, she had been impressed with the plaques of scriptures outlining his wall. There were sixty-six plaques representing a favorite verse of his from each book. His tiny bookshelf was aligned with concordances, bibles and pictures of Bishop and Mrs. Henry Freeman. He had not one, not two, not even three, but seven large statues of Jesus dying on the cross. Plastic doves hung from the ceiling and over in the corner was a life-sized statue of Jesus. Initially, Lisa saw all of this as symbolic of Eric's deep spiritual connection with God and she had been drawn to him. After the stunt he'd pulled at the park, it became apparent how all of these were warning signs of his insanity.

If Eric was surprised or happy to see her, Lisa couldn't tell by his expression. He stared at her blankly. "What can I do for you?"

She closed the door to give them some privacy. "Hi, Eric. I came—"

"It's Minister Freeman," he huffed.

Lisa chuckled, thinking back to the conversation when he'd asked her to call him by his first name, stating how he wasn't hung up on titles. "Look, I'm not here to get into it with you.

I think we both understand that our relationship is over. I wanted to give this back to you." She held the ring out to him.

"Romans 11:29 says 'For the gifts and calling of God are without repentance.'"

Despite her conscious screaming, "*Run!* He's crazy," curiosity prompted Lisa to ask him how in the world that scripture was relevant.

"Did I ever tell you my middle name?"

"No."

"It's Joshua. My name is Eric Joshua Freeman."

"O-kay. And your point would be?"

"The name Joshua has a very significant meaning. It is the equivalent of Jesus and means Savior. Don't you see? I am so connected with the Holy Spirit that, in many ways, I am God. If Jesus weren't Jesus, *I* would be. That ring was a gift to you because you are called to be my wife. But the devil has blinded you to the truth. I will—"

Lisa couldn't take it anymore. She tossed the diamond as he spoke and quickly got out of his office. Speed-walking to her car, in case Eric came after, she prayed under her breath. "Thank You, Lord, for allowing me to see his true colors before I made the mistake of marrying him!"

Later that evening, Lisa and Olivia met at The Cheesecake Factory at Easton for dinner. "I couldn't believe it when he said that!" Lisa shared with her best friend Eric's latest rantings. "Can you imagine how crazy he would be if we actually had gotten married? I tell you what, I'm going to listen to my mama the next time she warns me about a guy."

Olivia had remained quiet most of the dinner. She chuckled

slightly as Lisa filled her in on all the drama with Eric, but there was a heartiness from her laugh that was missing. "Liv, is everything okay?"

"Yeah, why do you ask?"

"This past week, you haven't seemed to be yourself."

"I'm missing my husband. He's back in New York now. I can't wait until he comes home, which probably won't be for about another month."

For some reason Lisa wasn't convinced by Olivia's explanation. They'd been friends for four years, since Lisa first moved to Ohio, and they'd weathered many of Isaac's business trips together. Though lonesome at times, Olivia never seemed to be this affected by his absences. Isaac and Liv appeared to be the perfect couple. Lisa hoped that his frequent traveling wasn't causing them to have major marital troubles that, perhaps, were too painful for Olivia to share. She would eventually get down to the bottom of what was bugging her friend. She and Liv normally didn't keep things from each other.

"You still haven't heard from Chanelle?"

"No," she admitted sadly. "The last text message RJ received from her said that she wanted to be left alone. Has Justin heard from her again?"

"She told him the same thing."

"I don't know what's going on with that girl, but it's officially out of my hands. She's an adult now and I'm going to let her live her own life, even though I see her headed down the wrong path. I really hope she starts school and doesn't screw that up."

"Chanelle has been giving you problems for a long time. Her behavior does not surprise me."

Lisa was a little hurt by Olivia's callous response, but she stuffed it and quickly changed the subject. They continued talking about various things over dinner. Olivia mentioned how excited Justin was about this year's football season. Their conversation was interrupted when Lisa's cell phone rang. She didn't recognize the number and had her daughter not been missing in action, she might not have answered it. "Excuse me for just a second, Liv...hello?"

CHAPTER 25
Down Right Ignorance

Lisa hung up the phone, horrified.

"Was that Chanelle?" Olivia seemed on edge.

"No, it was my nephew, Bryan. He said that Callie's in the hospital. She tried to commit suicide."

"Oh my!"

"I-I need to get there as soon as possible." Lisa pulled out the BlackBerry that Olivia had given her last Christmas and frantically searched for her boss's number. "I'll call and leave Neil a message. I'll call Megan, too. Hopefully, she can handle things while I'm gone. I need to get out of here. I don't know how I'm going to tell Mama about this. She's already worried to death about Chanelle and now Callie…It seems like my family is suddenly falling apart," she cried.

Olivia reached across the table and grabbed her hand. "Why don't you go talk to your mother now. Don't even worry about calling Neil or Megan. I'm going in for the board meeting in the morning so I'll talk to both of them for you."

As tears dripped onto her friend's hand, Lisa smiled. "Thanks, Liv."

"Now go 'head and get out of here. I'll call you tomorrow."

Lisa took her friend's advice and ran out of the restaurant. Already in a panicky state of mind, Lisa called RJ and asked if he'd come with her to her mother's house, sharing with him for the first time Callie's positive diagnosis in addition to the details of Bryan's call. RJ stepped up to the challenge without hesitation, meeting her at her home. They then rode to her parents' apartment together.

As expected, her mother broke down in tears when Lisa disclosed Callie's secret and suicide attempt. "You were right about Marvin all along, Mama," Lisa admitted. For years, their mother had professed that Marvin was "different."

"I wish I wasn't," she sobbed, uncontrollably. Lisa watched as her father held back his own grief and wiped her mother's tears. He appeared gentle, not at all like the alcoholic monster that had beaten her to a pulp.

From what Lisa was told, he had been sober since the incident last summer and was even attending church with her mother. Time would reveal if, in fact, he really had changed.

Escorted by RJ to the airport, Lisa and her parents were on the first available flight out to Sacramento that same evening. "Will you call and let me know how she's doing?" RJ asked.

Lisa nodded affirmatively.

"If I hear anything else from Chanelle, I'll tell you."

"Thanks for everything."

It was extremely late when their plane arrived, so instead of taking them to the hospital that night, Bryan took them all to Callie's home where they planned to stay. The three-hour time difference between California and Ohio had already taken a toll on Lisa's parents and they were soon off to bed, but Lisa and Bryan stayed up to talk for a while in the living room. Though Lisa was only about seven or eight years older than Bryan, they really weren't all that close, more likely because of the geographical differences than anything else. That night they both needed emotional support and thus, leaned on each other.

Bryan, who lived almost six hours from Sacramento in L.A., had been notified of his mother's suicide attempt by EMS. Apparently the mailman had spotted her seemingly lifeless body through the window. "I had no idea that she had even come back. I would call her cell phone and she pretended to still be in Ohio with you. I just feel so bad. I should have made it a point to contact you on a regular basis, but Mom was so adamant that no one knew about her condition I was afraid I'd somehow tip you off."

"It's not your fault. I should have been more attentive. I picked up funny vibes with her, but I've been so wrapped up in my own affairs that I sort of just ignored her. I mean, I prayed for her and all, but I never really sat down and gave her the attention that she probably needed. The night before she left we got into this huge argument and, in the heat of the moment, she told me that she was HIV-positive. I woke up the next morning and she was gone. I've been trying to call her ever since, but she wouldn't answer my calls. In retrospect, I should have called you as well, then you would have known that she was back and maybe this whole thing could have been avoided."

She and Bryan continued talking about Callie for a while, both feeling at fault. Lisa finally broke the cycle when she asked him how his wife, Tyra, and their baby girl, Naomi, were doing.

"Naomi's great." His face shone with pride as he pulled a picture of her from his wallet. Lisa's heart melted at the photo of the newborn dressed in a "Daddy's Girl" t-shirt. "This was taken the first day we brought her home from the hospital. She's ten weeks now. Tyra's got some new photos of her. She was supposed to have sent them off by now. Did you get one?"

"No, not yet. I did get one of the newborn pictures taken at the hospital. By the way, thank you for that."

"No problem. I'll remind Tyra to send you a recent one."

"When are they coming to see Callie? I'm looking forward to seeing Naomi in person."

Bryan sucked his teeth. "I don't think that's going to happen anytime soon. Honestly, Lisa, Tyra and I have been having problems." Pain peered through his eyes as he shared how Tyra insisted that Callie leave their house because she didn't want her to spread HIV to the baby. "I couldn't believe how ignorant she acted."

"It boils down to a lack of education."

"No, it was stupidity. The doctor even told her that there was no risk to the baby, but she listened to her ghetto cousin's boyfriend who said he saw on the news how this woman got HIV from drinking from a glass that an infected person had recently drank from. The glass had been washed, but supposedly traces of HIV were still on the rim."

"That's ridiculous. By now everyone should know that HIV can't be contracted that way."

"I tried to tell Tyra that, but she wouldn't listen."

"Give her some time; she'll eventually come around."

"We'll see. I need to call her. Part of me feels bad because I was pretty mad at her when I found out about Mom's suicide attempt. I really let her have it and I said some horrible things."

"Your emotions were running high. I'm sure when you call her she'll understand."

"Anyhow, the last thing you need to hear right now is about my marital woes. Congratulations, by the way. Mom told me that you are engaged."

Lisa laughed. "Boy, do I have a story to tell you."

Amazingly, Callie was in good spirits the next morning and pleasantly surprised to see Lisa and their parents since Bryan hadn't told her they were coming. After tears were shed and "I love you's" exchanged, Callie asked for the latest update on Chanelle. Eventually everyone settled in for what could be considered a "normal" hospital visit, under the circumstances. Their mother fussed at Callie for not eating, Callie complained about the hospital food, Lisa maintained the peace between them as best she could, and Bryan and their father talked about everything from sports to politics.

The next day was much of the same and on Thursday, Callie was released. Lisa had planned to go home first thing Saturday morning, but her parents were staying another week. Concerned that she hadn't really gotten any alone time with her sister, on Friday Lisa asked Bryan to take her parents out for a while so she and Callie could have some time together.

Callie was sitting on her bed reading her Bible when Lisa walked into the room. "You got a minute?" she nervously asked.

"Of course, I do. What's up?"

"I just wanted to say that I'm sorry for everything that I said to you the night—"

"Girl, don't even worry about it. I said some harsh things myself, so I'm sorry."

Lisa bent down to hug her. "I love you, Cal."

"I love you, too."

Seconds passed before their embrace ended. "I'm sorry for being so consumed with my life that I haven't been there for you. I love you," she repeated, making no effort to mask her quivering voice. "I will never let you down again."

"Girl, stop getting all mushy on me and making promises you won't be able to keep," Callie teased, but Lisa saw the water in her eyes. "Chances are you will let me down again, and I you, because we're human. But more than that, we are sisters and that's a bond we've both foolishly disregarded. *I* never want that to happen again." She smiled and her tears finally fell.

"Ditto," Lisa said in agreement. "So, then can we call a truce?"

"Yes, of course," Callie beamed, wiping her cheeks. "Now that we both got that off of our chests, what's up with you and Eric? I noticed you're not wearing your engagement ring. What happened?"

Callie laughed until she cried as Lisa unfolded the tale of Minister Eric Joshua Freeman and his mother, Mrs. Henry Freeman. Lisa had never told her sister about how her trip to Sandusky, OH to meet Eric's mom went. It seemed like each time Lisa told the story about Eric flipping out on her, the funnier it got. She and Callie laughed so hard that their stomachs hurt. "Oh my goodness," Callie continued bursting with laughter. "Can you imagine what he must've been like as child? That man didn't become crazy overnight. This has been a long time coming, and I'm sure it was his mother's fault. Somebody ought to put Precious and his mama on medication."

In all thirty-nine years of her life, Lisa could not recall a single time when she and her sister had shared such a joyous and intimate moment. "I'm going to make it a point to get out here and visit more often," she said.

"I was just thinking the same thing."

"I still remember the day Mama and Daddy brought you home from the hospital. I was like 'Finally! I have a sister.' My only regret was that they waited until I was nine to have you. It would have been nice for us to actually go through the same stages of life together. Regardless, though, you were my pride and joy. Somewhere down the line, life started getting hard for me and I got bitter. I think in many ways I resented you because you were everything that I didn't think I was. You were, *are*, beautiful—so slender and thin; and I'm so wide and fat. You seemed to have everything and I had nothing. The more life kept screwing with me, the more I resented you. I wanted children so bad, but because of what happened, I was unable to have any; and you were pregnant with Chanelle by age twenty."

"Girl, Bryan adores you."

"I know...and I him. For years, I'd dealt with the fact that my life was what it was and I moved on, but finding out I'm HIV-positive was a blow that even I wasn't ready to take. It definitely came from left field."

Callie began sharing with Lisa about the day her world fell apart. That day she had had a full teaching schedule. She had been at the college since seven that morning, lectured in five classes, and still held office hours for students who wished to speak with her.

It was about six in the evening when she left the campus. It was days like this when Callie appreciated all the more living within a ten-minute drive of the college and being able to take the back roads instead of the congested freeway.

"Let's have breakout sessions on various topics like single parenting, ways to enhance your marriage, life after menopause, etcetera," she'd brainstormed aloud to Sister Ellis, her co-chair for the church's Women's Retreat, while in route.

"That's a great idea! There are going to be women from all walks of life attending. It will be better for us to offer enough workshops that will minister to various needs. Do you have any speakers in mind for these sessions?"

"Yeah, I do, but I'm going to have to call you back. I just got home and I have company waiting for me."

Callie pulled into her horseshoe-shaped driveway, parking

behind the gold Chevy Avalanche that belonged to her late husband's best friend, Kelsey. He was sitting on her front steps when she got out. "Hey, Kelsey, I haven't seen you in a while. Come on in. What brings you by?"

Kelsey didn't budge. "I need to talk to you about Marvin."

Kelsey had taken her husband's suicide as hard as she did. He and Marvin had been friends since shortly after she and Marvin married. Having no family of his own, Kelsey had been adopted into theirs. "What about him?"

"I think I know why he killed himself."

Sweat immediately broke through her pores and her heartbeat flared up. Marvin's suicide note left no clues and the haunting question of "Why?" had been nipping at Callie's conscious and unconscious mind. "What are you talking about?"

Kelsey chewed his bottom lip before speaking. "I think he was positive?"

His explanation didn't immediately register in her mind. "Positive *about…*"

"Positive like in test results. I think Marvin had HIV."

Callie shook her head in disbelief. "Kelsey, why in the world would you make such an accusation? His death has been hard enough on me without factoring in this insane possibility."

"Callie, listen to me. I recently found out that I'm positive and I haven't been with anyone else since Marvin died."

Dizziness immediately began to circle around her. She willed her mind steady enough to ask for clarification. "Please say you're not telling me what I think you're saying? That you and Marvin were—"

"In love… We were for many years. He could never find the courage to leave you because of Bryan. I was faithful to him, but it's obvious that he wasn't to me. He wasn't to either one of us."

Hearing the word "us" brought with it so much pain that Callie physically became ill. She couldn't believe that she and this man, whom she'd welcomed into her family, had intimately shared her husband. She leaned over in the bushes to vomit as thoughts of the countless fishing trips and hunting getaways Kelsey and Marvin took several weekends a month filled her head. What she had thought were general male-bonding outings had most likely been homosexual *Brokeback Mountain* rendezvous. The more she recalled the many nights she'd slid into lingerie to properly welcome her husband back home, not knowing that he'd already given or received of the same, the more her stomach ached and the faster its contents hurled from her body.

"Are you okay?" He leaned over to assist her.

"Get off of me!" she screamed, punching and kicking him uncontrollably. He made several attempts to hold and comfort her, but she resisted, yelling and assaulting him until he got back into his truck and took off.

"I didn't want to believe him," Callie now said to Lisa, "But then a couple weeks later I found out that I was also positive and was devastated."

"How are you holding up now?"

"If you mean will I attempt suicide again, no way!" she swore. "Lisa, I should be dead. I took a *hundred* sleeping pills and I didn't die! While I lay on the kitchen floor, I could hear things going on around me, but I couldn't move a muscle. I remember screaming silently, 'Lord, just take me. I want to die,' but it was like God was saying to me that I still had work to do. I kid you not, Lisa, I begged to die and God would not allow me to do so. When I became conscious in the hospital, I promised the Lord that whatever He had planned for me, I would willingly accept the assignment."

"Wow…It's so awesome to hear you put a positive spin on it."

"I'm positive because God is positive. To be real, I still don't understand why this has happened, but I'm no longer at a place where I need to understand, because no matter what, God will work this out. It's a doozie of a job for Him, but He can do it. As long as I trust and serve Him, He'll handle all the rest. God has given me a second chance and I'm embracing it. What the devil meant for evil, God will turn around for good. I don't know how He will; I just know He will."

CHAPTER 26
Water Under the Bridge

As planned, Lisa returned home late Saturday afternoon after having an early morning breakfast with Callie. The two of them went to a twenty-four hour restaurant and had pancakes. Lisa wasn't all that hungry, but she enjoyed watching her sister indulge in her favorite morning meal. RJ was there to pick Lisa up from the airport when she returned home.

"How was your trip?" he asked.

"It was great. Callie is doing really well. She said to tell you hi. Last night she was very emotional, but it was a good thing. Tyra surprised her and Bryan by bringing their daughter to see Callie. That was Cal's first time seeing the baby. She didn't think she would even get a chance to see her."

"Why?"

"Tyra was paranoid about Naomi, that's the baby's name, getting HIV. Callie was supposed to stay with them for a while, but Tyra didn't want her at the house. That's why she came up here."

"Ouch...I know Tyra's reaction had to hurt."

"It did, but all is well now. Tyra, bless her heart, was so remorseful. She apologized and cried so much that I started crying. This morning she and Bryan dropped me off at the airport on the way back to LA. They were leaving the baby with Callie overnight and coming back tomorrow."

"How far is it to LA from Sacramento?"

"About six hours..."

"Whew, that's a lot of driving in a day's time."

"I know..."

"I'm surprised that Bryan and Tyra would leave Callie with the baby so soon after her suicide attempt. I guess it's okay since your parents are still with her."

"Mama and Daddy actually went as well."

"So Tyra and Bryan are leaving Callie *alone* with the baby?" He seemed worried. "I mean, I'm not saying she would try to hurt the baby or anything, but you never know what's going on in someone's head. Callie's not the type of person I'd ever thought would try to kill herself."

"Yeah, I know what you mean, but spending time alone with the baby will be good for her. Depression is an ugly thing."

"How's she doing now? Is she on any kind of medication?"

"She's taking things for her health, but not for depression. The doctor is concerned because most people don't have such a quick turnaround, but Callie is doing great. She's like a totally different person now."

"I figured she'd at least be on some type of antidepressant, but then again, I know firsthand how God can deliver a person."

"I hope He delivers Mama from gambling. She's likely to find her way to a casino while she's there. It amazes me that she doesn't think she has a problem."

"A lot of times we're blind to our own sins. We justify the things we do so we can keep doing them. It just goes to show that there's always going to be some issue God is dealing with us on."

"Yeah, but after all the years Mama has been saved she ought to know better. Seems to me like gambling was covered in Salvation 101."

"Maybe she was asleep during that course." RJ laughed, pulling into Lisa's driveway. He got out and helped her carry the bags inside the house as Lisa grabbed her mail on the way in.

"Would you like some water or something?"

"Sure."

Walking back into the kitchen, she asked him if he had heard anything else from Chanelle, but RJ had nothing to report. He took a seat at her kitchen table after she'd gotten some water for him.

Lisa began flipping through her mail that had built up over the week. "I cannot believe this!" She laughed aloud.

"What?"

"Remember when Chanelle was brought home drunk by the police officer? I couldn't figure out why the man was being so nice until he asked me to get him tickets to an Ohio State football game because of my connection with Olivia. Would you believe that officer put a friendly reminder in the mailbox for his tickets while I was gone?" She showed RJ the note.

"He knows their first game is coming soon and wanted to make sure you didn't forget. You better get on it. He gave you his telephone number and everything, so I'm sure he expects to hear from you," he teased.

Lisa rolled her eyes. "I'll mention it to Liv when I talk to her. He *did* go out of his way to help, even if he did have an ulterior motive. Speaking of Liv, I need to see what she's up to. I haven't talked to her all week long."

"You've been away. I'm sure she understands."

"Yeah, but something's going on with her. She's been acting a little weird lately. I'm concerned that she may be having marital trouble. I don't know why I'm telling you all of this, you couldn't care less."

"I don't mind listening to you. I'm surprised you're talking to me about this and not your fiancé. Have you guys set a wedding date yet?"

Lisa playfully glared at him. "Why are you asking me about him? Don't even try to pretend like you don't already know."

"Know what?" RJ smirked.

"You're not blind; you see that I'm no longer wearing an engagement ring." She wiggled the fingers on her left hand. "Plus, as much as you and Mama talk, I'm positive she's already told you about what happened with Eric."

"She said you should come forth and tell me yourself." He chuckled.

"Ha, ha, ha...," she said blandly.

"For what it's worth, I'm sorry that things didn't work out between the two of you."

"Yeah, I bet you're all broken up inside."

He reached across the table and grabbed her hand. "I meant what I said. I love you, Lisa. I'm sorry for everything I did to you. If I could take it all back, I would. I do love you; I've never stopped loving you."

She sat frozen, unable to break his gaze or pull away from his grip. There was no doubt that part of her still cared for RJ. How could she not? They were married for fifteen years. He was her child's father, first love, her first kiss...her first everything, of course she cared about him, but *love*? Maybe in a godly way as Jesus commanded or like one loves a puppy. But there was no way she could open her heart to him after all he had put her through. How could she trust him after he'd betrayed her so devastatingly? Yet, she couldn't explain why her heart fluttered when RJ spoke those words as if she had been waiting to hear them.

Lisa jumped when the phone rang. "I-I better get that." She fumbled with the kitchen phone receiver, hoping RJ hadn't noticed. "Hello."

"Um... Hi Miss Lisa." It was Gericka, Chanelle's best friend. "Did you get the messages I left for you to call me?"

"No, honey, I've been out of town. Is everything okay?"

"I promised Chanelle that I wouldn't say anything, but—" She started crying, "I think you should know."

"Know what? Is Chanelle okay?"

At the mention of his daughter's name, RJ came over to where Lisa stood and leaned his ear to the phone. "She made me promise not to tell," cried Gericka.

"Honey, if something is wrong with Chanelle, I need to know so I can help her."

Gericka sounded like she was going to hyperventilate, but she managed to spit out the most shocking statement. "She's... pregnant."

Lisa was relieved to have RJ with her as Gericka relayed the heartbreaking information to them. Poor Gericka had held in everything, but when Chanelle told her she was pregnant, it was too much for her to handle. She told Lisa where Chanelle was staying and explained to her how to get there.

RJ sped along the way while Lisa cried. "This is all my fault," she sobbed. "I did this to her."

"Baby, don't blame yourself. You're not responsible."

"You don't understand..." Lisa couldn't talk anymore. She just closed her eyes while RJ drove as her guilt overwhelmed her.

When they pulled up to the apartment building, Lisa said to RJ, "Let me go in by myself."

"Are you sure?"

She nodded. Lisa took a deep breath as she knocked on the door. Her stomach churned. She recalled the last unannounced visit she'd made back in May after Chanelle had skipped curfew twice because she had been hanging out with Kyle. Lisa had sworn Kyle was a bad influence on her daughter and so much as said that to his mother, Stacie. Now she stood there less boldly and self-righteous than she had been before. It was at a different apartment complex then. This neighborhood wouldn't have been a favorite pick of Lisa's, but it was a step up.

"Oh, it's you!" Stacie answered the door. She apparently had darkened her hair some because Lisa remembered it being more blondish the last time she'd seen her.

"Is Chanelle here?"

"Yes, but it's my understanding that she doesn't want to talk to you."

"Stacie, I know we didn't quite get off on the right foot before, but please let me in; I want to see my daughter." Lisa was shameless in allowing her tears to fall.

If Stacie wanted to remind Lisa of all the smug things Lisa had said to her during her previous visit, her expression certainly didn't show it. Stacie seemed to sympathize with every emotion Lisa was feeling without her having to say a word. "Come on in," she said.

Unlike Stacie's previous apartment, the front door to this one opened into the kitchen instead of the living room. Based on what she had seen before, Lisa expected to see a filthy kitchen with dishes piled up to the ceiling. It wasn't spotless, but for a woman with five kids, one grandchild, and one pregnant live-in, it looked pretty good.

"You can have a seat. Chanelle's upstairs. I'll go get her."

Lisa waited for at least twenty minutes before Stacie came back down the stairs. "I tried to get her to come down here, but she doesn't want to."

Lisa's heart broke. "May I go up and talk to her?"

"You're welcomed to try."

She told Lisa which room she could find her daughter in. Lisa knocked on the door. "Chanelle, it's me. I'd like to talk to you please."

"Go away!"

Lisa tried the door. It was locked. "Baby, please open the door." Lisa listened closely as she heard footsteps coming toward the door. When it opened, Kyle walked out. "You can go in." He brushed past her.

Chanelle lay in the bed, her back toward Lisa, who sat on the edge and hovered over her. "I'm so sorry, baby. I understand if you hate me. Right now I hate myself. I want you to know that you don't have to face this pregnancy alone."

"I see Gericka can't keep her mouth shut."

"She's worried about you, Chanelle."

"Is that all she told you?"

"No. She also said that Justin raped you the night of my engagement party."

Chanelle burst in tears. "I wanted to tell you, but I didn't think you would believe me. I just wanted to talk to Gericka that night. I'm sorry I called you a bi—"

"Shh...it's okay." She held her daughter in her arms. "Baby, not only do I believe you, but I'm going to stand with you every step of the way. He's not going to get away with this. We'll see to it that he is punished for his crime."

"I don't want to press charges."

"Why not? Justin deserves to be punished."

"But Miss Olivia's your friend."

"That has nothing to do with it. You're my daughter. Besides, Liv is a good person; she'll understand. We'll do whatever's necessary to take care of you."

"You're not in this alone, sweetheart." RJ's deep voice penetrated the atmosphere. Startled by the sound of her father's voice, Chanelle looked his way. "I've been waiting anxiously in the car, so I came in. I was with your mother when she got the call. I want you to know that we will both be there for you."

"But, Mama, Miss Olivia—"

"I'm not worried about Olivia. I'm worried about you and I want you to come home."

"I don't know about that. Stacie said I could stay here as long as I need to."

"You're officially grown now, so I can't make you come with me, but I want you to. Home is where you belong."

It took some convincing, but Chanelle ultimately decided to go with Lisa. As they were headed out, both Kyle and Stacie hugged Chanelle. Lisa still wasn't crazy about Kyle's baggy pants or the cornrows he sported, but she was impressed by his compassion. "Take care, Shorty," he said to Chanelle. "Call and let me know how you are, okay?"

Chanelle nodded and Kyle looked like he wanted to hold her in his arms and never let her go.

"I love you and I'm here whenever you need me," Stacie added.

"Thanks, Stacie...I love you, too."

Under any other circumstances there might have been a twinge of jealousy as Lisa witnessed the obvious bond between her daughter and Kyle's mother. But, feeling as if she, herself, had let Chanelle down, Lisa was thankful that Stacie had been there for her. Sure, Stacie was young, too young to have five children and be a grandmother in Lisa's opinion, but there was obviously a warm-hearted side to her that Lisa hadn't taken the time to understand.

Before walking out, Lisa turned to Stacie and said, "Thank you..." The woman she once deemed an unfit and neglectful mother had unselfishly opened her home and heart to Chanelle, and for that, Lisa had a new sense of admiration for her. "I'm sorry for the way I acted toward you.

"Don't worry about it. It's squashed. As far as I'm concerned, it's water under the bridge. Chanelle's well-being is all that matters now."

CHAPTER 27
Just Stuff

RJ and Lisa wanted to take Chanelle immediately down to the police station, but she wasn't ready and wanted to go home. RJ drove separately and Lisa rode home with Chanelle in the used Honda Accord that she had bought herself with her graduation money. Chanelle was virtually silent during the ride and Lisa couldn't help but blame herself for Chanelle's rape since she had practically forced her daughter into Justin's arms. It had been almost two months since Lisa had seen her daughter. She thought back to the night of the engagement party and how withdrawn Chanelle had been. Lisa wished she had asked more questions instead of buying Justin's answer that Chanelle was tired. It sickened her to think about how charming he'd pretended to be, complimenting her that night, all the while knowing that he'd sexually assaulted her daughter. If she could get her hands around his neck…

Justin had hurt two of the people she loved dearly. Not only was she worried about Chanelle, but she was worried about Olivia as well. Lisa was going to have to be strong for the both of them. Justin had violated everyone's trust, including his mother's. Liv was going to be devastated by her son's actions, and Lisa needed to do her best to remain strong because Olivia, and especially Chanelle, needed her to be.

When they got to the house, Chanelle asked to be alone and went straight to her room while RJ stayed downstairs to comfort Lisa. "Are you okay?"

"No," she said honestly.

Pulling her into his chest and kissing her forehead, he whispered, "This is not your fault."

"But I'm the one who—"

"Shh...I'm not going to let you do this to yourself."

Lisa cried, securing herself in RJ's arms for several moments until her cell phone rang. RJ got a peek at her caller ID. "Is that who I think it is?"

Lisa nodded.

"Under the circumstances, I don't think you should talk to her."

Lisa shrugged. "Sooner or later I will have to anyhow. I know this is going to kill her." She took a deep breath before answering. "Hey, Liv."

"Are you back in Columbus?"

"Yeah; I got back a few hours ago."

"Have you heard from Chanelle?"

Lisa thought it was a little weird that Olivia would immediately ask about Chanelle and not ask about Callie or her trip. The last couple of weeks, Liv had been obsessed with whether or not Lisa had spoken with her daughter. Lisa now wondered if Olivia knew more than she had been letting on. "Yes, I have heard from Chanelle. As a matter of fact, she's home now. Why do you ask?"

"B-because...I'm concerned about her and you. You're my best friend and Chanelle is like a daughter to me. I've been worried about her, too."

Lisa felt a slight twinge of guilt about her suspicions. "I'm sorry,

Liv. You're right. I guess I'm on edge because Chanelle told me some very disturbing news."

"What did she say?" Olivia spoke cautiously.

Lisa took a deep breath, hating that she had to break this news to her best friend. "She said that Justin raped her the night of the engagement party."

"That's all she said?"

"That's *all?* Liv, that's a whole heck of a lot."

"I'm sorry; I didn't mean it that way. I just wondered if she said anything else...like has she gone to the police?"

"Not yet. RJ and I are hoping to take her later today. She doesn't want to go right now."

"Sounds to me like she may not be sure that it was rape. The party was nearly two months ago; if my son raped Chanelle, surely she would have said something before now. Does she have any proof of this accusation?"

"So you think Chanelle's lying?"

"It's possible. I mean, c'mon, Lisa, Chanelle hasn't been an angel. This wouldn't be the first time she lied to you."

"True, Chanelle has lied before, but not to someone else's detriment. She knows that Justin risks facing legal trouble and I can't imagine that she would make this up. I don't think she's lying. I believe her."

"Justin is a college football star and is destined for the pros after next year. Girls are literally falling all over him. He wouldn't have to rape someone to have sex, so Chanelle's story doesn't add up to me."

"What would she gain by lying on him? What would be her motive?"

"Jealousy. She's mad because Justin broke up with her, so now she wants to ruin his career by falsely accusing him of rape."

Lisa burned hot with anger toward her best friend, but she remained calm. "Liv, I understand you're upset and I would be too if I were in your position. The fact is that I believe Chanelle and as soon as she's ready, we're going down to the police station. I know you love your son and no matter what he's done, you shouldn't stop loving him. The bottom line is we're going to file a report and let the justice system determine Justin's guilt or innocence."

"I'm warning you...don't go to the police with this dumb and unfounded accusation," she said viciously.

"Are you threatening me?" RJ quickly snatched the phone from Lisa and hung it up. "What did you do that for?"

"I felt the conversation getting way out of line. Until we talk to the police you don't need to have any further communication with her."

RJ went upstairs and spoke with Chanelle alone. During which time Olivia had tried to call Lisa several times, but following RJ's instructions, she didn't answer. About an hour or so later, they were headed to the police station.

When they got there, RJ took the lead in speaking with the officers. Lisa was glad not to have to be the strong one; RJ was doing it for her. After finding out exactly where they needed to go to make the claim, Chanelle was taken into a room, accompanied by RJ and Lisa.

"Hi, Chanelle, I'm Detective Troy Evans. I'll be the one investigating your case." Lisa apparently watched too much television because she expected to see a somewhat heavyset, bald, white man eating a doughnut and drinking coffee. But Detective Evans was just the opposite. He was tall, dark and built with muscles like an action figure. He looked to be in his mid-to-late-thirties and spoke with a slight Southern twang. "I want you to take your time and tell me everything that happened the night you were raped. If it gets too hard for you to talk or you want to take a break, just let me know."

Chanelle nodded.

Lisa's heart ached as she listened to her daughter's story.

"Miss Olivia was planning a surprise engagement party for my mom. The night before I spoke with Justin and he asked if I'd be willing to help him and his mother set up things for the party. I said 'yes.' Justin and I went out a lot, but we weren't really dating. Anyhow, Miss Olivia told Mama that she and her husband were having a banquet, so when Justin picked me up, I told my mom that I was going to help with that. Miss Olivia had us running back and forth from their house to the hotel. I'd brought my clothes with me because I thought I would change at the hotel, but we finished much earlier than expected, so I went back to their house with him since we still had some time." Tears began to well in Chanelle's eyes as she recanted her story.

That day they had listened to music while hanging out in the huge entertainment room the Scotts had in their basement, which was decorated with a large theater-like television, a pool table, arcade machines and a ping pong table.

"You think you're gonna go to more of my football games this year?" Justin had asked.

"Probably. You know Mama and Miss Olivia will be at your games all the time. I'm sure I'll come with them."

"I'm surprised you even agreed to go out with me. I didn't think you liked me. You've only been to a few games before."

"No offense, but spending the afternoon with thirty- and forty-something-year-old women is not my idea of fun."

"So it had nothing to do with me, then, right?"

"No."

"Good." He leaned closer and kissed her. They'd kissed several times, but Chanelle wasn't really overtaken by his kisses. Justin was cool and she liked him, but not really in that way. Secretly, her heart still longed for Kyle, but he was no longer interested in communicating with her. Justin was fun to hang out with and she didn't know how to tell him that she didn't like him in *that* way. With only a few more hours before the party started, she would suffer through his non-hormone charging kisses, but before they went out again, she was going to find some way to let him know that she just wasn't interested in him romantically. He was a nice guy. Hopefully they could remain friends.

They were both laid back on the couch when Justin blurted, "Have you ever had sex?"

"No," she answered uncomfortably.

"You and that Kyle dude that your mom hates never done it?"

"No."

"Y'all never did *anything?*"

"We've kissed and stuff, but we never had sex."

"What do you mean by 'and stuff?'"

Chanelle shrugged her shoulders. "Just stuff."

"Has he ever put his hand down here?" He made an attempt to touch her privates, but she blocked him.

"I think we should go back to the hotel and see if your mom needs us."

"If she did, she would've called us by now. Besides, we've worked hard all day and so has she. She's probably in one of the hotel rooms taking a nap. So what has stopped you from doing it?"

"I just didn't want to." Truth was, all those daggone scriptures her mother had inbred in her scared her into abstinence. Plus, though Chanelle enjoyed the kissing and touching she and Kyle had done, sex was serious business. She didn't want to give her body to anyone unless they would be together forever. She and Kyle were too young to make that kind of commitment to each other. Kyle wasn't a virgin, but the one thing Chanelle liked about him was that he respected her.

"Maybe you were waiting on me." Justin began kissing her again. This time he took it a lot further, groping her breasts and rubbing that sensitive spot between her thighs.

Chanelle squeezed her legs together. "Stop it!" She tried shoving him off of her, but his football-chiseled body was much stronger than her petite one and he remained fixed.

"I'm not going to hurt you, just relax."

"I don't want to do this !"

"Why not?"

Chanelle had planned to save her big lecture for another time, but she had to get it out now. "I just don't like you that way!"

"You're kidding, right?"

"No. I think you're a really cool person and I enjoy hanging out with you, but I don't like you enough to do this. You're more like a brother to me."

Justin laughed wickedly. "Thanks, but if it was meant for me to have a sister, God would have given me a biological one. Besides, if you were so interested in just being friends, why have you allowed me to stick my tongue in your mouth?"

"I don't know...I guess I didn't know how to tell you." Chanelle was still pinned between him and the couch and she couldn't get out from under him.

"I can stick my tongue other places if you'd like."

"No, thank you!"

"You know what I think..." He began planting kisses on her neck and grinding on her. "I think you're just scared your mom's going to find out. I'm not going to tell anyone; it'll be okay."

"Get off of me!" She tried pushing him again, this time digging her nails into his shoulder.

He grabbed her fist so hard it hurt. "Don't do that again or I'll kill you." There was something in his eyes that made Chanelle believe him.

"Justin, please...I don't want to do this," she pleaded as tears trickled from the corners of her eyes.

"Quit trying to pretend like you didn't know what we were coming here to do. You've been leading me on for weeks now, wearing your hip huggers and tight shirts that show off your breasts. You've been trying to give it to me; now I want it."

Chanelle tried to fight back, but ultimately gave up as Justin ripped her clothes from her body. She continued pleading with him not to do this. She even tried to negotiate a deal saying she would have sex with him another time, but he didn't fall for it and against her desire, he forced her out of her clothes and spread her legs apart as he thrust himself into her repeatedly, panting and kissing her as though she enjoyed his actions.

Chanelle lay paralyzed as his clammy body scrubbed against hers and his rough lips gnawed on her neck. His sweat dripped onto her as he continuously shoved roughly inside her. "Say my name..." he ordered, but Chanelle remained silent. With even more force he pushed himself in deeper. "I *said*, say...my...name!"

Her tears shot in all directions as she forced his name out.

"Yeah, baby, that's right."

Blood was everywhere by the time he finished. Justin seemed pleased with his deed. "You weren't lying when you said you were a virgin. It was nice and tight...just the way I like it."

Chanelle's privates hurt badly, like she had been prodded with a knife.

"There's a restroom around the corner. You go take a shower and I'll clean up this mess," he commanded, panting heavily.

The water burned the part of her that had been violated, but she scrubbed hard, making it hurt worse as she tried to wash the experience away.

"No one ever has to know what happened with us, right?" Justin said to her as they sat in the car outside the hotel getting ready to go in for her mother's party.

She just looked at him.

"I can't risk you going in there trippin' and saying stuff that's not true. No one is going to believe I did anything to hurt you. But, if you lie and say I did, it's going to cause a lot of unnecessary trouble. This is our secret. I'm not trying to brag, but there are a lot of girls who wish they were in your position right now. Girls throw themselves my way, but I like the way you play things. I like the girls who are conservative and play like they want to wait."

"I wasn't playing," she spat, attempting to get out of the car, but he grabbed her.

"Yes, you were. You wanted it just as much as I did. Are we clear on that?"

"Yes..." she whispered.

"Good, now put a smile on your face and let's go in here like we had a great time."

"So," Detective Evans, continued jotting down notes, "have you spoken with Justin Scott since that night?"

"A couple of times. My mom and I got into a fight that same night and I left. The next day Justin left messages for me to call home and quit trippin'."

"Did you save any of those messages?"

"No, Sir."

"He left you messages, but did you actually speak with him."

"A couple of weeks ago when I found out I was pregnant."

"What did he say?"

"He talked to his mom and she took me to get an abortion."

"That wench did what!" belted Lisa, bewildered that her best friend had neglected to share this information.

Chanelle continued speaking. "I couldn't go through with it, but Miss Olivia thinks that I did. She took me to the clinic, but she didn't go in with me because she didn't want anyone to recognize her, so she waited outside."

Hours soared by and it was getting late. Chanelle was visibly getting frustrated as well. A couple of times she sighed irritably during the interview. When the detective began to verify facts from Chanelle's story for what seemed like the umpteenth time, Chanelle snapped. "Why do you keep going over that night? Either you believe me or you don't, but I'm done talking."

RJ looked as if he was about to say something, but Detective Evans spoke up first. "You've done a great job, Chanelle. Please don't take tonight as any indication that I don't believe you." He spoke gently. "It's my job to interview victims as thoroughly as possible. I need to make sure I have all the facts."

"I've told you everything that happened."

"Thank you...it took a lot of courage for you to come down here. Again, you've done a great job. I have enough information for tonight."

"So then we can go ahead and take her home?" asked RJ.

"Yes, but..." Detective Evans hesitated for a moment. "There is one more thing that could possibly help. Though it's been several weeks now since the attack, I would recommend that Chanelle goes to the hospital to have a sexual assault kit done. Obviously, there wouldn't be any semen found, but it's possible that there may be other evidence of an assault. Chanelle, it's totally up to you. I can't make you go. Even if you do go, I can't get the results unless you sign a medical release giving the hospital permission to share them with me. You don't *have* to go tonight, but since it's already been a while, I would suggest the sooner you go, the better."

Lisa watched as Chanelle, though noticeably tired, nodded her head in agreement. "I'll do it tonight," she answered.

Detective Evans seemed pleased. He even agreed to meet them there. He also gave Chanelle some pamphlets and other literature on rape crisis centers in the area. He had one last word of advice to share before they walked out. "Since Justin Scott thinks you've had an abortion, let's keep it that way. I'm going to bring him in for questioning. Unfortunately, this sort of thing happens more than I'd like to admit. I want you to know that it's not your fault and you did absolutely nothing wrong. I'm proud of you for coming forth; most victims keep silent. Is there anything else you have to tell me before we get going?"

"No, but I brought these with me." Chanelle seemed more at ease now that the interview was over. She reached in her bag and pulled out some clothing. It was a lime green tank top with blue jean capris. The shirt was torn in several areas and there was blood on both it and the capris. Chanelle had even brought her underclothes; her panties were also covered with blood.

Detective Evans looked surprised. "Is this what you were wearing the day of your assault?"

"*Yes,*" Chanelle answered in a way that indicated she didn't want to continuously be asked about this. Detective Evans was pleasantly surprised that she had thought to keep those items. He explained how her clothing would be turned in to the property room and then sent to the lab for processing. Lisa was also proud of the way Chanelle handled things. She remembered the outfit very well and her heart thumped with anger as she pictured Justin ripping off Chanelle's clothes so he could have his way with her. It wasn't the type of image that any mother wanted in her head.

CHAPTER 28

Conflict of Interest

Despite Lisa's protests that she and Chanelle would be fine, RJ still insisted on crashing on her couch. It was well into the wee hours of the morning when they finally got home and Lisa didn't feel like protesting. Plus, she really did feel more secure with him there. This whole series of events had shaken her up quite a bit and it felt good having RJ around to console her.

The three of them slept right through Sunday morning service. Had Lisa been up, she probably would have gone to church with RJ instead of going to her own. She wouldn't have wanted to risk Chanelle seeing Justin at their church and she would have wanted to avoid Olivia as well. She was still baffled over Olivia's involvement in the situation.

The hospital staff wasted no time reporting the results of Chanelle's examination to Detective Evans, who called to inform them as he'd promised. As expected, there was no semen found within Chanelle, but the examination did confirm that she was several weeks pregnant. The timeline correlated exactly to the night the rape occurred. In addition, the test revealed that Chanelle had a great amount of scar tissue, which was indicative of some type of aggressive intercourse.

Later that Sunday evening Lisa's mother called to tell about her trip to LA. She was bummed out about losing money in some slot machines, but she was elated to learn that Chanelle was home. Lisa knew she would have to fill her mother in on what was going on sometime, but she didn't think it would be wise to do so over the phone. Lisa didn't even tell Callie, who, of all people, would be able to handle the news considering she had had a similar experience to Chanelle's. Lisa just didn't feel like worrying anyone else right now.

That night RJ camped out on Lisa's couch once again, leaving from there to go to work. Lisa got to the office about thirty minutes earlier than normal that Monday. Chanelle had asked if it would be okay for Kyle to come over. Lisa didn't mind, especially because she didn't want to leave Chanelle alone, but she had to come in to work since she'd missed the entire previous week due to her trip to California.

"Hey, welcome back. I was wondering what happened to you last week." Megan burst into her office.

"I had to go to California to see my sister."

"Is everything okay with her?"

"Yes, she was hospitalized, but she's fine now. Sorry I left on such short notice. I hated to leave you hanging. Olivia said she'd let you know."

"She came in several times last week and did some work from your office a couple times. She said she was trying to help the board get some stuff together. I asked about you, but she just told me that you would be off for a while."

"I'm sorry, Megan. I should've called you myself. I was with Liv when I got a call about my sister, so I left at a moment's notice."

"That's okay. Nothing happened last week that I couldn't handle. I'm guessing Mrs. Scott won't be here for the board meeting today, considering the circumstances. I saw the news this morning."

"What news?"

"They said Justin Scott was brought in and questioned about rape allegations brought against him yesterday."

"Really?" The police moved faster than Lisa thought they would.

"They're saying it's possible that he'll be suspended from playing football if charges are filed. I figured you would have already known since you and Mrs. Scott are such good friends."

"I didn't speak to Olivia at all yesterday."

"Do you think it's true...that he really raped someone?"

Lisa shrugged her shoulders casually. "That's for the police to figure out."

Megan looked at her suspiciously. "I'm surprised you're not more upset about this. Are he and Chanelle still dating?"

"No, they are not."

Megan looked like she was waiting for Lisa to volunteer additional information, but when Lisa remained silent, she said, "Oh...well, I guess I'll get to work."

"Enjoy your day."

Lisa waited a few minutes and then closed her door. She called both RJ and Chanelle to see if they had heard the news. Chanelle hadn't, but RJ had caught wind of it on his way to work. Lisa went to the lounge and tried to appear nonchalant as she and co-workers watched the "breaking news" report. A clip played of Isaac giving a statement proclaiming Justin's innocence. Reporters asked the Ohio State football coach whether or not Justin would still be able to play in the upcoming game this Saturday. He said, "As of now, yes, because Mr. Scott has not been charged with any crime. If that should change, then the Athletic Department will take appropriate action."

After the report, Lisa quickly returned to her office. Though she had plenty of work to do, she wasn't making any progress. She tried to focus, but she kept wondering how things had gone down at the station. It was around one when Olivia called Lisa on her cell phone. She struggled with whether or not to answer it, but ultimately did out of curiosity.

"Hey, Lisa. I'm so glad you answered the phone. We really need to talk."

"I don't have anything nice to say to you."

"I know you're upset, but we need to clear the air."

"I don't understand how you could look me in my face, knowing how worried I was about Chanelle and not tell me that you'd taken her to get an abortion."

"Do you think I liked lying to you? I know this is hard for your family, but you have to realize it's hard on mine, too. Lisa, we've been too close to let our friendship be destroyed by this. Will you please come by after work so we can talk? I'm hoping we can mend some bridges."

"I can't come over after work; I want to get home and be with Chanelle."

"Then leave work early and come."

Lisa mulled the idea over a few seconds. "I guess I can do that. Give me about an hour or so and I'll be over."

Lisa could have walked out of her office and been within ten feet of Megan's desk, but she called her on the intercom instead. "Hey, Meg..."

"Yes?"

"Olivia called and asked me to meet her. I know I was gone all last week; do you think you can handle things or do you need me to stay?"

"No, go ahead. I'm sure Mrs. Scott needs you with everything that's going on. I'll be fine."

"Thanks, Meg, you're the greatest."

Before leaving, Lisa also called Detective Evans. "Don't go," he warned her. "I understand that the two of you had a close friendship prior to this, but there's clearly a conflict of interest. Justin has given a sworn statement saying that he's never touched Chanelle. He's denied our request to voluntarily give a DNA sample, so we have to get a court order to obtain it. Chanelle's clothing is awaiting processing for anything that will link to Justin. The more he denies having had sex with her, the better it will be for our case. It's not a good idea for you to talk to anyone—especially his mother—while we're in the middle of an investigation."

Lisa did not heed Detective Evans's advice and headed to Olivia's suburban home in Delaware County. Mending her friendship with Olivia was not her main concern, but after all they had shared over the years, Lisa felt obligated to at least hear her out. She felt partly responsible for Liv not believing Chanelle was raped. Lisa had been the sole culprit in planting her daughter as a bad seed in Olivia's head. It was logical that Olivia would believe Justin over Chanelle since he had always been the "good boy." Lisa could understand that. What she didn't understand is how Liv could secretly try to terminate Chanelle's pregnancy.

Walking up to the brick sidewalk, Lisa quickly took a trip down memory lane, thinking about the many occasions when she had visited the Scotts' home. With Isaac traveling a lot and Justin gone most times, she and Liv often hung out like schoolgirls, engaging in sleepovers and good old-fashioned fun. Part of Lisa mourned their friendship, realizing that no matter what happened with the case against Justin, things between her and Liv would likely never be the same.

"Thanks for coming by." Olivia reached out to hug her and Lisa stiffly returned the gesture. Though there were small lines of tension creased in her forehead, Liv seemed to be in good spirits.

"Come sit out back." She followed Olivia to the back patio and they sat at the table. Lisa's mind quickly went back to Memorial Day when she and Isaac sat out here and he'd told her about the surprise engagement party Liv had thrown for Eric and her. Things were so different then. Liv had been more than a best friend; she had been like her sister, but now, she wasn't someone that Lisa could trust any longer. "I know how much you love half and halfs, so here's some lemonade-iced tea."

"So what did you want to talk about?" she asked, giving in to the invitation for a drink and treat. Liv hadn't done a bad job making Lisa's favorite drink and the brownies smelled way too pleasant to pass up no matter how mad Lisa was.

"I want to talk about everything that has happened. The police questioned Justin about Chanelle's allegations."

The brownies tasted just as good, if not better, than they smelled. Lisa finished her bite before responding. "I know…I spoke with the detective right before coming over."

"So you know this thing is very serious. Justin may be suspended from playing football this season. This could be bad for him if it's dragged out much longer."

Lisa took the liberty and got another brownie. "I know, Liv, but it's out of our hands. I wish to God this had never happened."

"Me, too. There's a lot at stake here, but there's a way we can work it out. It's not completely out of our hands, you know?"

"I'm not sure what you mean."

"Well, between you and me, how much would it take for Chanelle to change her story?"

Lisa nearly choked on the treat. "You can't be serious? You

think you can pay us off and make this all go away? Justin committed a crime and, like it or not, he will pay. That's non-negotiable."

Olivia's grin turned evil. "In this world, everything is negotiable. I really like you, Lisa, and it's unfortunate that something like this has come between us. I can't allow your daughter to ruin my son's future. Before you walk away from the offer, think about it. Isaac and I are prepared to pay you any amount. We'll take care of Chanelle's college tuition, pay off your mortgage, anything you desire; name your price. This is the one opportunity you have to get anything you want in life."

"What I want is my daughter's rapist to be punished. No amount of money is going to change my mind about that. This conversation is over." She stood up so forcefully that the chair she was sitting in fell over.

"Not so fast..." Liv quickly got up and blocked her path as she headed for the door, grabbing her by the arm. "I'd advise you to take the money and have Chanelle drop this thing."

"This *thing?*" Lisa jerked away. "That's what you're calling it. Your son raped my daughter and you're calling it a thing? It's a crime and I'm quite shocked that you're not more appalled by it."

She laughed wickedly. "Yes, rape is a crime, Lisa, but Justin never raped her. In fact, he never so much as touched her at all. It's his word against hers. Now who do you think a jury is more likely to believe, a college football star with an impeccable record or a rebellious teenager who has been giving you one problem after another? I'm sure somewhere the police have a record of bringing Chanelle home drunk."

"That has nothing to do with your son violating her!"

"All I'm saying is drop it."

"If you're so confident that Justin is innocent and will be cleared, then why are you trying to pay me off?"

"Because it's a nuisance to have to go through this process." Liv retreated back to her seat while Lisa continued standing. "It's a waste of everyone's time. We have more important things to do. These allegations, though they are false, can ruin my son's life. As his mother, I can't sit back and let that happen. A mother will do anything to protect her child."

Olivia's words hit Lisa like a two-ton truck. *"A mother will do anything to protect her child."* That's the same line Olivia had spoon-fed Lisa when she talked her into confronting Stacie. Lisa thought it was good advice back then; now it seemed devilish.

"The good thing about all of this is that Justin is a junior. If he's suspended because of Chanelle's absurdities, he'll still have a chance to play his senior year. Honestly, he doesn't need this shadow hanging over his head. It will be much easier on us all if she drops these ridiculous allegations."

"The only thing that's being dropped is this conversation. We're through!" Lisa started to the door once again when suddenly she began to itch very badly. It was as if a swarm of invisible mosquitoes had attacked her.

At first Lisa thought it was her nerves until Olivia said, "Are you feeling okay? I hope you're not having an allergic reaction to anything around here...say, like the brownies."

Lisa halted dead in her tracks and stared in disbelief at her former friend. "You put peanuts in those, didn't you?"

"Only a cup or two...I ground them really fine so that they couldn't be detected, then I added M&M's to mask the taste. I had a feeling that you'd be too righteous to accept my offer, so I wanted to know that I mean business...I will not allow my son to go down without a fight."

"How could you? You know I'm allergic to peanuts."

"Do I?" She pretended to be shocked, placing her hand over her chest as if hearing this for the first time.

"Liv, we've been friends for years. You, of all people, know that I can't have any products with peanuts in it! You did this on purpose!"

"Prove it. Hypothetically speaking, say I did know and I purposely put peanuts in the brownies. You would claim that during our numerous conversations, you told me of your allergy. The problem is that in a court of law there would be no evidence to support this theory. You have to remember, my husband makes his living as a defense attorney. If you can't prove it, I didn't do it. The wonderful thing about the justice system is that the burden of proof lies with the accuser. You say I knew, I say I didn't. It's your word against mine, just like it's Justin's word against Chanelle's."

Lisa took a few steps closer to Olivia who was now standing again and glared straight into her eyes. "You think you're so clever, don't you? You thought you could hide Justin's crime by taking Chanelle to the clinic to have an abortion."

"Did I?"

Lisa was doubly agitated by the smug grin on Olivia's face. "There is proof that Justin raped Chanelle. DNA doesn't lie. I'm sure you know that, which is why Justin won't voluntarily give a sample. That's okay, though. Eventually the police will get what they need, especially since Chanelle is still carrying his baby; I know a paternity test will discredit anything Justin has said." Lisa would have given money for an instant replay of Olivia's prideful grin turning sour. She had never seen her sweat under pressure and quite frankly, Lisa got a sense of satisfaction about having one up on her. "Now who do you think the jury will believe?" As the look of horror rested over Olivia, Lisa gave her own wicked smile and left.

CHAPTER 29
Malicious Intent

Lisa managed to hold it together like a lioness while in front of Olivia, but as soon as she made it to the rehabilitation center where RJ worked, she broke down. Inside RJ's closed office she cried hysterically as she told him about what had happened with Olivia.

"I messed up everything," she sobbed into his chest.

"Shh! It's okay. I'm going to see if I can find you some allergy medication and then we need to call and let Detective Evans know what happened."

RJ left the room and Lisa lay there, thinking about her daughter and how strong Chanelle had been during the weeks she had been away from home. Chanelle had even continued planning to attend college when classes started in a few weeks. The only difference is that Chanelle would stay at home instead of living on campus now. Lisa was so proud of her daughter for persevering, despite the circumstances. Lisa had promised Chanelle that justice would be served. How could she tell her that she had obstructed it?

Lisa itched uncontrollably while waiting for RJ to return. Her eyes roamed his office. This was her first time being inside there.

His walls were decorated with biblical scriptures and pictures of Chanelle and her. It wasn't creepy like Eric's office has been. Lisa felt flattered and got the sense that both she and Chanelle were important to him. Lisa was surprised by the newspaper clipping that hung among the family photographs. It was a photo from the night they had gotten arrested. The clipping showed RJ being escorted out of the drug house in handcuffs and his boxers. RJ had framed the picture and wrote Genesis 50:20 across it. Lisa couldn't think of the scripture off hand, but she made a mental note to look it up later.

"I found some medicine for you." RJ walked in, carrying the medicine and a cup of water. "I also spoke with Detective Evans. He'll be here in a few minutes."

"Thank you. I'm sorry to come barging in like this. I know you have a lot of stuff to do. I didn't know what else to do."

"It's okay." He was gentle in assisting her as she swallowed the pills. "I have a great staff that, honestly, does the bulk of the work. I'm just the overseer."

"You're not *just* the overseer. You run the place, Mr. Director."

RJ shrugged his shoulders nonchalantly. "The title itself isn't important to me. I'm at a point where I realize that the only ones impressed with titles are people. When I get to Heaven, if anything, the only title Jesus will have for me is servant. I used to be caught up in doing and being what everyone else expected me to be, but now my top priorities are fulfilling my God-given purpose and being there for my family."

Lisa recalled how excited she had been back in the day about RJ taking over his father's ministry. She wondered if he had included her in the "everyone," but she didn't have the courage to ask. Instead she inquired about the unusual picture. "How does Genesis 50:20 relate to that newspaper clipping?"

RJ smiled proudly. "Remember when Joseph's brothers worried that he would seek revenge on them after Jacob died for selling him into slavery, but Joseph said to them, 'You thought evil against me, but God meant it unto good?' That article reminds me that the things meant to destroy me are now being used to God's glory. Being a pastor caught up in a drug scandal could have and should have been the end of me, but God placed me in a position to help others, despite everything that I went through. As crazy as it sounds, I'm proud to be able to relate with the people who come through here. Only God can do something like that. I keep the article up because it's a testimony to everyone who walks through this door that God is capable of doing the impossible."

Lisa was rendered speechless. She had once accused RJ of being a charlatan and now he had spoken a Word so powerful that it gave her goose bumps.

"Excuse me..." Detective Evans knocked on the door, walking in and closing it behind him. "I take it that your visit with Olivia Scott didn't go well."

He was a lot cuter when he wasn't being sarcastic. Lisa held RJ's hand for strength as she recounted that afternoon's events.

He looked tense and drew in several heavy breaths before speaking. "I knew talking to her would not be a good idea. It doesn't surprise me that she tried to pay you off. Had she given you a check, we could have used that as proof, but she's way too smart for that."

"But, what about her intentionally flaring up my wife's allergies?"

Detective Evans looked as surprised as Lisa was by RJ's reference to her as his wife. "I hate to say this, but Olivia's right. There's no way to prove that she had malicious intent when serving you the brownies. From now on, stay away from her. Don't answer any of her phone calls. I doubt she'll be stupid enough to leave you voice messages, but if she does, save them. You should seek a restraining order against her."

"So how strong is Chanelle's case now? Did I mess things up really bad?"

He sighed heavily. "I won't say 'really bad,' but you've definitely made things more difficult for us."

Lisa was ashamed and hung her head low. RJ gave her a reassuring pat on the back.

"Justin has wasted no time changing his story. On my way here I got a call that he is now saying that he and Chanelle had consensual sex and she started bleeding because she was a virgin. No one is going to be surprised now if his DNA is found on her clothing and he's confirmed as the baby's father."

"Doesn't the fact that he changed his story show that he's guilty?"

"To us, yeah…but Isaac Scott is one heck of a defense attorney. If this goes to court, I'm sure he's going to file a motion to try and keep the jury from finding about Justin's conflicting statements. Let's hope the judge will see things our way. The only concrete evidence we have of forced sexual activity is Chanelle's torn clothing. Most people don't rip their clothes before having consensual sex, so that's a clear sign of an attack. I just wish there was some way to prove she was wearing that outfit the day Justin raped her."

"I may be able to help you with that," Lisa said confidently.

CHAPTER 30
Section 105.13A

RJ was concerned about Lisa driving because the allergy medication she had taken was known to cause drowsiness. Even though she declared she was "fine," he left his car at the center and drove Lisa home in hers. Also concerned about Olivia's threats, RJ first stopped by his place to get some clothes for the remainder of the week. He didn't ask, but rather told Lisa that he would stay with her and Chanelle until the whole thing blew over.

When they got to the house, Chanelle was sitting in the living room watching television. Kyle was no longer there, but evidence remained of his presence. There were no dishes in the sink when Lisa went to work this morning, but now there were two of everything waiting to be washed. She didn't like to come home to dirty dishes, but she wouldn't dare make that an issue in light of the more serious matters at hand. Lisa felt obligated to tell Chanelle that she had told Olivia about the baby and gave her daughter a very abridged version of what happened earlier, eliminating Olivia's deliberate attempt to flare up her allergies. She didn't think her daughter needed to be concerned with that. She apologized profusely to Chanelle who replied that she wasn't going to "sweat it" and then retired to her room for a nap. As RJ worked to change the locks on the door and the security code on the alarm, Lisa busied herself emailing Detective Evans the pictures from the day of the engagement party that Olivia had sent to her. Among the bunch were images of Chanelle wearing the exact same outfit she had turned in to Detective Evans.

Just as Lisa had hit "send" the phone rang and Callie's home number showed up on the display. "Tell me Chanelle is not the one Justin Scott is accused of raping!" her mother wailed. Lisa could hear her father and sister in the background trying to calm her down. "Dear Lord, he raped my baby!" Lisa's heart tumbled as she heard her mother drop the phone and cry out in pain.

"Daddy, get her some water," Callie ordered before picking it up. "Lisa, what's going on? Mama's having a fit. We heard on the news that Justin Scott has been questioned about rape allegations."

Lisa was at a loss for words.

"Oh no, it was Chanelle, wasn't it?" Callie seemed heartbroken.

"Yes…" Lisa wasn't surprised that Justin being questioned made the news in California. Justin was only *the* key running back for a Big Ten college, and his parents were famous. She just hadn't expected it to reach *her* family so soon.

"Is Chanelle at home? How is she doing?"

"Yes, she's here." Lisa told her sister about the call from Gericka that led to this revelation. "Please don't tell Mama about the pregnancy. This is already a lot on her. I'll tell her when she gets home."

"I won't. I'm so sorry this happened to her. I know exactly how she feels."

"She's doing better than I thought."

"Look, we've debated this topic before, but I really think she should be in counseling. Chanelle has gone through a lot in her young life. I know you said she appears to be fine, but honestly, Lisa, that's an inherited defense mechanism that our family tends to have. Mama does it, you do it and I do it as well. I hope Chanelle knows that she can talk to us any time, but it'll be good for her to talk with someone professionally trained to deal with these types of issues."

"I agree. The police gave her some information to a rape crisis center, but I want to get her someone she can talk to about everything. You were right, Cal. I should have listened."

"This is not about me being right. I want to make sure Chanelle gets the help that she needs."

"I'm going to talk to her and see if it's something she wants to do. It's not something I can make her do, but I'll look into it just in case. I don't know where to start. I'll see if I can get some recommendations from the church."

"I have someone I can refer you to. You know how I was gone every Tuesday running errands? I was actually going to counseling. My therapist here recommended a wonderful psychiatrist; I can give you the name and number if you'd like."

Lisa got the information from her sister and then Callie said she needed to go to check on their mother who could still be heard crying as though she was having a nervous breakdown. Before hanging up, Callie said a prayer for her and Chanelle with more "oomph" than Lisa had heard from her sister in quite some time.

RJ also thought Chanelle attending counseling would be a good idea and Lisa wasted no time calling Dr. Lancer who stated that she still had Callie's slot open the next afternoon if Chanelle wanted to accept it. RJ and Lisa pitched the idea to their daughter who wasn't enthusiastic, but didn't refuse.

Tuesday morning, Lisa dropped RJ off at work since he had

left his car and driven her home the day before and then drove to her office. As usual, she spoke to her assistant who peered up at her with a horrid look. Megan always looked sad and never wore a joyous expression, but the look she had today was eerie.

"What's wrong?"

Megan struggled to speak and then Lisa saw Neil Criton, Brentson's CEO, walking out of her office with a couple of security men carrying her computer and other items.

"What's this all about, Neil?"

"Hello, Lisa. I wish I was here under better circumstances... Um, let's step inside here so we can talk." He motioned toward the doorway of her office.

Lisa's wobbling knees made her too weak to move. She leaned on Megan's desk for support. "Just tell me what's going on?"

"Very well then." He took a few steps closer to her. "You're being placed on administrative leave without pay, pending an investigation into pornography allegations."

"What!"

"We've received an anonymous tip that you have been downloading porn onto your computer at work."

"That's absurd! Where did this tip come from?"

"I'm sorry, I can't tell you that. It was anonymous."

"C'mon, Neil, think about how ridiculous this sounds. If I wanted to look at naked people on the Internet, why wouldn't I do it on my own personal computer? Why would I do it at work?"

"Why do thieves rob banks in broad daylight? It doesn't make sense, I know, but we have to investigate it. I'm just following orders."

Lisa knew somehow Olivia had set her up. The only person who had access to her login information was Olivia; and Megan did mention that Olivia had done some work in her office last week.

"Pornography isn't the only allegation against you, Lisa. It's also been reported that you've been taking time off of work without submitting leave slips."

"But, Neil—"

"You were off all last week and yet, your absence has not been officially documented."

"You want me to fill out a leave slip for last week? Fine...I have no problem doing that."

"I'm sorry, but at this point filling out a slip won't do you any good. Last week isn't the only time you've left without submitting leave. You did it yesterday and numerous times before. And then there's an issue about your taking extended lunch breaks."

"Who doesn't have extended lunch breaks around here? You and every other company executive have taken time off without it officially showing up on the books. I apparently had the board's approval to do those things. Most of the time I was with Olivia. I distinctly remember several occasions accompanying her to business lunches with you knowing full well I was on company time and now you want to hold that against me!" Lisa was outraged that all of a sudden this was a problem when she'd definitely had Neil's unwritten approval.

"According to section 105.13A of the Brentson Employee Handbook, all employees are required to submit the appropriate leave form when taking time off of work, including additional time during lunch. Any employee found violating the rule is subject to disciplinary action."

Lisa was sickened by his politically correct jargon. "Neil, why are you doing this to me?"

"Please don't take it personal. I'm simply following the established rules of Brentson Technologies."

"I know Olivia's behind this whole thing." Anger corroded her insides. "Her son raped my daughter and now you're doing her dirty work!"

Megan gasped. "Oh my goodness, Lisa...I didn't know..."

"I wasn't aware of any personal issues that you and Mrs. Scott have. I'm strictly following company policy."

"This is bull! You've become her spineless puppet." From the corner of her eye, Lisa observed Megan turn bright red, ready to cry as if she had been the one reprimanded. Technically, Megan's job could also be in danger because she, like Lisa, had enjoyed the extra "perks" of having a connection with Olivia Scott. Lisa wouldn't dare bring Megan into it and she was glad that her assistant's job hadn't been affected, but she did have some advice for her. "Watch your back around here. As you see, no one can be trusted." She gave Megan a stern word of warning before angrily stomping away.

CHAPTER 31
Church Issues

Lisa was livid! Instead of racing over to have it out with her ex-best friend as part of her wanted to, she rushed to update RJ on the latest happenings. When she got to his office he was in a meeting with Pastor Burlington.

"Lisa, it's so good to see you!" Using his cane for assistance, Pastor Burlington immediately stood and hugged her. "I saw you at church Sunday, but you ducked out before I got a chance to speak." The sunlight from RJ's window bounced from the top of his hairless dome, making it glisten.

"Yes. I'm sorry about that. I didn't really feel like lingering."

"I understand. Robert has told me about what's going on. I want you to know that I'm praying for all of you."

"Thank you."

"Well, you're here to see Robert, not me, so I'll mosey on out so the two of you can talk. I'll be around in the building; have someone page me when you're done with the misses here and we can finish up."

"No, don't leave on my account. I'm sorry to interrupt. What I have to say can wait until later." Lisa began to back out of the room.

"Are you sure?" RJ spoke up.

"Yes..."

"Lisa, if you were coming to ask RJ for a slice of bread, you have precedence over me." He winked. "I'm going to leave so you can speak with your hus—Robert."

"You don't have to leave, Pastor Burlington. Seriously, this isn't a do or die situation. I just came to vent because I lost my job today."

"What!" exclaimed RJ.

"Well, technically I've been placed on administrative leave without pay, but it's all the same. Olivia and her husband practically run that place."

"What happened?" Pastor Burlington asked. Lisa had obviously sparked his curiosity as well.

She shared with both of them the event that had taken place moments ago.

"Olivia's trying to coerce you into making Chanelle change her story. You, downloading pornography? That's absurd!" RJ quickly came to her defense.

"I know...," spewed Lisa.

"If Olivia and the other board jerks approved your absences, it's not fair for them to use your time off against you."

"Robert, we all know that the Devil doesn't fight fair. The minute Lisa accepted privileges that went against company policy, she made herself a pawn. You can best believe that a record of your unofficially approved absences has been kept as insurance in case you ever went against the grain and they wanted to get rid of you."

"I can't believe these people are being so ruthless!" spat RJ.

"I can't believe Olivia. I thought I knew her so well...I thought we were friends. Apparently I didn't know her at all."

"I can believe everything," inserted Pastor Burlington. "Some people with money think the rules don't apply to them."

"But Olivia is supposed to be a Christian. She was supposed to be my friend," cried Lisa.

"The key words there are 'supposed to be,' and only the Lord truly knows. He will take care of her in His time. Sometimes it's the people close to us who hurt us the most. As David said in Psalm 41:9 'Even my close friend, whom I trusted, he who shared my bread, has lifted up his heel against me.' Some of the hurt we experience from our friends is because we failed to ask for discernment before letting them into our lives in the first place. Even in those situations, God is capable of using those people to get us to where He wants us to be. Listen, I'm not gon' start preaching. Lisa, I don't want you worrying 'bout money. I'm sure Mr. Director over there can find something for you around here. If there's no open position, perhaps he can create one."

"Thanks, Pastor Burlington. We'll see if I'll have to ask RJ to take you up on that."

"Meanwhile, I want you to take some time to rest and be with Chanelle. She needs you and your entire family needs time to heal. Robert can take off whenever he needs to in order to be with you. Have you spoken to your pastor about any of this?"

"No..."

"Well, I suggest you do. From what I understand, the Scotts are very active in the church. As the head of Hope Ministries Rehabilitation Center, I'd want to know if one of my leaders was behaving in such a manner."

Chanelle went to her appointment alone that same afternoon. Lisa asked her how it went and she just said, "It was fine." Lisa didn't press her daughter for more information than she was ready to give. Later that day, Lisa decided to follow Pastor Burlington's advice and she called the office to see if she could speak with Pastor Ross. As expected, she wasn't able to get in that same day due to such short notice, but she was able to set up a meeting on Thursday afternoon.

Lisa confided in her sister about Olivia's latest tactics at work, but once again withheld the information from her mother. She pulled into the church parking lot Thursday afternoon. While waiting to see Pastor Ross, she spotted Eric walking down the hall. Thankfully he didn't see her. At least if he had, he pretended not to and that was fine with her.

Pastor Ross was a very chubby and petite man with a gray Afro. Standing several inches taller than him, Lisa looked down when he stood up to greet her as she was granted permission to enter his office. "Sister Hampton, what is it I can do for you?"

"I wanted to speak with you to let you know about what's happening with one of the leaders here at the church." She took a seat and went into her story about the rape, the peanuts, the attempted payoff for Chanelle to change her story and the incident at work.

"And what would you like me to do about this?" he asked cynically.

"I would think it's something you would like to speak with her about."

"Regarding everything you told me, it's your word against hers. Sister Scott does a lot for this congregation. The police are handling the rape allegations. I'm not sure the other alleged incidents are things I need to get involved in."

"I get the impression that you really don't care."

"Sister Hampton, you interrupted my day and set up this urgent meeting with my secretary. I had other things planned during this time, but because you *insisted* this was an emergency, I rearranged my schedule. I have patiently listened to your complaints and that's the best I can do. I'm neither judge nor jury. There's nothing I can do to help you. This is an issue for the courts."

"But you are the pastor of this church."

"Yes, but I make it a point not to involve myself in matters that occur outside of the church walls."

"Isn't it your responsibility to correct leadership when they are out of line? Though these are not technically church issues, like it or not, Olivia's behavior is a direct reflection on this church."

"Again, it's your word against Sister Scott's. No offense, but I don't know you very well. In fact, I don't really know you at all. If it had not been for the fact that you participated on the anniversary committee, I might not even know your name. Thank you, by the way. You all did a wonderful job commemorating my time at this church. Anyhow, I've known Olivia for quite some time and she and her husband—"

"Have done a lot for the congregation," Lisa said grudgingly. "I knew money controlled politics, but I didn't think the Scotts would have this church in their back pocket, too. I'm sorry for wasting your time. I see this is something that you're not willing to address." Lisa had so much she wanted to say, but she politely got up and walked out while she could keep her mouth shut.

CHAPTER 32
A Permanent Fixture

Within several months, Justin had been officially charged with rape. Consequently, he had been suspended from playing football for Ohio State indefinitely. As the weeks turned into months, things eventually settled to some form of normalcy for Lisa. Her parents had long ago come back from California and naturally had been heartbroken upon learning of Chanelle's pregnancy. News of Justin's arrest still made headlines and the trial date had been set for early next year. Lisa was surprised at how quickly the date had been set. She thought it would take a year, if not more, before this all came to a head, but apparently Justin had waived his right to a preliminary hearing and Isaac had pulled some strings to get a date as soon as possible. Lisa was sure that the Scott family wanted to make sure this trial was far behind him by the time football season started next year. Justin going pro was the only thing that family seemed to care about.

Chanelle, who was now twenty weeks pregnant, had agreed to testify at the trial next year, and was still attending counseling every other week. She still didn't really share her feelings about the rape with Lisa, but she seemed to be adjusting well. Lisa was glad that she was at least talking to someone professional; and she was also continuing forth as planned. She'd started college back in the fall and had been doing great. Lisa marveled at her daughter's strength. She had endured such a horrible ordeal and still wore a smile. The relationship between the two of them had grown tremendously. Gone was the rebellious daughter constantly bumping heads with the overwhelmed mother. Chanelle had shown considerable growth, not just in her personal life, but her spiritual life as well. Lisa no longer had to fight with her daughter to get up for church Sunday mornings or attend mid-week Bible study because Chanelle was often more eager to go than she was. They were now regular attendees of Pastor Burlington's church. It was a much smaller congregation, but the close-knit family environment was what they needed. Even Kyle seemed to enjoy the hospitality and had become a frequent visitor.

The whole ordeal with Justin had brought Lisa and Chanelle closer together. In fact, it had brought everyone in their family closer together; and Lisa couldn't have been more excited as she strolled down each aisle in the grocery store gathering items for the Thanksgiving dinner she was hosting. She shared her menu plans with her sister, talking on her cell phone with her Bluetooth earpiece.

"Dang, girl, it sounds like you're trying to feed an army."

"Well, it's better to have too much food than not enough. RJ said he spoke with his brother. He and Sheila are driving up. Pastor and Sister Burlington have also been invited."

"Is Kyle still coming? Or as Mama calls him, 'Kelvin.'"

"She's finally gotten his name right. She's still calling Stacie, Stasha, though. But, as far as I know, he's coming. I told Chanelle to make sure she also invited his mother and siblings." Lisa had developed a soft spot for Stacie and Kyle ever since she found out how they had looked out for Chanelle. Lisa saw Kyle regularly because he had become just as much of a permanent fixture around the house as RJ. If he wasn't at work, and Chanelle wasn't at school, then Kyle was likely to be by her side. He was polite and generous, always calling before he showed up to see if Lisa or Chanelle needed anything.

One day Kyle had gotten to the house before Chanelle had made it home from class. Lisa took the opportunity to engage in a conversation with him and learned that he wasn't as thuggish as she'd originally thought. Yes, his pants were still a little too big, in her opinion, and she didn't appreciate hearing his loud stereo system blocks before he got to her home, but overall, she found him to be a nice and intelligent young man. He had hopes and dreams like anyone else, just not the means to see them through. He wanted to go to college, but Stacie couldn't afford to send him, and Kyle had a plan to work all this year, save up some money, and hopefully start school next fall. Lisa admired his determination and respected the fact that he was willing to work hard for what he wanted.

Over the months, Lisa and Kyle became so comfortable with each other that she didn't mind giving him "motherly" orders to pull up his pants and he always obliged without a mumble.

"Didn't you say that Stacie has four other children and a grandchild?"

"Yep."

"Girl, you *are* gonna have a lot of folks in your house. Now I see why you are buying so much food."

"I don't mind. I'm just glad that everyone can get together."

"Well, don't feel like you have to buy all the food yourself. I'm going to give you some money when I get up there."

"No; that's okay. And anyhow, how are you going to pay for anything? You don't have a job either," teased Lisa.

"There's a difference between being self-employed and un-employed such as you."

"Hey...I work...sometimes." Lisa had formally been let go from Brentson Technologies. The pornography allegations were thrown out because the incidents occurred when she was in California, so it was obvious that she could not have been involved. But, Lisa could not dispute all the time she had taken off of work. Pastor Burlington had been right. Lisa didn't know that there had been a list kept and it was presented against her and used to accelerate her termination. Overall, she was glad to be out from under Olivia's reign. Every now and then Lisa kept in touch with Megan, who stated she wanted out of Brentson as well and was emphatically looking for another job. Currently, Lisa worked on an "as needed" basis, helping RJ at the center. She didn't get paid much, but it kept her utilities on.

"Is working sometimes enough to feed everyone?"

"Yes." As proud as Lisa was of her daughter, she was also proud of her sister. Callie had decided not to continue her tenure at the college where she taught and had applied for several grants looking to begin The Callie Jamison Foundation, a non-profit organization whose primary mission was to help people living with HIV find healthcare and other resources needed to live a healthy lifestyle. Things were still in the beginning stages, but all was going well. "RJ gave me money for most of the stuff," she explained, putting several packages of dinner rolls in her cart. "Mama called earlier and said that she would pick up the turkey and green beans. She won some money the other day, so I guess she's feeling extra generous."

"When is that woman going to give up gambling?"

"You got me...I'm done preaching to her about it. She's just going to have to learn the hard way."

"It seems to me like she should have learned already. Anyone who takes bill money to play scratch offs has a problem. I couldn't believe it when you told me she'd played the lottery with the money Daddy gave her for bills."

"Daddy is a better person than I could ever be because I would've been right back in Maryland. He's sticking it out, though. He's been trying to get her to get some help."

"That just goes to show how much he has changed."

"I'm starting to see that. At first I thought it was all a charade, but he really is a different person. I guess it took Mama leaving him for him to get it together. He's been very active in the church as well, although he has been down that road before." Their father had previously been one of those who served the Lord in spurts. It was sort of like a three-three rotation: three months walking with the Lord, and three years backsliding.

"Well, I think he'll be alright. I'm sure Mama's gambling addiction will keep him coming to Jesus, because Lord knows she has to be driving him crazy."

"Speaking of Jesus, did I tell you I got an email from Eric the other day?"

"What did he say?"

"Just that he was aware of everything and wanted to let me know he was praying for us."

"Aw…that was nice. I hope you responded."

"I did, but it was short and sweet. All I wrote was 'thanks.'"

Callie laughed. "I'm sure he was hoping for a little more. After all, the man *called* you to be his wife."

"Girl, I thank God that He did not let me make the mistake of marrying that man because it would have been awful."

"Your prayer life would be the bomb though, because he would have made sure of that with his morning ritual."

"You're silly. Anyhow, let me let you go so I can hurry up and get out of this store. My goal is to get everything I need because I am not trying to come back out tomorrow. You know the store is going to be packed tomorrow night with it being Thanksgiving Eve."

"Yeah, I need to finish packing before Bryan and Tyra get here. I look forward to seeing you tomorrow."

Lisa spent about another thirty minutes or so shopping, and stood in line for what seemed like forever. She was in the parking lot loading bags into her trunk when she heard the wicked voice. "Well, well, well...look who I've run into."

Lisa's muscles tightened and she silently prayed, "Father, in the Name of Jesus, deliver me from evil." She ignored Olivia as she had done the last several times they'd run into each other. Lisa was starting to get the feeling that these meetings weren't coincidental. This was about the sixth time she'd seen her former best friend in the last couple of weeks since the trial date had been set. Olivia didn't live on the same side of town as Lisa and yet she kept popping up. This was the first time Olivia had spoken to her. She normally just gave Lisa the evil eye. Olivia approaching her and actually speaking was, to Lisa, a definite sign of nervousness and fear.

After the first couple of "run-ins," Lisa had stopped telling RJ about them because he was being excessively protective of her. He had finally given up the guest room at her house and was back with Pastor Burlington, but he was still over every night. His presence didn't bother Lisa, though. For the first time since their divorce, she could actually say they had become friends and she enjoyed his company.

"How's the little pregnant slut of yours doing?"

She had some nerve calling Chanelle a slut! Lisa took a deep breath and shot a piercing glance Olivia's way. For a brief milli-second, Lisa felt sorry for her. Liv's birthday had been in September and she had turned fifty. Lisa would be thirty-nine next month and Olivia used to pass for someone her age or younger, but today she looked every bit of fifty and then some with the large bags and dark circles under her eyes. Even her cheeks seemed to sag. She looked awful! No one in their right mind would guess that the figure dressed in a jogging suit, baseball cap and not a stitch of makeup, was the wife of multimillionaire Isaac Scott. Liv always had a Kodak-moment-ready appearance. Lisa con-tinued unloading the cart, praying that God would enable her to move quickly so she could get away from this woman before she gave in to the urge to attack her.

"It's not too late to end this, you know?"

"No thanks!"

"C'mon, this is ticking me off, Lisa. Justin has missed out on playing football this year because of this stupid ordeal."

Even without Justin on the team, Ohio State was doing very well. They'd only lost one game and that was after going into over-time. Yeah, Justin had been a great player, but the team had learned to survive without him; and the cop who'd brought Chanelle home drunk earlier this year hadn't been by to bug Lisa for tickets anymore. "How dare you make this about football! Justin is a rapist, so his playing sports is not high on my list of priorities."

"It is on mine. He'll be allowed to play next year once he's cleared of these ludicrous charges. You better hope that happens."

"That'll be up to the jury."

"My husband has been practicing law now for over twenty years. He knows the ins and outs of the legal system. How do you think he was able to get a trial date so quickly? Don't you think he knows how to stack a jury?"

"If Isaac stacks the jury, then they'll vote in Justin's favor, so you don't have anything to worry about, do you?"

"My son's reputation and future are at stake! Tell Chanelle not to testify. We will make sure that she and the baby have enough money to last them for the rest of their lives."

Lisa got irritated at Olivia's reference to their grandchild as "the baby," as if Chanelle had been impregnated by a stranger. She laughed cynically as she wheeled her shopping cart to the designated area. Olivia followed to her annoyance. "We don't want your money; we want justice."

"Remember…justice can be bought."

"Maybe…but peace can't be. That's obviously something you don't have. You continue to rely on your money and we'll continue to rely on God. No matter what the outcome of the trial, we will be at peace—will you?" Lisa slammed her cart in with the others and jogged back to her car, not giving Olivia a chance to speak further, and quickly sped off.

CHAPTER 33

Woulddas, Shoulddas, Coulddas

Thanksgiving morning, Lisa got up early to start dinner, assisted by Chanelle and her mother. RJ ran around making sure everyone got picked up from the airport. Between Lisa's home, her parents' apartment and Pastor Burlington's place, all the out-of-town guests had places to stay, so no one would need to stay in a hotel. RJ was still staying with the Burlington's most of the time, and was giving up his guest room to his brother and sister-in-law. RJ could really afford to get his own place, but it seemed like Pastor and Sister Burlington enjoyed his company.

Dinner was ready around four and everyone was present; Kyle and his family had just arrived. The men had set up tables in the basement so that all twenty something people could fit comfortably for dinner. Callie, Tyra and RJ's sister-in-law, Sheila, were down there putting on tablecloths and place settings, while Chanelle was busy playing with baby Naomi, Callie's granddaughter. Lisa's mother was in the kitchen with her putting all the food into serving dishes when Kyle came into the kitchen carrying a pan. "Where should I put this, Miss Lisa?"

"What is it, sweetie?"

"Some baked beans that Stacie made."

Lisa still cringed when Kyle referred to his mother by her first name, but that was an issue she didn't have the right to correct him on. Lisa was, in many ways, a young parent; not as young as Stacie, but young nonetheless, having Chanelle when she was only twenty. But Lisa was "old school" when it came to raising children. She believed in butt whuppins, saying "Ma'am," and "Sir," and she definitely believed in drawing the line between parent and friend. Friends call each other by their first names, but children called their mamas, "Mama" or something similar. "You can just sit it on the counter and we'll take it downstairs with the rest of the food."

"Hello..." Stacie poked her head into the kitchen.

"I'm sorry, I was coming out to properly greet you guys." She gave her a hug. "Thanks for the baked beans. You didn't have to bring anything."

"I know...I wanted to throw in something Chanelle said you weren't making. I didn't feel right coming empty-handed with all the mouths I brought to feed."

"Girl, please, I knew how many people you were bringing when I invited you. I do appreciate it, though. Kyle, hang up their coats for me, please. Then you guys can get settled downstairs. We're going to bring the food down in a minute."

When Kyle, Stacie, and the rest of the Lewis crew were safely out of earshot, Lisa's mother leaned over to her and whispered, "You're really not going to put them baked beans out with the rest of the food, are you?"

"Yeah, why?"

"Humph...you don't have to worry about me eating any of them. Lord knows, I don't eat no white folks' food. It just don't taste the same as ours."

"Mama...," Lisa said with as much patience as she had left after having been up since four this morning. "In case you didn't know, every time you eat out, unless it's a Soul Food restaurant, you're eating 'White Folks Food,' so don't even start that mess."

"What mess, Skeeter?" Her father rounded the corner.

Lisa rolled her eyes. "I don't even want to repeat it. Here, carry this downstairs, please?"

Everyone gathered in the basement, holding hands as Pastor Burlington said grace. Dinner turned out to be great. All the food was delicious and even though several people had commented on how good Stacie's baked beans were, Lisa's mother stuck to her word and didn't have one bite.

After eating, everyone talked, laughed, and a few people even dozed off a bit. Pastor and Sister Burlington were the first to leave, followed by Stacie and her kids. Kyle, unsurprisingly, stayed behind with Chanelle. Eventually, the women trickled upstairs into the living room and left the men in the basement watching a basketball game.

"Anyone want to go shopping with me in the morning?" asked Lisa. Shopping on the Friday immediately after Thanksgiving was one of those traditions that she and Olivia had started together that she was now forced to continue on her own. She used to go for fun, but now she was going because of necessity. If anyone was going to get anything from her for Christmas, in light of her current employment situation, it would definitely have to be bought on sale. "I plan to be there as soon as the stores open."

Callie was the first to speak. "Girl, naw. Tomorrow is one of the biggest shopping days of the year. I never go to the store then; and anyhow, you know I don't like dealing with crowds."

"I'm with Callie," echoed Tyra.

"You know better than to ask me," scolded her mother. "I am not that much of an early bird."

"What about you, Sheila?" Lisa asked David's wife who was always so quiet and reserved.

"I won't be able to. David and I are headed back in the morning."

"Chanelle, are you going shopping with me in the morning? I want to leave the house no later than five." Lisa hollered out to her daughter who was sitting in the kitchen playing a game with Kyle.

"No, I'm straight."

"Why all of y'all have to be such party poopers?" she sulked.

"At least we'll be some well-rested party poopers," snorted Callie, playfully, and stuck her tongue out at Lisa.

Later that night, RJ lay on the sofa bed in the Burlingtons' living room, thanking God for allowing him another chance to spend this day with his family. It had been an extremely long time since both sides of their families had gathered together for a holiday. When he and Lisa were married, it used to happen at least once a year, but their separation and subsequent divorce put an end to all of that.

Hearing someone stir in the kitchen, RJ turned to see his brother. "Hey, man…could you possibly be any louder? I'm trying to sleep, you know?"

"Hold on…" He turned the garbage disposal on and quickly back off. "Did that help you out some?"

RJ sat up. "I see one thing hasn't changed…you're still my pesky little brother."

"Whatever…this little brother of yours can take you on any day."

"Is that right? You and what army? I got you by both height and weight." Despite the fact that he hadn't followed through on his good intentions to get to the gym regularly, RJ still had a nice, burly build. David was a few inches shorter and not as muscular.

"Man, that's okay. All I need is a slingshot and rock. I'll take you out like David did Goliath."

RJ laughed. "You would bring the Bible into this."

David came and sat on the sofa bed next to his brother. "I had a good time today. I wish we could stay until Sunday, but I need to get back to handle some things."

"Hey, man, I'm just glad you could make it. I enjoyed having you."

"It seems like things between you and Lisa are going well. I was watching the two of you interact. Aw...it was so cute, like two little love birds flirting with each other," he mocked.

"I don't know about all of that. We are getting along well, but we're a long way from going down the aisle again. This whole trial with Chanelle has brought us closer together."

"Is Chanelle still going to testify when the trial starts next year?"

"Yep... Lisa blames herself for everything that has happened and I hate when she does that because it's really my fault. The whole chain of events started with me. I'm the one who messed up. It was because of my mistakes that they moved up here in the first place." RJ had pretty much been able to hold it together for Lisa's and Chanelle's sake, but now, talking one-on-one with his brother, best friend and confidant, he released his tears that had accumulated like fluid inside a blister. "This is all my fault," he cried. "I let my family down."

"Bro, don't blame yourself. This is not your fault. This is the work of the enemy."

"He wouldn't have had a chance to work had I not messed up. I failed my family. I failed my wife and my baby girl. What if God is punishing them because of me?"

"RJ, hush. You know that God is not like that. He's not going to hold Lisa, Chanelle or anyone else accountable for your actions. Besides, He's already forgiven you. Why are you backtracking now?"

"I know He's forgiven me. It doesn't mean that there aren't consequences resulting from my actions. People think they can go out and do whatever they want, ask for forgiveness, and not have to deal with the consequences of their sin. Yes, it was *my* sin, but unfortunately when one person sins, it not only affects that person, but it can affect others as well. I mean, if that weren't true, then we would not have to suffer because of Adam and Eve. It doesn't just stop there. You've read the book of Joshua. Look at what happened to Achan's family in chapter seven. His children and everything he owned were destroyed because he sinned. Likewise, my getting arrested affected everybody...Lisa and Chanelle, the most."

"You're right, your actions affected everyone, but RJ, you've been given something that Achan wasn't...a second chance. You have to believe that, no matter what transpired in the past, God is able to mix all of it together and make it work out for your good in the end."

"It seems like we would all be better off if I had just kept preaching. Lisa wouldn't have had to start life from scratch; and Chanelle..." He swallowed hard. "Chanelle would not have been raped." Hearing that any person had been violated by rape, be it an adult or child, was heartbreaking enough for RJ, but the thought of his daughter being victimized was bone-crushing.

"Now you're falling into the trap of the woulddas, shoulddas, and coulddas. The reason you were so frustrated preaching is because it wasn't your purpose. Any time we're operating in something that is not our God-given purpose, there will be a great deal of tension."

David was right. Preaching was never something RJ felt God had intended for him to do. It was something that everyone else expected him to do because he was the eldest child and his father's namesake. From the time he could remember, his parents talked about him taking over his father's ministry and everyone else jumped on the bandwagon, including him. RJ was on his way to making it "big time." He'd rubbed elbows with some of the well-known, prominent television ministers of the day. But, night after night, sermon after sermon, RJ left the pulpit feeling empty. He was always striving to take his ministry to the "next level," thinking that doing more would make him feel better and maybe even validate the call that others had put on his life.

The drug outreach program he implemented at his church was supposed to get dealers and users off the streets and into the church. Though he was the pastor, RJ didn't believe in delegating everything. He led by example, working hard like the other church members and gladly making visits to the homes of known drug addicts. He really wanted to help...he really tried to help. One day he was interviewing a user and he listened to how she described the euphoric experience with smoking marijuana.

"Come on, preacher man...try it," she had enticed him. *"You come here every week all stressed out. I can see the tension lines on your face. I know you're trying to help me, but let me help you."*

That particular day had been hard. RJ had officiated a funeral earlier that morning of a thirteen-year-old boy who was beaten to death by gang members. RJ wasn't particularly fond of attending funerals, let alone officiating them, but that was part of his "duty" as the pastor. In a moment of spiritual weakness, RJ took a hit. The user had been right. The drugs did help with his stress level, but only temporarily. Every time his high ended, he couldn't wait for the next one to occur. He'd listened to the voice inside of him telling him that marijuana was a mild, harmless drug. "Everyone has a vice...even preachers," the still voice would say. He thought that he'd stick with marijuana, but over time, his high didn't last as long and the desire to do stronger drugs overtook him; and his recreational drug use with this woman evolved into an adulterous affair.

Her name was Delilah, which should have been a red flag by itself seeing how, in the Bible, there was a woman by the same name who tricked Sampson into telling her the secret of his strength, only to turn him over to the Philistines. Looking back, the whole thing was pure insanity. No man in his right mind would cheat on his wife with a drug addict. He learned one hard-nosed lesson about sin: it would always take you further than you meant to go. RJ was so focused on keeping up his preacher appearances for everyone else; and ironically it was the drugs that enabled him to do it.

"Look how God has even used your drug experience," David continued. "It's no coincidence that you are here in Columbus. God knew Lisa would move up here with Chanelle. He knew this would happen to her and He has planted you here for them."

"Man, if God knew it would happen, why didn't He just stop it in the first place?"

"Unfortunately we live in a world where bad things happen, which are beyond our control. That's the destructive nature of sin. Don't start blaming yourself for everything bad that happens. Yeah, you made some mistakes, RJ, so what? Who hasn't? Now, just be there and let God use you the way He wants to. Use this opportunity to be the man of God that you wanted to be for your family all along."

RJ soaked in his brother's words and once they resonated in his spirit, he did feel better. At least good enough to get a good night's sleep, something that had been eluding him. David also said a powerful prayer of encouragement over him.

"Thanks, man. I really needed that."

It was about one or so when RJ and David finished talking. Four hours later, Lisa was calling him to see if he was still on his way to pick her up so they could go shopping. "I don't know how I let you talk me into this one," he mumbled as they rode on the freeway.

Still sleepy herself, Lisa half-smiled. "Thank you…"

"Did your mom call you last night?"

"No. I went straight to bed after everyone left. I didn't even stay up to talk with Bryan and Tyra. Why?"

"She left a message for me with a few things that she and Callie want us to be on the look out for and get for them."

Lisa looked at him and laughed. "Nuh-uh, they are wrong for that. I'm not buying anything for them. They should've come themselves."

CHAPTER 34
No Further Questions

The remainder of that year flew by quickly. Lisa had turned thirty-nine in December and she, Chanelle and RJ drove to Baltimore to bring in the New Year with David and Sheila. Reporters and photographers swarmed the front of the courthouse as Justin Scott was escorted in by his parents. Lisa watched from afar as her former best friend did not appear to be camera shy. She couldn't make out what was said, but she was sure it was along the lines of proclaiming Justin's innocence. Olivia was camera ready, looking way better than she had the time when Lisa saw her at the store.

"Come this way." RJ grabbed her arm and they proceeded in another door.

The Scotts had really used the media to their advantage and Lisa was slightly worried about whether or not there would be a "fair" trial with all the exposure. Columbus was Ohio State football crazy and her daughter had pressed charges against one of the star players. Thankfully, Chanelle hadn't received any backlash from this ordeal that Lisa was aware of. Her identity was supposed to be kept anonymous, but somehow information about her being Justin's accuser mysteriously appeared on the

Internet. They'd started receiving calls from reporters to hear "Chanelle's side of the story." After a few days of being bombarded with calls, Lisa was forced to change the home telephone number.

Twelve jurors lined the wall looking intently as the prosecuting attorney, Richard Griggs, instructed Chanelle to tell the ladies and gentlemen about the night Justin had raped her.

It was the second time Lisa had heard her daughter repeat the story, but it was still as painful as the first. She couldn't help but feel responsible for allowing the Scotts into their lives—for hand delivering her daughter to a rapist! Tears welled in her eyes as Chanelle, who appeared confident and strong, recounted the events.

Holding her hand, RJ whispered in her ear, "Are you okay?" His breath was warm and his lips lightly touched her ear, causing a slight sensation.

She nodded. It was just the two of them there. Initially, Lisa's parents had attended, but her mother would get so emotional that neither Lisa nor her father thought it would be good for her to sit through the entire trial. Several times Stacie, Kyle, and Chanelle's best friend, Gericka, had accompanied them, but she and RJ had been the only ones there daily.

"It's not your, fault," he said.

She wanted to scream, "Yes, it is!" but instead silently turned and looked at him. Her stomach tickled with his lips inches from hers and she was once again aware of the temptation she'd been fighting for quite a while to allow their lips to reunite. Though the timing to respond to the urge was all wrong, she was encouraged by his comfort and smiled and said, "I love you."

That didn't quite come out right! What she meant to say was "I love having you here." *Here*, like in Columbus, so she didn't have to experience this alone. *Here*, like in the courtroom holding her hand. Having made no secret how he felt about her, RJ looked pleasantly surprised. He smiled, then quickly refocused on their daughter.

"Chanelle, is it fair to say that you didn't come forth with charges against Mr. Scott because you felt your credibility wouldn't hold up against that of an Ohio State football player?"

"Objection!" yelled Isaac before Chanelle got a chance to answer. "Prosecution is leading the witness."

"Sustained…" ruled the judge.

"Sorry, Your Honor, I'll rephrase the question…Chanelle, please tell the court why you waited several weeks to make these accusations against the defendant."

"Because I was scared that no one would believe me."

"Just for the record, other than the allegations of rape, do you have any personal vendettas against Justin Scott that would prompt you to falsify your testimony as a way to get back at him?"

"No, sir, not at all…"

"Thank you; no further questions…"

Isaac looked at Chanelle like a hungry bear ready to tear her apart. He took his time rising up from his seat, obviously a theatrical performance. "Ms. Hampton, how many intimate relationships have you been in prior to meeting Justin Scott?"

"Objection!" Attorney Griggs jumped out of his seat. "The question is irrelevant and has no bearing on the current case."

"Your Honor, I'm not trying to violate any confidentiality laws. I'm simply attempting to establish a motive as to why this young lady would claim she was raped. If I can be permitted to continue, I will quickly get to the point."

"Overruled," the judged ordered. "The witness may answer the question."

"Again, Ms. Hampton, how many intimate relationships have

you been in prior to meeting Justin Scott?" Isaac seemed even smugger now that the judge had ruled in his favor.

"I had never had sex before, if that's what you're asking."

"How many boyfriends did you have?"

"One."

"Were your parents, particularly your mother, supportive of this relationship?"

"Not at first."

"Please just answer yes or no from now on," Isaac instructed. "Did you ever lie in order to spend time with this other individual?"

"Yes, but—"

"So it's safe to say that you have a history of lying when it suits your purpose."

"Objection! Defense is being argumentative!" Mr. Griggs shouted.

"Sustained. The jury is instructed to disregard counsel's last statement."

"Ms. Hampton, is it true that you and your ex-boyfriend are back together now?"

"Yes."

Isaac continued grilling Chanelle, asking questions suggesting that she accused Justin of rape because he broke up with her. He even went so far as to say that Chanelle made up the rape allegation because she had cheated on her ex-boyfriend and didn't want him to be upset.

Of course, Mr. Griggs objected to many of his questions and the judge ruled in the prosecution's favor in most cases. Detective Evans assured the family that Richard Griggs was the best prosecuting attorney in the state. "I've worked with Richard for a long time. If anyone can hold up in court against Isaac Scott, it's him," the detective had said. Mr. Griggs was doing fine, but Lisa had watched enough reruns of *Matlock* to know that Isaac was trying to plant reasonable doubt with his questioning and that worried her.

Isaac tried his best to break Chanelle down or trip her up with trick questions, but she really held her own. She appeared fearless, speaking clearly and not hesitating to make eye contact.

"Prosecution, do you have another witness?"

"No, Your Honor, the State rests its case."

It was now the defense's turn to present and Isaac called Lisa as a hostile witness. He badgered her about all the problems with misbehavior she'd previously had with Chanelle. Every single thing that Lisa had told Olivia in confidence was being used to build Justin's defense.

Lisa was embarrassed by all the damaging remarks about Chanelle being thrown up in her face. She wondered how hurt Chanelle felt listening to them, and in the midst of her interrogation issued a tearful apology to her daughter. Isaac, in turn, said something to the judge, which caused him to order Lisa to keep her comments directed to the court. Once the grueling process was over, Lisa again apologized to her daughter, who amazed her by being so carefree.

"Mama, chill out. We both said some things about each other. It's over now, so I'm not taking anything you said to heart."

Lisa smiled. Chanelle seemed so much more mature than she had given her credit for being. Though the circumstances of her pregnancy were not ideal, she was confident that her daughter would make a wonderful and loving mother.

It wasn't a surprise to Lisa that Justin took the Fifth Amendment and refused to testify in his own defense. She would have loved to see him try to explain to the jury why he'd changed his initial statement to the police of not having any sexual contact with Chanelle to having consensual sex. Isaac had tried to get that information suppressed, but the judge ruled in favor of the prosecution. In his closing argument, Richard Griggs reminded the jury of Justin's discrepancy.

He also brought back to their attention the evidence supporting the fact that Chanelle had been wearing the torn clothing the night she accused Justin of raping her and the result of the sexual assault examination. As far as Lisa was concerned, Mr. Griggs had done a wonderful job trying the case and giving a convincing closing, but Isaac proved that he was a force to be reckoned with.

When it was his turn to speak, Isaac glossed over Justin's conflicting statements, arguing that Justin did what many young boys full of potential with a bright future would do. "He lied because he feared the damage that these false accusations would do to his reputation." Isaac also claimed that the scar tissue reported in the doctor's analysis was the result of Chanelle, a virgin, agreeing to have "rough sex." To discredit the pictures proving that Chanelle had worn the clothes, he suggested that perhaps she had torn them herself. He proposed the ridiculous theory that Chanelle was a vindictive teenager who became angry when Justin wasn't interested in pursuing their relationship any further. "She conjured up this story of rape as a way to get back at my client," he had said. "Chanelle Hampton did not say that Justin raped her until after he broke up with her. It is only then that she regretted becoming sexually involved with him. The last time I studied the law, regret did not equal rape. Ladies and gentlemen, I ask you not to punish my client because this young lady changed her mind weeks *after* the consensual act of sex occurred. Justin's only mistake was believing that yes meant yes."

As much as Lisa loathed the fact that Isaac knew his son was guilty, part of her had to admit that the man was good at what he did. It's no wonder that he'd gotten high-profile clients acquitted of some pretty tough charges. Lisa just hoped that this jury didn't buy into all of his antics.

Court was dismissed so the jury could deliberate. On the way out of the courtroom, she noticed a young Caucasian woman slip out quickly. Lisa had seen the woman once before and wondered what her interest was in the case.

In what seemed like the six longest hours of her life, Lisa was relieved when the prosecution called to tell them that the jury had reached a verdict. She, Chanelle and RJ made all the necessary calls for family and friends to meet them at the courthouse. On their way, Lisa also called her sister in California to give her an update.

"No matter what happens, we know that God is in control. Call me as soon as you get out of court," Callie ordered. "I love you guys and I'm praying for you."

Chanelle's supporters were deep in numbers at the courthouse, comparing well to friends and family of Justin's. Among Chanelle's advocates were Lisa's parents, Kyle, Stacie, Gericka and dozens of spectators anxious to hear the conclusion. Both Detective Evans and Attorney Griggs had even brought their wives, Natalie and Sylvia.

"Has the jury reached a verdict?"

"Yes, Your Honor," answered the foreman.

Lisa clutched one of Chanelle's hands while RJ held on to her other one. The paper with the jury's decision was handed to the judge who asked that everyone control their reactions until after the verdict was read. Lisa had never been more nervous in her life. Her chest caved in and out heavily. She wasn't sure if such a quick decision meant good or bad news.

"We, the jury, find the defendant, Justin Scott…guilty…"

"Nooooo!" Olivia wailed, zoning out the foreman as he gave the specifics of the guilty charge. "That slut ruined my son's life!" It didn't take long for her to be removed from the courtroom.

"Bailiff, take the defendant into custody. Sentencing will be pronounced in twenty-one days. Court is adjourned."

Tears of relief fell over Lisa, Chanelle, and many who came to support them. RJ first held Chanelle into his arms and then grabbed for Lisa to join them. For the first time since the news of Chanelle's rape had come out, Lisa witnessed tears fall from her ex-husband's eyes. "I promise to do whatever I can to protect you both from now on," he pledged.

They thanked Richard Griggs for successfully prosecuting the case.

"No, thank you, Chanelle, for having the courage to come forth. A lot of victims are too afraid to face their assailants, but you did great."

"He's right…" came the voice of the young Caucasian lady that Lisa had seen earlier. "Justin raped me well over a year ago and I've been tormenting myself ever since because I didn't go to the police. I admire your courage. I may not be able to get justice for myself, but I'm glad you did." Tears rolled down her cheeks and she walked away before anyone could give a response or learn her identity.

Outside the courthouse, reporters swarmed to Mr. Griggs who was poised in giving very diplomatic responses. Chanelle was asked how she felt and the eighteen-year-old smiled. "I'm just glad it's over."

CHAPTER 35
All Too Familiar

Justin was sentenced to six years in prison for his crime. In Lisa's opinion, he should rot in jail for the rest of his life, but the law was the law and serving six years was better than him getting off scot-free.

Now, the first week of March, Chanelle was only about six weeks shy from her due date, which was in mid-April. Lisa, her mother, and Stacie were planning to throw Chanelle a baby shower in a couple of weeks.

Lisa had come to grips with the fact that she was going to be a grandmother and was even looking forward to the birth of the baby. Chanelle had learned the baby's sex and had already picked out a name. Kyle had continued to stand by Chanelle's side. He was stepping up and filling the role of the baby's father. He'd accompanied them to several doctor appointments, carried a picture of the sonogram in his wallet and even helped RJ paint the nursery.

Chanelle told Lisa that Kyle wanted to adopt the baby after it was born. What surprised Lisa more than Kyle's willingness to take on such a large responsibility was her daughter's mature response. Chanelle had actually rejected his offer. She said that though things were great between the two of them, she realized that he was still young and may eventually have a change of heart. She didn't want to burden him with such a long-term commitment until she knew for sure how things would work out between them.

Lisa was in the kitchen making bowls of ice cream for RJ and herself when Chanelle walked in and kissed her on the check. "Bye, Mama," she said.

"Bye, sweetie. You be careful; I know it's warmed up a bit, but there may still be some ice out there on the road."

"Okay; I love you."

"I love you, too, baby."

She headed out to meet one of her friends.

Lisa heard the same type of exchange between Chanelle and RJ, who waited in the living room as Lisa got their treats. It could probably be said that Lisa and RJ were dating. They continued to spend a lot of time together and had even shared a few passionate kisses since her Freudian slip of confessing her love at the courthouse.

Long ago, Lisa had originally fell in love with the idea of being a "preacher's wife." She loved the V.I.P. treatment she had received from people who recognized her as "First Lady Hampton." She got special attention at beauty salons, reserved seating at special events, and gifts and letters of appreciation from different members of the congregation. Though she would never assume responsibility for RJ's actions because he did have a choice in the matter, she did acknowledge her own prideful and materialistic behavior. Thus, her *First Lady* charm necklace that she'd taken off the night Eric proposed to her stayed buried in her jewelry box, replaced by the heart locket RJ had given her last month for Valentine's Day.

Lisa continued to help RJ at the center when he needed her

and she still struggled at times to make ends meet, but she had obtained pure joy. The kind of joy that having high-profile friends couldn't buy. The kind of joy that allowed her to love RJ for his character rather than his position. RJ helped her out financially, but it wasn't like he had loads of money to spare. He paid bills at the Burlingtons' and was also still paying off some of the debt that he'd accumulated while they were living in Maryland. The one thing that he did have for her was true, unconditional love, and despite the mistakes he had made, she knew that for sure. It was the fear of learning to trust again that she still needed to overcome. The drug addiction was one thing, but the adultery seemed much harder for her to overcome.

Cold now after having eaten her ice cream, Lisa nestled into RJ's arms as they watched a DVD that he had rented. The movie, a suspense-thriller, was long, boring and predicable! Lisa was disappointed that she was able to figure out the storyline about thirty minutes into it and tried to get RJ to turn it off, but he was a die-hard let's-see-the-movie-through-to-the-end type of person so she suffered through it. When it was finally over, she went into the kitchen to microwave some popcorn while RJ put the second movie in.

"This one better be good or else you're going to be banned from picking the movies from now on," she playfully warned him. "You should have gotten a comedy or something because that was awful!"

"Oh, don't give me that. When I asked you what you wanted me to get, you said, and I quote, 'It doesn't matter…get whatever.'"

She threw a kernel his way as he reached in the bowl for a handful. "Well, clearly 'whatever' meant a comedy, duh?"

RJ laughed. "Next time I'll try and do a better job of reading your mind." He leaned in confidently for a kiss. He released her mouth long enough to whisper the words, "I love you..." and then embraced her lips again with his tender ones. She could taste the salt of the popcorn on his mouth as she allowed herself to get deeper into the act.

Though they spent a lot of time together, they didn't engage in kisses like this too often. Lisa wanted to "take things slow" and every time his lips met with hers, she was reminded of their times together. RJ had always been a great kisser. Right now, he was dangerously great, because her mind played reruns of how his lips had often explored her from head to toe during their previous relationship.

Lisa didn't allow her thoughts to run away. When they finally came up for air, she deflected the moment by saying, "I hope you don't think that lets you off the hook for picking a crappy movie."

RJ smiled, warmly. "I'm sure that had to count for something." He grabbed the remote and started the movie. He definitely exhibited patience with her. He seemed to know when to quit and she appreciated that.

The second movie was much better than the first. It was full of action and held Lisa's attention with every scene. They were about halfway through it when flashing blue and red lights soared through the living room window. The scene had been all too familiar to Lisa and she panicked, recalling how fearful she'd been the first time she'd seen these lights nearly a year ago when Chanelle had skipped curfew. RJ was the first to the door with Lisa at his heels.

"Officer, what can I do for you? I'm Robert Hampton and this is my wife, Lisa."

Calling her his wife was still a habit that RJ hadn't shaken, even though they had been divorced for nearly six years now. It no longer bothered or surprised Lisa when he did.

"Do either of you know this young lady?" The officer held Chanelle's driver's license.

"Yes, she's our daughter. What's wrong? How'd you get that?"

"Sir, I'm afraid I have some bad news…"

Lisa's father walked into the hospital room. "Skeeter, I wanted to let you know that Kyle and Stacie are out in the waiting room. You want me to tell them to come back here?"

"Yes, that's fine, Daddy. How's Mama?" she asked, her face felt sticky from dried tears. They'd been at the hospital all night, waiting…hoping…praying for something to change.

"Not good. I'm going to take her home to get some rest. I'll be back in a few hours after I pick Callie up from the airport."

"Baby, do you mind waiting a few minutes before allowing Kyle and Stacie to come back here? I would like to be alone with Chanelle for a minute," requested RJ.

She nodded. "I'll walk out with you, Daddy."

People had been in and out all night—Hattie, Raymond, Pastor Burlington, Chanelle's best friend, Gericka and her parents, Lisa's former assistant, Megan, plus others from the rehabilitation center and church. RJ just wanted a minute alone with his daughter. He continued leaning over her comatose body, his tears splashing on her cheeks. "Chanelle, if you can hear me…I want you to know how much I love you. I'm so sorry, baby. I'm so sorry that I haven't always been a good father. I'm so sorry…" He broke down. The tubes and monitors connected to his baby girl reminded him of his guilt for failing his family years ago. Traces of the conversation he'd had with David Thanksgiving night still played in his mind, but those memories didn't stop the nagging question: Would Chanelle be in this position had he made different choices? Was he Achan and had his entire family been destroyed because of his sins?

"God…" RJ sobbed. "I'm sorry I let You down; I'm sorry I made so many mistakes. God, do whatever You have to do to me, but please…*please* don't punish Chanelle for anything that I have done."

CHAPTER 36
A Few Choice Words

Stacie walked with Lisa as she escorted her parents to their car. Kyle, the vibrant young boy Lisa had grown to love, had stayed behind in the waiting room; all the joy drained from his eyes. He made no attempt to hide his pain as tears freely flowed down his face when Lisa hugged him.

"My nerves are too messed up. I need a cigarette before going back in. I'll meet you up there," said Stacie.

Lisa wasn't crazy about engulfing secondhand smoke, but she stayed outside with Stacie anyhow.

"How is she?" Stacie wasted no time lighting up.

"Not good. She was conscious for a little while before we got here, but she's been in the coma ever since."

"And the baby?"

"He's hanging in there. I pray he pulls through. He's so tiny."

Stacie blew circles with her smoke. "It's all over the news. Thank you for calling and telling us."

"I know how much you guys care about Chanelle. I didn't want you to find out about this through the media."

"The police better catch up with Olivia before I do because I swear if I see her, I'm going to kill her."

Lisa identified with Stacie's anger, remembering the gut-wrenching feeling she had when the police officer stated that Chanelle had been involved in a drive-by shooting. He gave her and RJ all the information that he had at the time. The "friend" Chanelle had gone to meet was Olivia. The police have a 9-1-1 tape of Chanelle calling for assistance from her cell phone after having been shot. During the call, Chanelle stated she had agreed to meet Olivia at a restaurant because Olivia wanted to make amends and be in the baby's life.

According to what Chanelle told the police, she was in the process of following Olivia home so she could pick up some things that Olivia had bought for the baby. As they were about to get on the freeway, Olivia's car came to a complete stop and another car pulled alongside Chanelle. When the passenger of the other car began firing into Chanelle's vehicle, Olivia sped off. Chanelle was able to give the operator her location, which helped them find her quickly. Lisa and RJ were told that Chanelle was able to talk to the officers when she was initially brought into the emergency room; and when she was no longer able to speak, she wrote sketchy notes, scribbling Olivia's name repeatedly. Unfortunately, RJ and Lisa never got a chance to speak with their daughter because she had slipped into a coma minutes before their arrival. The last words RJ and Lisa ever heard their daughter say to them were "I love you."

Chanelle had been shot four times: once in the head and neck; and twice in the abdomen. It was by the grace of God that the bullets missed the baby. He was delivered via an emergency C-section. The doctors were still concerned about him, though, since he was six weeks premature and had been born under stress.

"That woman is ruthless to do something like this, especially to the baby, who is her own flesh and blood." Stacie continued puffing her cigarette.

"She obviously doesn't care. I've learned the hard way that Olivia is vindictive. I bet this is her way of trying to take my child from me since she blames us for Justin being in jail. The crazy thing is, I do feel responsible…not for Justin, but for Chanelle. Maybe if I had reported the times I suspected Olivia of following me…"

"What! When was this?"

"Last year sometime, before the trial started. I mentioned to RJ that I had seen her a couple of times, but after a while I stopped telling him. He was being very protective, and I appreciated it, but I guess I really didn't consider her a danger; and I didn't want him getting all worked up about nothing. I didn't see her anymore once the trial really got underway, so I figured it was over. I should have known she was capable of something like this. I remember—"

"Remember what?"

"Nothing…" Lisa thought back to the day when Olivia sat in her office listening to her vent about Kyle and jokingly told Lisa that a hit could be arranged. In retrospect, Lisa believed that Olivia was serious and had she shown genuine interest, Olivia may have arranged for something similar to happen to Kyle. "I feel like I should have seen this coming."

"Lisa, this isn't your fault," Stacie said along with some other things. She called Olivia a few choice words that, quite frankly, Lisa had thought, but hadn't spoken out loud.

"I really appreciate how much you and Kyle have been there for Chanelle. I don't know if I can ever thank you enough."

"You don't have to. I've liked Chanelle from the first time I saw her. She was so sweet. Then, when she and Kyle broke up and she started hanging with Justin, I didn't hear from her for a while. I'll never forget the night she called and asked me if I would pick her up."

"Was that the night she and I got into a fight?"

"Yeah…truthfully, I planned to bring her home, but when she told me what Justin had done to her, I identified with her pain in more ways than one." Stacie lit another cigarette. "I was raped by my mom's boyfriend when I was thirteen. I told her and of course he denied it. She'd only been going out with him for a month, but he wasn't the one she kicked out; it was me. She sent me to live with my alcoholic grandmother who didn't care whether I came or went."

Stacie's voice cracked and Lisa sensed that she was still dealing with some issues in her childhood. Guilt briefly came over her as she was reminded how she immediately made assumptions about her based on her outer appearance. Having had the last several months to see glimpses of her heart, Lisa knew that she had completely misjudged her; and learned that judging a book by its cover wasn't always wise.

"I'll be the first to admit that I've done a lot of buck wild things. I got pregnant by a man thirty-four years older than me when I was fifteen. I wasn't necessarily a good mother at first. It took a few years for me to get my act together. Sometimes I feel like I failed. I mean, I'm freakin' thirty-three and I have an eighteen-month-old granddaughter. I wanted better for my kids than I had and I don't seem to be able to give them that. I work night and day to make ends meet, but I can't afford to send my son to college." Stacie swallowed hard. "My point for saying all of this is that I could immediately tell that Chanelle came from a good home. She wasn't the type to experiment with drugs or do any of the wild things that I've done. I know she got drunk that one time and all, but for real, that's mild compared to my teenage years. Chanelle is a good girl. It's just messed up that something like this happened to her."

Lisa admired Stacie's compassion. "Thanks for being there for her when I wasn't."

Stacie put out her second cigarette butt. "This is not your fault," she repeated. "We all make mistakes with our children, but you're not responsible for what happened to Chanelle."

Stacie sounded extremely sincere and Lisa wanted to believe her, but she still felt an overwhelming amount of guilt. She forced a smile. "Thanks...C'mon, let's go back in. We left Kyle in the waiting room. Seeing how upset he was, it's probably not good for him to be alone."

CHAPTER 37
Any Given Day

P astor Burlington mounted the pulpit slowly, leaning to the right with his cane. "Ladies and gentleman, we're gathered here today because Robert and Lisa Hampton have been forced to lay their one and only daughter permanently to rest." Chanelle's lifeless body rested in a charcoal-colored casket amidst various floral arrangements just a few feet from where RJ and Lisa were sitting. "I've done a lot of eulogies in my life. I've buried both of my parents, one of my sisters, my best friend and countless others. Yet, no other service has challenged me like this of eighteen-year-old Chanelle Hampton."

"As I began to prepare for this service, I wondered, 'Why do bad things happen to good people?' It's the same question that the prophet, Habakkuk, had asked God; and the same question I know many of you have recently asked after learning of the circumstances surrounding this young lady's death."

Deep moans and groans echoed throughout the sanctuary. Chanelle's grandparents, friends and other family members seemed to be the most affected, though people who didn't know the family well were also moved to tears. Several surprise guests included Detective Troy Evans and his wife, Natalie; Attorney

Richard Griggs and his wife Sylvia; and even the Ohio State head football coach came to offer his condolences.

RJ kept his arm snugly around Lisa who had been holding up much better than he had expected. Chanelle never came out of her coma. It was just Lisa and him in the room, in addition to hospital staff, when the doctor had pronounced her dead, making Chanelle's murder the sixteenth one of the year thus far.

RJ will never forget that moment. "Time of death: 11:41 am," the doctor had said. Those were the most ear-piercing and horrifying words he'd ever heard. Yet, he believed that the Lord had prepared him for what was to come. During the time he'd spent alone with Chanelle when Lisa walked her parents out to their car, the Lord had settled in his spirit that Chanelle wasn't going to pull through. Initially, RJ went into a crying and praying frenzy because he felt like he was responsible for what had happened to his daughter. "It should be me! I should be the one fighting for my life!" he pleaded. God allowed him to vent while at the same time ministering words of encouragement to his spirit. It was in that moment when RJ was freed from bearing the burden of guilt. He had a choice: to wallow in self-pity over his mistakes or to trust that God was in control of all things and to stand on His Word to make it through.

Not wanting to upset Lisa any further, RJ never spoke about what would become of their daughter. Perhaps the Lord had prepared him because He knew that Lisa would need to be comforted by him. Whatever God's reasoning for the revelation, RJ stayed glued to Lisa's side. When Chanelle passed away, instead of calling friends and family immediately, he took Lisa off alone and held her as she wailed in his arms. In such situations most people would have tried to think of something spiritually deep to say, but RJ didn't utter a word. He allowed Lisa the time to grieve, just as God had allowed him.

"I look down into this casket…" Beads of sweat dropped from Pastor Burlington's bald head as sorrow drenched his countenance. "And I see potential that never got to be. I see a young girl who was unfairly snatched from this life when, in many ways, life was just beginning for her. Ladies and gentleman, Chanelle's death is proof that we live in a fallen world—a world in which evil is present. There used to be a time when we as a society collectively took care of our senior citizens. Now the elderly have become prey…easy target for thieves. On any given day we can turn on the news or open the *Columbus Dispatch* and find cases about robbery, sexual molestation and as in Chanelle's case, murder."

RJ pondered a moment on how many things had transpired over the last year.

Just twelve short months ago, he had begun settling into Columbus and his new position as the Director of Hope Ministries Rehabilitation Center. Chanelle was driving Lisa crazy and he would have likely sold his right arm to be this close to Lisa again. Now he and Lisa had a bond that he was sure was much stronger than the one they had during their marriage. He was a grand-parent, and his baby girl—the only seed he had planted—was dead, courtesy of Lisa's ex-best friend who had been arrested and charged with conspiracy to commit murder. RJ truly had been delivered from his drug addiction; Chanelle's death would have been enough to push him over the edge had it not been for God guiding every step he made.

"I'm sure by now you are all aware of the high-profile nature of this case," Pastor Burlington stated. "Though each of us have our own opinions about what should be done to the individuals responsible for such a heinous act, there's one thing we must agree on. What happened to Chanelle Hampton was purely a work of evil! In Ephesians, six, verse twelve, Paul tells us that we don't wrestle against flesh and blood. In other words, the true enemy in this case, or any case, is not those who have been arrested for this crime, but our *real* enemy is the devil. And he will do whatever and use whoever is willing to try and destroy us. Men and women who engage in evil are too ignorant to realize that they are actually doing Satan's bidding. The Devil can't make anyone do anything. What he does is entice people with things like power, money and revenge, all the while luring them into sin. And sin, no matter how small it may seem, will always take you further than you meant to go, and leave you longer than you meant to stay."

"Folks, the devil is knocking at every one of our doors, waiting for us to give him the opportunity to come in. Robert and Lisa, you have walked a very tough road. I want you to take all the time you need to grieve. You have every right to be hurt. To be honest the pain may never go away, but hopefully, over time, it will diminish. You also have every right to be angry about what happened to your daughter. What I encourage you two, and the rest of y'all, not to do is allow your anger to turn into resentment or bitterness. It's during tough times like this when we are tempted the most to question God. We think 'God, if You're so powerful and mighty, and You have the whole world in the palm of Your hands, then how did this happen?' Sometimes people go through things and turn their backs on God, but the Psalmist tells us in chapter nine, verse nine that the Lord is our refuge in times of trouble. Robert and Lisa, I want you to know that this is the time when you need God more than ever. Not only will you need Him, but you will also need each other."

Lisa squeezed RJ's hand as if to affirm Pastor Burlington's last point of them needing each other. Perhaps that was her way of letting him know that she needed him. RJ patted her hand softly as if to say that he would be there with her every step of the way. He'd let her down before, but never again.

Not only did she need him, but so did their grandson. Chanelle had picked out his name weeks before her death. Both he and Lisa wanted to honor her wishes and so they named him Chandler Robert Kyle Hampton like she'd wanted. Chandler was still in the hospital, but he was a fighter and his prognosis was very good. That didn't surprise RJ. He knew his little man wouldn't give up easily. He came from a long line of headstrong females and determined men who didn't give up without a fight. Chandler was going to make it. He had to...

"We may never understand why God allowed this to happen to Chanelle," Pastor Burlington continued. "I want everyone here to understand that Chanelle's murder was never part of God's plan for her life. In Jeremiah 29:11, God says 'I know the thoughts I think toward you...thoughts of peace, and not evil, [thoughts] to give you an expected end.' So, if God thinks only good toward us then we're still left with the question of why do bad things happen? The only answer I have to that is sin. God doesn't ever promise that bad things won't happen, but Jesus promises to be with you always, even until the end of the world. Despite all of your unanswered questions, I implore you to continue trusting in God. I've walked with the Lord long enough to know that the Devil's plans never thwart God's power. Keep trusting God and over time you'll see that what the Devil meant for evil, God will ultimately work out for your good."

"Fortunately for Chanelle, she is with Jesus right now. Let her sudden death be a warning to all of you who don't have a relationship with Him. Tomorrow is not promised. Death does not discriminate. It can come at any moment in your life. Ask yourself this one question: if you were to die right now, would you be ready to meet Jesus?"

CHAPTER 38
Knight in Shining Armor

L isa's family gathered at her house after the service to help her polish off some leftovers. She appreciated all the food that was brought over, but she didn't think she would be able to eat one more piece of fried chicken or chicken casserole for quite some time. Lisa laughed silently to herself as she watched her mother devour one of the casseroles, claiming how good it was, not realizing that Stacie had made it. Had someone told her beforehand, her mother would have claimed not to eat "white folks' food," and if someone told her now, she would probably swear she was sick.

"Lisa, someone just pulled up in the driveway for you," her sister announced, walking into the kitchen.

"Who is it?" Callie laughed and whispered in their mother's ear, who also giggled.

Lisa went into the living room and noticed RJ's goofy grin. "Who's here?" she pressed.

"It's a bird...it's a plane...it's super Christian!" He busted out laughing just as the doorbell rang.

"Hello, Sister Hampton." Her ex-fiancé, Eric, stood at the door. "I hope I'm not interrupting anything."

"No, you're fine. Come on in. May I offer you something to eat or drink?"

"No, thank you." Eric took a seat on the sofa, acknowledging RJ and the rest of her family who had gathered around.

"Guys, would you mind giving us a few minutes alone?" Lisa inquired of her family who stood like spectators at a carnival.

Even in the hours after their daughter's funeral, RJ couldn't stop his testosterone from taking over. He apparently wanted to make it known that he was the man in Lisa's life now and so he obliged her request to speak with Eric alone, but kissed her on the cheek and said, "Baby, I'll be in the kitchen if you need me."

Eric stared blankly. "I heard about what happened to Chanelle and I wanted to personally offer my condolences."

"Thank you, Eric. I mean, Minister Freeman. I appreciate you stopping by."

"How are you doing?"

"My emotions fluctuate throughout the day, but right now I'm fine."

"I want you to know that I was praying for you and Chanelle during the rape trial."

"I know…I received your email. Thank you so much."

"No problem. Are you sure you're holding up okay?" He seemed genuinely concerned.

"I really miss her. We had grown so close. It's difficult not having her around. I'm glad to at least have a part of her left with me."

"I'm assuming you're talking about the baby. Is it going to be all right?"

Lisa didn't like her grandbaby being referred to as an "it," but she knew Eric didn't mean any harm. "Prayerfully so. He's still in the hospital and will probably be there for a while, but things are definitely going in his favor." Lisa picked up her digital camera from off the coffee table. "Want to see some pictures of him?"

"Sure…" Eric eagerly flipped through the images. "Wow… what a tiny little fellow. What's his name?"

"Chandler Robert Kyle Hampton."

Eric seemed surprised. "Kyle as in that young man she was seeing?"

"Yep; and Robert, of course after RJ. Turns out that Kyle isn't so bad of a kid after all. I was just too stuck on outward appearances to give him a chance."

"Looks like there has been some spiritual growth taking place, huh?"

Lisa wasn't sure if he had meant that as a compliment or not so she simply nodded.

"I'm glad you shared these pictures with me. He's adorable."

"Thanks…"

"I heard on the news that Olivia was arrested. Do you think she's really behind this?"

Lisa nodded sadly. "That's the way it's looking. She didn't actually pull the trigger, but the police found the gunman who turned her in. The prosecutor said it may take a while for her case to go to trial because of all the injunctions Isaac is filing, but they are actively pursing the case. In the meantime, I've filed a restraining order against her so she can't come anywhere near Chandler or me."

"Who would have thought she would do something like this? It's horrible. I've known Olivia for over a decade through the church, and I never saw such a wicked side of her. I'm no longer part of the ministry at Abundant in Christ. These last few months, I've been gone almost every weekend. I started my own church in Sandusky."

"Really? Congratulations! What's the name of your church?"

Eric gave a proud look. "The Tabernacle of Jesus. It's so awesome. I'm really looking forward to the move. I've only been able to make it on the weekends, so I've been missing choir rehearsal and midweek Bible study. I'm looking forward to attending those things from now on. Services are held at Mother's house for the time being. She leads Bible study and directs the choir in my absence."

"Wow, you have enough members for a choir already?"

"We are a blessed congregation, for sure. Mother and I are the only members now, but God is faithful and He will increase our numbers."

It took all the Holy Ghost power Lisa had to keep from cracking up.

"There's too much corruption in churches nowadays. The Lord is looking for honest people to do His will. I have a very unique calling on my life. I am anointed."

"I see... RJ, can you come here please?" she yelled. It didn't take her knight-in-shining-armor long to appear.

"Is everything okay?"

"Yes, sweetheart, Minister Freeman was just telling me about the church he has started. I thought you would like to sit in on the conversation. It's rather interesting."

"Oh, really..."

"Yes. I started my own church. It was a big step of faith."

"Good for you...God will reward you for your faithfulness. Isn't that what Hebrews 11: 6 says, that without faith it's impossible to please God for he that comes to God must believe that He is and He is a rewarder of them who diligently seek Him."

Creases immediately folded into Eric's forehead and Lisa nudged RJ in the side for picking with him. "Brother Hampton, you were close, but the scripture actually states 'he that com*eth*' not comes, it's 'com*eth*.' Pardon if I seem agitated. Sister Hampton can tell you that I take it very personally when people misquote the word of God."

"My bad...for some crazy reason I thought *comes* and *cometh* were pretty much the same, but clearly they are not." RJ may have appeared sincere to Eric, but Lisa could tell that he barely restrained himself from laughing.

"Well, I think it's time for me to go. I need to prepare for Sunday's sermon anyhow." Eric got up and walked to the door quickly without waiting for Lisa or Eric to escort him. "Sister Hampton, you're in my prayers. Brother Hampton, I'm praying for you as well," he said as he let himself out.

Lisa playfully hit RJ. "Why'd you run that man out like that?"

"Don't blame me...you're the one who called for help."

CHAPTER 39
Under the Rug

Spending her days at the hospital sitting with Chandler had become a daily routine for Lisa. As expected, RJ and her parents called several times throughout the day to check on him. Each time, Lisa pretty much said the same thing: Chandler was doing fine. Actually, he was great. He was breathing without the respirator now and doctors said he might be able to come home in another few weeks. When she wasn't at the hospital, Lisa was busy at home getting the guest room together, which had been converted into a nursery.

Chanelle's bedroom continued to stand as is. Lisa wasn't ready to do anything with her daughter's room yet. It had only been a couple weeks since they'd buried her and she was going to give herself time to grieve, as Pastor Burlington had been sure to tell her many times. Days were still up and down emotionally for her. Chanelle's funeral was the first time she had to bury someone close to her who had died so violently. Lisa didn't understand it and she stopped trying to. It would never make sense.

Lisa was in the process of gaining full custody of, and adopting, Chandler. Considering that his dad was in jail and his paternal grandmother was out on bond and facing murder charges, she didn't think she'd have any problems getting the courts to rule in her favor. Neither Justin nor Olivia had shown any interest in Chandler's well-being.

Lisa sat in the waiting area, putting together a scrapbook with pictures of Chanelle that she wanted to give to Chandler. The scrapbook would chronicle each stage of Chanelle's life. Hopefully through this and other mediums, Chandler would have a sense of who his mother was.

Lisa was staring at a kindergarten picture of Chanelle nostalgically when someone walked in the waiting room.

"Hello…the nurse told me I could find you in here."

Quickly wiping her tears before they fell, she looked up to see Pastor Ross, the leader of her former church, coming her way. For a split second Lisa's muscles contracted, recalling how he had blown her off the day she went in to speak with him about Olivia. She breathed deeply, hoping to swallow those feelings of resentment. She faked a smile, standing up to shake his hand. "Hi, how are you?"

"I'm good, thank you. What about yourself?"

She shrugged. "I've had better days and I've had worse. What brings you by here?"

"I owe you an apology. I wish I would have done more that day you came by the office."

"I don't know what you could've done to stop this. I'm not really sure what I was expecting when I came to see you. I guess I just wanted you to listen."

"You handled yourself quite professionally. I'm ashamed to say that I haven't been true to the gospel that I've been preaching." He let out a heavy sigh. "The Bible says that God is no respecter of persons. He doesn't deal with people based on outward appearances, positions, or wealth and He really doesn't care about titles that people parade around church. Yet, day-after-day, week-after-week, our churches are packed with people—with leaders who operate with the 'I'm better than you are' mentality. I was one of them and unfortunately, I treated people differently according to their status."

"I've always known that Olivia Scott was the sweetest person to be around as long as she was able to get her way. When the chips didn't fall in her favor, things got ugly. I can't tell you how many members have come to me with issues—serious issues—about one thing or another and, not wanting to rock the boat or risk not getting those huge tithing checks, I did nothing—absolutely nothing. I was supposed to be representing God and I let Olivia and even others, because of their status, influence what went on at Abundant in Christ, rather than God."

Lisa wasn't sure what he expected her to say. She definitely was not going to take on a prideful spirit and pour salt in his wounds. She'd made misjudgments about character based on external circumstances as well. "Everyone makes mistakes in judgment from time to time. At least you're acknowledging it," she said.

"It wasn't just Olivia. There were other people in ministry that I should have talked to or sat down with because of some disturbing things. I'm not saying that as the pastor I should have reprimanded every person for every complaint I received because I'm sure not all were legit. But, I've been very good at sweeping things under the rug. There are many times when I've received letters from members about things that I ignored. God is not pleased with me and I'm not pleased with myself. For what it's worth, I want to again say I'm sorry. I could have written you a letter or called you, but I felt the need to do this face-to-face."

"Thank you, Pastor Ross. It was very big of you to come here."

"Bless you, but this is not about me getting brownie points. It's something I'm doing because it's the right thing to do. I'm sure you probably never want to be a member of Abundant in Christ again, but if you ever decide to come for a visit, you will always be welcome."

"Thank you."

"Things will be different if you do come. I've cleaned house, letting a lot of individuals who had been key leaders go. As a result, I've lost a lot of my big contributors and my staff is virtually non-existent. We'll likely have to sell the building and move into a smaller place; financially, we're sinking quickly. But you know what? I have peace." He chuckled. "I'm sorry...I'm unloading all of this on you and you're probably like 'why is this man telling me all of this?' I guess I just feel so bad about how I responded to you; I just want you to know that God has dealt with me. He has literally whupped my behind and it has been nothing pretty."

"Well, like I said, apology accepted."

"Hug?"

"Sure, why not?" She smiled.

"Mrs. Hampton, it's time for Chandler's next feeding. Do you want me to go ahead and do it since you have company?"

"I'm sorry, Pastor Ross, but I really don't like to miss his feedings."

"No problem. I said what I needed to say. You take care and I'll see you around."

Lisa gathered up all her photos, said good-bye to him and then headed off to feed her grandbaby.

Epilogue

One year later…

The media frenzy was stirred again when Olivia finally went to trial for her part in Chanelle's murder. Lisa got to the point that she didn't watch the news much because day in and day out, every station and news reporter seemed to rehash Justin's rape case before leading into Olivia's. Lisa got enough of hearing about Olivia whenever she and RJ sat in court during the trial. Lisa thought the pain of losing Chanelle had indeed diminished in some capacity, but she learned that it had only been suppressed. As soon as the trial began, Lisa found herself mourning her daughter's death again as though it had just happened—and she still hadn't been able to do anything to Chanelle's room.

Olivia had refused to acknowledge any wrongdoing despite cell phone records proving communication between her and her co-conspirators, who had taken plea deals, agreeing to testify against her. Documents showed that Olivia had spoken with the gunman minutes prior, and after, he had opened fire on Chanelle. In addition, bank statements confirmed that she had paid him large sums of money. The state had a strong case against her, but she apparently refused any plea deals and wanted to take it to a jury. Perhaps she thought Isaac's fame and fortune would buy her some sympathy votes.

Each time Lisa saw her former friend come into the courtroom dressed like she was attending some fundraising gala and sitting smugly in the defendant's chair, she thought about the scripture in Proverbs 16 which talks about pride going before destruction and a haughty spirit before a fall. A lot of things under the Scotts' reign were beginning to fall apart. There had been talk of money laundering investigations against Isaac, and Brentson Technologies' CEO, Neil Criton, was arrested for fraud.

Megan, Lisa's former assistant, had managed to find a job prior to the company's downfall. She still kept in touch with Lisa every once in a while. On days when Lisa wanted to feel sorry for herself because her daughter had been murdered, she often thought about Megan who had continued to persevere through life despite having lost her husband in the war. If Megan, who did not yet know Christ, could make it through, Lisa who, had Jesus as her personal Lord and Savior, was certain she would make it.

One of the most difficult parts of sitting through the trial had been when the prosecutor played the 9-1-1 tape of Chanelle calling the police for the jury. Lisa had been told of the tape, but for the first time she had heard the desperation and pain in her daughter's voice. Though she was praying daily for God to teach her how to forgive Olivia, her progress had regressed quite a bit after that day. She was still moving forward, but Lisa realized it wouldn't be an automatic or immediate process. Forgiving Olivia was something she had to do continuously, and definitely something she had to work hard at doing.

Despite all the heartache she had gone through as a result of losing Chanelle, Lisa still managed to have joy. At forty, she was the proud grandmother of one-year-old Chandler who kept her on her toes. With a house full of guests, everyone gathered around as Chandler dove into his birthday cake.

"Baby, hurry, get the camera and take the picture!" Lisa yelled to her husband. In a private ceremony back in the summer with just family and friends, Lisa and RJ had remarried. There was no fancy engagement party, only a simple announcement and a backyard barbecue. Lisa didn't know who was happier about the wedding, her or her mother, who had never stopped loving RJ. Lisa couldn't have been more honored to have her father walk her down the aisle—rather grass—as Pastor Burlington stood to officiate. Lisa's relationship with her father had come a long way. He definitely had more patience than Lisa had ever given him credit for because her mother was still gambling away their money. She was currently on a very expensive losing streak, and Lisa prayed that God would deliver her from this addiction before things got any worse.

RJ's brother, David, was his best man and Callie stood up as Lisa's maid of honor. A year after learning she was HIV-positive, Callie was still very healthy. She was taking her medication and not having a single problem with it. She was no longer in therapy over her husband's suicide and the Callie Jamison Foundation was well on its way to making a mark in the nation. Callie had already received broad recognition for her work after sharing her story on several national television talk shows. In addition to helping RJ at the center when she was needed, Lisa worked behind the scenes helping Callie keep track of all her speaking engagements and donations. The internet and email made it easy for Lisa to assist her sister despite the distance between them.

Once RJ snapped the picture of Chandler, Lisa reached down to wipe his hands when he grabbed a lock of her hair with the other one, decorating it with yellow cake and buttercream icing.

"Now that's a Kodak moment." Stacie laughed. She and Kyle, who was now enrolled in college, had continued to be present in Chandler's life and on a few occasions, Lisa had allowed him to stay overnight with them. Lisa didn't like to let Chandler out of her sight too much, but she trusted them and she knew that he was always in good hands. Even Chanelle's best friend, Gericka, was at the party and babysat him at times.

She and RJ made sure to take Chandler by the Burlingtons' once in a while as well, especially since RJ's moving out apparently left a void in the couple's lives. The Burlingtons didn't have any children of their own, so RJ and Lisa attempted to include them in every family event they had.

"Lisa, watch ou—"

Callie tried to warn her. She must have seen the intent in Chandler's eyes. As Lisa was trying to free her hair from his grip, he had taken his other hand and smeared icing on her cheek.

RJ, along with everyone else, laughed and continued taking pictures. "These are some great photographs for his baby book." Sensing the crowd's reaction, Chandler chuckled heartily, smashing in his cake and blowing spit bubbles.

"Real funny when it's not you," Lisa said, trying to clean up his mess quickly, getting assistance from those nearby.

"I'll take him upstairs and wash him off real good," Callie offered, lifting him from the high-chair and heading up the stairs.

While Callie was tending to Chandler, Lisa took a paper towel and wet it in the kitchen sink so she could wipe her face.

"Here, let me help you with that." RJ snuck over and seductively nibbled on her cheek.

"Stop it!" she playfully scolded him, sensing all eyes in their direction.

"Come on, y'all. Let's go in the living room so the newlyweds can be alone," teased her mother. Embarrassed, Lisa protested, but her guests gathered plates of chips and other goodies and then scattered.

"See what you did!" She threw the wet paper towel at RJ.

He allowed it to fall to the floor and gently grabbed her by the waist, leaning her against the sink. "I love you, Mrs. Hampton."

"I love you, too," she replied sincerely. RJ leaned in for what Lisa suspected was intended to be a passionate kiss, but she stopped him short with a peck. "Uh-uh, don't you start anything."

"I'm not...I'm just adoring my wife." He massaged his lips on her neck. It felt good—real good—and Lisa knew that this afternoon's foreplay was merely an introduction to what RJ had planned for that night.

"Excuse me, but this is a birthday party, not your honeymoon." Callie walked in, holding Chandler. He giggled along with everyone else as if he had really gotten the joke.

Lisa gently pushed RJ aside and grabbed Chandler, who reached out to her.

"I look forward to the after-party," RJ whispered in her ear, then quickly kissed her on the cheek and joined the rest of the guests in the living room.

Callie rolled her eyes playfully. "I can only imagine what he said. Bryan and Tyra may have to stay with me at Mama's and Daddy's because something tells me that you two may be turning in early." She winked.

Lisa was sure her cheeks were red from blushing. Thankfully Chandler diverted both of their attention. He was pointing to a magnet picture frame on the refrigerator with Chanelle's photograph in it.

"Ma-ma." He smiled.

Lisa got teary-eyed as she stared at her daughter's picture. It was taken shortly before Chanelle's murder in front of the rehabilitation center. Her mind quickly went over everything that had happened with her family in the last few years and she was amazed at how God had brought joy out of so many painful situations.

Callie must've been thinking the same thing because she said, "Everything the devil meant for evil has backfired against him, you know? Chanelle's death, my being positive, Mama and Daddy's previous marital problems, your and RJ's divorce...all that stuff was meant for our destruction, but look at how God has brought us through. It's definitely a testament to His glory."

"Amen to that!" cheered Lisa.

"Ma-ma," Chandler continuously repeated.

Lisa kissed him and held him close. "Yes, baby. That's your mama."

DISCUSSION QUESTIONS FOR
In Times of Trouble

1. How do you handle disagreements when you and your child's grandparents (maternal or paternal) don't agree with your methods of discipline or child-rearing?

2. Depression is something that many of us may experience at times, to varying degrees. What are some ways to overcome this joy-stealing spirit?

3. In Chapter 3, there's brief mention that Lisa previously had a run-in with the law. What are some ways that a criminal record affects a person's entire life? How do societal responses differ from the Word of God regarding our pasts?

4. What do you think of Lisa's punishment of Chanelle? Was she too harsh, too lenient, or just right? How would you have handled the situation?

5. Would you be attracted to a spiritually mature man or woman even if his/her looks weren't all that great?

6. Are you a product of, or have you been divorced? In what ways do you think divorce affects children? Do you think therapy for children is a good or a bad thing?

7. Hattie makes a comment about Lisa being "super holy" when Lisa doesn't support the fact that she plays the lottery. What is your take on their friendly debate? Do you tend to side with Lisa or Hattie?

8. Do you think Olivia gave Lisa good advice in chapter 9? Would you have followed it? Why or why not?

9. What do you think of Eric?

10. Isaac mentions a downfall of being wealthy is that many of his relatives often look to him for freebies. How would you suggest dealing with family members or friends who are always looking for a handout?

11. Though she obviously feels wronged by Tyra, Callie encourages Bryan not to let her situation come between him and his wife. As Bryan's mother, this is a very noble act. Would you be able to give your child the same advice if you felt wronged by your son/daughter-in-law?

12. Read Matthew 19:9 and Matthew 5:32 and discuss them. What is your interpretation of these scriptures?

13. What do you think of Eric's point of view about the word "luck?" Does he have a valid argument?

14. Do you think the close relationship between RJ and Hattie is healthy or counter productive to Lisa being able to move on with her life?

15. In chapter 19, do you think Lisa responded to Chanelle in a way that is symbolic of how many parents would have responded or did Lisa overreact? Please explain.

16. Do you personally know anyone who suffers from the same thing that Callie suffers from?

17. Both Eric and Olivia suggest that Lisa do something to get her mind off Chanelle. What are some things you do when you find something or someone constantly worrying you?

18. Reflect on Chapter 23. In your opinion, did Lisa do anything wrong at the restaurant? Why or why not?

19. What are some signs to look for in a person who's suicidal?

20. In chapter 26, RJ says, "A lot of times we are blind to our own sins. We justify the things we do so we can keep doing them." Do you agree with his statement? Why or why not?

21. In what ways has Lisa helped to create a negative image of Chanelle to Olivia?

22. RJ states that he should have been destroyed by the actions of his past, but notes how God has used his past to enable him to help others. Has there been something in your past that you can look back on now and see how God has used the painful events of your life to help you minister to another person?

23. What do you think of Pastor Ross' explanation to Lisa about why he won't get involved in her situation?

24. Have you ever suffered because of the wrong committed by another or has anyone ever suffered because of your wrongs?

25. Lisa had previously painted a glamorous picture of being a pastor's wife. How much do you think the reality of the role coincides with the beliefs that she once held?

26. What do you think motivated Olivia to take such drastic measures in chapter 36?

27. Read Ephesians 6:10 – 18. What has been your experience with spiritual warfare?

28. What is your opinion about other translations of the Bible such as the New International Version, The Amplified Version or the New Living Translation? Do you think any of the original meaning of scripture is lost with the different translations or do they assist with understanding difficult passages?

29. What are some problems in today's churches and what are some things we can do to resolve them?

30. Reflect on the book title, *In Times of Trouble*. Think about situations in your own life and how this can apply to you.

About the Author

Yolonda Tonette Sanders attended Capital University where she majored in Political Science and Criminology and then received a Master's degree in Sociology from Ohio State University. In 2008, she started Yo Productions, LLC, a theatrical entertainment and literary services company, which she used to launch her first stage production, *Soul Matters*, based on her debut novel. Besides writing, Yolonda enjoys reading, singing, spending time with her family, and working out. Her favorite sports are volleyball and basketball, despite being no good at either. Ultimately, she's very grateful that her writing abilities tremendously outweigh her athletic ones and that she's been given world-wide opportunities to share her work. Yolonda currently resides in Columbus, Ohio with her family. Readers can connect with Yolonda online at www.yoproductions.net, www.facebook.com/yoproductions, or on Twitter @ ytsanders.